Image

By Jamie Magee

Enflame: Book Three of the "Insight" Series

ISBN-13:
978-1466492219

ISBN-10:
146649221X

Cover art rights owned by Jamie Magee
Cover art design by Marek Purzycki
First printed copy, May 2011
Created in the United States of America

"Love is much like a wild rose, beautiful and calm, but willing to draw blood in its defense" ~ Mark Overby

Happy Birthday Amanda ~ your enthusiasm for this story is behind every word....

Chapter One

Make peace, not war. That's what we're told. If only it were that simple. What we're never told is that – invariably – throughout the history of mankind, war always comes before peace.

It's been one week since we moved through the souls in the city of Delen, since Donalt lost his life...one week... you'd think in that amount of time, the message of Donalt's death would have spread throughout the dimension of Esterious, that people would have thrown down their black cloaks and began to cheer.

Instead, the city of Delen, the largest in Esterious, is now seen as demented. The surrounding cities are in the process of building a great wall. In their ignorance, they believe that if there is a wall between them and the people of Delen, they'll be protected. Protected from what? That's what I wanted to scream at them.

Rumors led us to believe that Drake was at the estate in which I'd been held, on the other side of the world. People now looked to him for direction. I could only imagine what he was telling them: that it was I – not him – that had betrayed them. That he would continue to fight for my heart so they would all be redeemed. We'd heard from the people in Delen that, before we came, the world was warned that a false leader would emerge, but that he wouldn't be powerful enough to move them all. Only Drake and I would be, together. I accused Drake of misinforming them, but August, Landen's grandfather, told us that it was Donalt that had said those words in his last speech.

Landen I and were sitting on the wall that surrounded the palace. The dark storm in which it had been immersed days ago had diminished. The people of Delen were painting the gray stones white and planting beautiful gardens throughout the court. We could see their intent: they thought that if they made it beautiful, Landen and I would stay there. Neither of us had stepped foot inside since we ran from the roar of Donalt's death. Landen feared that if we went in, the city would see it as a promise to rule them – which was something we refused to do.

In the distance, we could see the neighboring cities building their walls as fast as they could. Our first effort to hinder them was to move through the builders, encouraging them to join us. We'd managed to save just over a hundred more people, but now armed guards stood behind the workers – with every intention of killing anyone who even seemed to smile. We held back from helping any others. The risk to their lives was just too great.

Landen slowly reached his hand over and gently

placed it on my knee, I felt a numbing calm ease through my soul. I looked up into his waiting blue eyes to find him smiling at me.

"You're going to wear yourself out trying to calm me all the time," I thought.

He grinned and looked into the distance. *"You know my only intent is to keep you happy,"* he thought, wrapping his arm around me.

"What are we going to do, Landen – wait for another planet?" I complained.

"One day at a time. You need to take time to appreciate what we've done," he answered.

"It's not enough. We have so much more to do. Beyond this world, there are others…I don't have time to be grateful."

"You have to be grateful for what you have if you want to bring more things to you that will make you grateful."

"Wise words…did you just make that up?" I asked bleakly.

"That's the law of the universe, the law of all faith," he answered, pulling me closer to him and immersing me in a blissful calm.

I smiled at myself, realizing that my impatience was ruling me again. I then sighed and looked up at him. "I'm grateful," I whispered.

He leaned down and gently let his lips rest on mine. *Me, too,* he thought.

Brady and Dane came to the base of the wall where we were sitting and looked up. They were both covered head-to-toe in ash. Our family had spent every day in Delen, helping the people begin to build homes that showed their individuality.

"Are you guys ready? It's almost dusk." Dane asked.

I looked to the West and saw the sun lowering itself into the gray clouds. Dane was like a human clock. He would always appear at my side at dusk. He never wanted me here when it was dark. The nightmares I had as a child seemed to haunt him just as much as they haunted me… maybe it was because he had to watch me suffer growing up. Between him and Landen, I wasn't even allowed to yawn here.

"Whenever you guys want to go," Landen answered.

"Everyone else already left. Let's go," Brady said.

Landen wrapped his arms around my waist and let us fall. He'd gotten really good at using his energy to move him wherever he wanted to go. As we walked through the streets to our passage, the people all smiled and bowed their heads. Their affection always made us uncomfortable. Landen and I both feared that they'd never really know how to live on their own. They'd rebuilt Patrick's home. The rusty staircase was replaced by beautiful white wooden steps. There were usually flowers running across each one, leading our way. Landen had asked Patrick several times not to allow people to mark a path. Yet, the flowers re-mained.

The string was calm. It had been since we'd managed to dismantle the looking glass. I walked in front of the others. I could sense that Brady wanted to talk to Landen. Brady, who'd always defended our right to do what we wanted to do – which was to help others, no matter the risk – had been wavering lately. He'd never stand in our way, but he feared – just like all of us – that each time we faced the conditions of a planet we'd risk our lives.

We stepped inside our dimension, Chara. Landen had driven his Jeep to the passage that morning because we knew we were going to August and Nyla's for dinner, which was a distance way too far to walk. On our way there, we drove Dane and Brady home. Marc and Stella's house was just before August's. Landen slowed as we drove by. They hadn't come out of their house since their celebration. I knew they needed time to themselves, but I was anxious to show Stella all of Chara, her new world. I noticed that all the drapes were still pulled. I sighed and glanced at Landen – who was laughing under his breath. He may have teased me about my impatience, but at times I thought it was one of the traits he loved most about me.

"It won't be too much longer," he promised.

I knew he was missing Marc, too.

Nyla was waiting for us on the porch. Somewhere in the house I could feel August. The frustration he was feeling stung the air.

"He must still be trying to read the scroll," Landen thought.

When we were told that there were eight beyond the sun and the moon, we thought that each time one of the planets orbited, we'd face the trial of that planet's influences. August wasn't so sure of that conclusion anymore. It seemed that the time of day that we'd redeemed Delen, in Esterious, was twelve hours before Mercury had orbited. To August, as well as to all of those that were raised in Chara, that was a distance that could span a lifetime. In the stars above, with each moment that passes, the universe moves. According to theory, the five minutes between Landen and Drake's birth decided who I'd love, who would see through all dimensions. I personally wouldn't have cared who was born first or last or in which dimension in which they were raised – because I knew it would be the soul inside of Landen that I would have loved.

It was an odd thought, though: what if it was reversed?

What if Landen's soul had been born in Esterious as Livingston's son? What if Drake had been born in Chara? In that case, in theory, Landen and I would have been able to redeem the entire dimension without even really having to try. In that scenario, Drake would have been raised in Chara, without any knowledge of me. Soon he would be searching for his soul mate. It seemed that would have been easier. I mean, if we're up there free to "choose our path," then why didn't it happen that way? Now, with the path we'd chosen, I must hurt Drake and he must hurt Landen and me. I took refuge in the idea that with great suffering comes great reward.

Nyla reached up and hugged Landen then me. "I'm glad you two are here. Now maybe he'll come out of the study," she said in a lighthearted tone.

"Has he been in there all day?" Landen asked

"I haven't seen him out of there in two days. That's why I called you this morning. He'll come out for dinner if he knows you're here," Nyla said, extending her arm to lead us in.

Their house was the most unique out of all of ours. Every single wall in every single room was bookshelves. From the floor to the ceiling, row after row there were books. August prided himself on having read all of them. Each book mapped out the history of all the cultures in each dimensions. August was fascinated with how similar dimensions responded to the same issues – and how differently.

We made our way to the dining room. Nyla already had dinner on the table. She left us there to go down the hall to August's study. I felt his surprise and joy as she told him we were there. He came swiftly to greet us. Landen and I both stood and hugged him before sitting again.

"You've been in there a while, huh?" Landen said, looking over August. "Any answers?"

August's smile faded. He cleared his throat before he answered, "Only more questions. But I'm most certainly convinced that it's not the orbit that compelled the trial."

"Then what is it?" Landen asked.

"I don't know…maybe the influences of the planet in the order of the orbit…I just know that the time between the orbit and your action was too great for it to be linked as a source," August replied.

Nyla tapped her finger on the table to get our attention. "Now, now, that's enough. After dinner, you two can lock yourself in the study with him – but right now we're going to have a discussion without all of this anticipation of the unknown," she said, looking at all of us.

She picked up her fork and began to eat her salad. I laughed under my breath. I'd never seen her so bold, demanding. I began to eat my salad and Landen started a conversation about all the progress that had been made in Delen. Nyla seemed happy to hear about that topic.

I helped her clean the kitchen after dinner and Landen disappeared into the study. Nyla had made two trays to take to Marc's house. I thought about taking them for her – but I didn't trust myself to leave them there and walk away. I knew I'd knock on the door and call them out.

I shuffled through the living room, looking at all the books and wondering how it could be possible for August to recall them as individuals. There was a dark purple book just above my eye level. I reached for its tattered bind and gently turned through the pages. I didn't recognize the language the words were written in, but every few pages had illustrations of symbols. As I turned the pages, the symbols seemed to grow more evil – so I slammed the book closed and squinted my eyes, trying to block the memories of my nightmares, the weight of the demons on my chest.

I went down the hall to August's study, letting my fingers dance across the bookshelves. At the end of the hallway, I could see Landen leaning over a table, looking at the scroll with August. Keeping my distance, I leaned in the doorway. When they looked over documents from my first life, I always felt haunted, like there was a voice from then screaming at me – my voice. I reached for the charm on my neck, a sun with a crescent moon. My thumb outlined the star that now rested behind them. This charm had seen more than I'd ever be able to recall. I felt like it was a part of me, that somehow it would unlock the past and help me face my future.

"Any luck?" I asked them.

Landen glanced up at me then back down. "No. It's all symbols and letters, a combination of four languages…it doesn't make any sense," he answered, feeling frustrated as he continued to study it.

I took a deep breath and walked closer. This scroll was with our birth charts, the charts that we'd left here for our family over four million years ago. As I let my fingertips run across the edge of the scroll a familiar rush of déjà vu came over me, haunting me.

My eyes searched over the scroll with Landen and August. I didn't recognize the script or symbols, which were of every shape, mocking man and animal, water and fire. I did notice, though, that surrounding one of the larger circles were what looked like numbers. At the top was a one, to the right and left there was a one. At the bottom there was a nine: 1119.

"Do you know what these numbers mean?" I asked.

Landen and August leaned in close enough to see the

tiny numbers. August then ran his fingers around the circle. Inside it, there was an illustration of a flower. The flower was not detailed. Just a series of dots. Time had faded them. Some were darker than others. I imagined if someone didn't have an eye for art, they would easily be dismissed as random marks.

"What's today?" August asked

"Eleventh month, sixteenth day," Landen answered.

I took in a deep breath and stepped back. I'd been so lost in everything that I hadn't remembered that my birthday was just days away – that I'd be nineteen. It seemed impossible that the year had slipped by so quickly, without warning.

"My birthday is November nineteenth: 1.1.1.9," I whispered into the room.

As Landen and August both looked at me then down to the scroll again, I felt the tension rise and a heavy anxiety growing. I stared at August. He was the one who was full of dread.

"What is it, August?" Landen asked, knowing that it had to be more than my birthday that had him so concerned.

"This circle is Venus. There are nineteen petals on the flower, nineteen stems, and nineteen dots marking the ground they're growing in. It's your birthday. That's when we'll have to deal with Venus," August declared.

Landen and I leaned forward and let our eyes rush over the flowers, finding the number nineteen over and over again. August then ran the magnifying glass over the other planets.

"Each of these planets has an image, a coded number, designed within them – and I'd guarantee you that I'd find the twelve-hour difference in the image of Mercury,"

August said.

"What are you saying? You just found a map of everything we're going to face?" Landen asked.

"Not what – *when*," August corrected. "This is remarkable. I mean, I have a lot I'm going to have to decode, but this may be a way to navigate away from war," he said as he filled with hope.

Landen and I couldn't share his joy. We were more focused on the fact that I'd be nineteen in three days – and that something was going to test us. Landen walked around the table to where I stood and wrapped his arms around me. I hid my face in his chest, trying to hide my fear. Someone always seemed to get hurt when my heart was tested. I hadn't had time to overcome my last experience with Drake. I still struggled with the vision of his eyes full of pain and his argument that I'd been taken from him.

It didn't take August long to notice that we weren't celebrating with him. His emotion then returned to dread and he cleared his throat. "I want to take these to Perodine. If anyone can help me understand the codes locked in this scroll, she'd be able to," he said to us.

As I felt Libby and Preston's enthusiasm, I looked up from Landen's chest to the doorway. I heard a loud knock and suddenly felt concern coming from Ashten, then my father. August walked to the door, but Preston opened it before he could reach it. His blue eyes shined in the dark room full of bookcases.

"Are you ready?" he asked us all.

"Ready?" Landen questioned.

"Wait just one minute," Ashten said, reaching to hold Preston back. "I've already told you not tonight," he huffed, trying to catch his breath. I imagined that he'd chased Preston all the way there.

"What's going on?" I asked, knowing that Preston and Libby had the intent of getting us to Esterious right then and there.

"Preston is convinced that you and Landen need to see Perodine," my father answered.

"It's important," Libby said, stepping forward and pleading with her eyes. I knew that she believed every word she said.

Landen let his arms fall from around me, then reached for the scrolls and began to roll them gently.

"You're not going anywhere tonight," Ashten said to us.

Landen slid the scrolls into a long tube, then turned and looked at his father. "We only have three days," he said, taking my hand and leading me to the door.

"What do you mean? We have longer than that," Ashten said, following us out onto the front steps.

"We were wrong about the orbit. Every time is mapped out on here. She will help us," Landen answered. "Where is she?" he asked Preston.

"In Delen. In the palace," Preston answered.

"Are you sure? We were just there," I said.

Libby and Preston both frantically nodded 'yes.'

"You stay here," I said to Libby.

She sighed. "I knew you were going to say that," she said, looking solemn. Landen nodded for Preston to go back to Ashten.

"She's in the observatory," Preston said to Landen, who nodded in response.

August climbed into the backseat of our Jeep and Landen drove off in the direction of the passage, not allowing any more arguments.

August slid in the middle to talk to us as we drove. "I

don't want to concern you, but we may have less than three days. It's well into the seventeenth day in Esterious and Delen is in the same time as Willow's birthplace," he said, looking at Landen.

Landen tightened his jaw and increased his speed. There was no doubt he was in shock. He thought we had more time. He longed for the peace in which he wanted us to live. Sensing that I felt guilty for being the reason we had to live through this, Landen reached his hand over and let it rest on mine. He then looked at me and shook his head 'no,' reassuring me that there was no reason for my guilt.

Chapter Two

Once we reached Delen, we could see that all of the palace lights were burning brightly. People were lining the streets, anxious to see what had brought Perodine back so abruptly. As we walked through the large iron gates, flashes of the storm came to me. An overwhelming emotion of grief flooded me. The girl kissing Landen…the pain in Drake's eyes as I hurt him once again…those memories were worse than any nightmare I'd ever had.

The front doors were open. A young woman dressed in black was standing in the shadows. She intended to lead us to Perodine.

Inside the palace we grudgingly climbed eight flights of stairs then turned down a short hallway that led to a vast open room. In the center of the stone room there was a square pool. Stars from above reflected in the dark water. Perodine was standing near the center of this cosmic mirror. The water was clinging to her waist. She waded carefully backwards as she moved the water grew shallower. She was wearing black slacks and a black T-shirt. I'd never seen her so informal. It made her seem more real, approachable. I could feel her anger, frustration, and absolute dread as she gazed at the reflection of the stars.

August walked in front of Landen and me. When he reached the pool he quietly slid his shoes off and slowly stepped in, trying not to move the stars on which Perodine was focused.

Landen and I cautiously walked to the pool, anxiously watching them, wanting any help we could get from the stars above.

"Perodine," I said quietly. She looked up as if I'd screamed her name then noticed August in the pool for the first time. Around her neck, I could see dark bruises – as if she'd been severely choked by someone. "Who hurt you?" I asked, horrified.

As she held back tears that wanted to surface, her eyes seemed to turn to glass. She then waded through the pool toward me, filling with absolute defeat. As she leaned across the edge and put her hand on my face, her eyes carefully studied my every feature. "I'm afraid, my child, that he is more powerful dead than he ever was alive," she whispered to me.

I felt as if the wind was suddenly knocked from my body. My heart thundered in my chest. *What did she mean? Donalt was a ghost, a demon?*

"He's been planning this for millions of years," she continued.

"Planning what?" Landen asked, terror consuming him.

Perodine let her hand drop from my face, then slowly turned around and sat on the edge of the pool. August was now quietly studying the starry reflections.

"He knew all along where Guardian's soul would be born, where you'd be born. He orchestrated this entire dilemma – just so he could return again," Perodine answered. "I'm such a fool."

"It's not your fault," I muttered, sitting down next to her.

"I just don't know why I didn't see it in the stars," Perodine said, letting her face rest in her hands. I put my hand on her shoulder and so did Landen. Together, we tried to give her a sense of calm – but she refused to succumb to the emotion.

"Absolute genius," I heard August say in a disgusted tone.

Perodine looked up from her hands. August waved her over to see the reflection he was studying. She approached carefully. August began to point to the water. As Perodine studied the stars, I felt an anger come over her with an intent of revenge.

"What do you see?" Landen asked them.

"In the stars, I saw conflicts in Willow's path. A man, darkness keeping her from you. I thought it was Drake – but Donalt weaved his intentions alongside Drake, hiding himself," Perodine said, shaking her head and smiling – almost deviously.

"I don't understand," I said, looking around at all of them.

"When I saw danger in your path, I thought it was Drake. I never thought it would be Donalt. I'd already considered him dead. I never considered the idea that he'd linger between lives," she said, looking around the room in the dark shadows. She let her anger overturn her fear then glared into the darkness.

"How can he take the power if it's her heart?" Landen asked, bewildered.

"I'm afraid he's had four million years to plan – and I've had only moments to understand it," Perodine said, concentrating on the stars again.

She and August waded in the water for countless minutes, then at the same time they said, "Three days."

August looked back in our direction. "Just like the scroll."

"What scroll?" Perodine asked.

"It was found with their charts," he said, wading toward us.

Perodine looked at me and smiled. "You did manage to steal it," she said as relief overcame her.

"You know what it is?" I asked, stepping out of her way.

She reached for a towel wrapped it around her then led us to a doorway. On the left, it led to another vast room. Two of the walls were books from ceiling-to-floor, one was a wall of windows and in the center of the third was a large fireplace. Two doorways framed either side of it, leading to more of the palace. Three couches framed the fireplace. A large round table was in the center of the room, circled by six chairs, and books and scrolls were open all over it. As Perodine walked over to it and began to clear a space for the scroll we'd brought, we followed her, eager to get her interpretation.

"We knew that Donalt had the most trusted stargazers of that time study the heavens above at the time of your birth we knew that it held the path of all of your lives. The night you were pushed into the string was the night you intended to steal it," Perodine explained as she moved open books from the table to make room for the scroll. "I never knew if you had it or not. I think I've looked for it every day for the past four million years," she continued, reaching for the scroll.

As Landen handed it to her, his eyes met mine. Perodine then gently unrolled the delicate cloth. If she could read this, our lives would be told to us before we had a chance to live them – which was something that everyone and no one wanted. I could feel disappointment coming from Perodine.

"What is it? Is it the wrong scroll?" I asked.

"No, it's the right one – but it's been altered," she said as she leaned in and looked closely at the symbols. "It looks as if you sought advice on how to decode it. There are answers around the planets, written in code along with foreign words," Perodine said.

"Those are answers?" August asked. Having seen the document as an original, seeing the division now was astounding to him.

"Well, what someone *thought* were answers," Perodine said bleakly.

"If Donalt is a ghost, how dangerous is it that Willow is here?" Landen asked.

Perodine seemed to freeze as her eyes raced back and forth. She then looked to the doorway that led to the pool, then back at us. "Where's Allie?" she asked.

Allie, Brady and Felicity's infant, was someone I felt would lead us all one day. Perodine had said as much when I saw her last.

"In Chara, where she belongs," I answered.

As I spoke, Perodine shook her head no. "No, he knows about the passage you made to Evelyn and Stella, the one that rests next to your home…Donalt knows everything," she said in a rush. Landen and I looked at each other. It had escaped our attention that we'd left an obscure gate inside Chara.

"You must go there and take everyone with your bloodline to Pelhan. I'm sure he's expecting them. Return here with your shields – it's the only protection I think we have," Perodine said, walking to us then guiding us to the doorway.

"What do you mean 'shields?'" Landen asked, stopping her.

I could feel her impatience and urgency. "The Cancers, the ones who have lingered at your side your entire life," Perodine said breathlessly.

I took Landen's hand and pulled him to the doorway. I knew what Perodine was saying: return with Dane and Marc, the two that had unknowingly guarded Landen and me throughout our lives.

"Landen," August said to stop us. He then took a sheet of paper from the table, wrote a quick note and rushed it to Landen. "Tell Nyla to give you these books – and make sure she gets to Pelhan."

Landen nodded. We knew August intended on staying there and trying to unravel the scroll so he could protect us.

The people of Delen were lingering on the streets, wondering what was about to happen. Landen raised his hand and said, "We'll be right back," over and over again, trying to assure them that they were all safe.

When we stepped in the string, my heart felt like it was pounding through my chest. I couldn't breathe and not finding breath sent me into a panic: I started to see black spots.

A dizzy sensation swept through me. Landen reached his arms around me and held me as tightly as he could against his chest, rushing a calm through me. *"It can't get any harder, Landen...I'm not over the last time. I can't go through something like that again,"* I thought as the panic faded in his embrace.

He leaned back and looked into me. I found myself mesmerized by the diamond blue eyes that the light of the string had created.

"We love each other. They cannot tear us apart."

"I'm not as strong as you. I get weaker every time."

"You get stronger. We both do," he thought.

He swayed me with the flow of the string. I closed my eyes and took in the overwhelming power of energy flowing around us, as well as the calm that Landen was giving me. I slowly began to catch my breath. When the tightness in my chest began to release I let my hand fall inside of Landen's. He smiled at me and gently kissed my forehead.

In the distance, we could feel the string filling with emotion, an anxious emotion. Landen tightened his grip on my hand and we began to run to Chara – fearing the worst. When the first hazes of Chara came into view, we saw hundreds of people crossing out of Chara into the neighboring dimension, Olence. We passed by them, eager to make sure our family was safe. Inside our passage we saw Chrispin and Olivia waiting with their travel bags.

"What's going on?" Landen asked Chrispin.

"Preston and Libby told your dad to make everyone on this side of Chara move for three days. They told them to go to Olence. Do you know what they're talking about?" Chrispin asked, bewildered.

"We have to return to Delen with Marc and Dane and take the rest of you to Pelhan," Landen answered.

"What? You're not hiding me away and taking Marc off to battle! I should be there – wait, why Dane?" Chrispin asked, feeling betrayed.

"I didn't choose. That's what Perodine said. Look, Donalt is in-between, like your Dad – only in a dark way. He's the threat this time. I have to listen to Perodine's advice," Landen said, pulling me to our Jeep. "I need you to get everybody here for me. I'll get Nyla and Marc," he finished as we began to pull away.

Chrispin nodded and ran to his Jeep, then drove off in the other direction. Landen stopped at our house and ran in to grab our bags then we sped through the streets to Marc's house.

All of their lights were out. We could feel the calm of sleep coming from them. I felt so guilty. We were about to charge in and separate them after they'd had only days to know one another.

"If he wants to stay with her then I'm going to tell him to," Landen said as we turned into Marc's yard.

I knew Perodine believed that the Cancers would protect us, but I didn't want to ask either of them to return with us. I let the intent of giving Dane a choice to stay too come to me. Landen grinned weakly as he sensed it. We hesitated for a moment, staring at the dark house, feeling the love between Stella and Marc. It was so beautiful. Landen sighed heavily then opened the Jeep door. Anxiously I followed him to the porch.

Landen knocked quietly on the door and we waited. We then felt them waking up, wondering who had the boldness to disturb them. Marc opened the door and squinted in our direction, then closed it behind him, keeping us all on the porch. "It's a little late for a visit, don't you think?" he said, stretching and smiling at Landen. When Landen didn't smile back, Marc knew something was wrong. "Already?" he asked.

Landen nodded. "Three days. Perodine told us to take our families to Pelhan and return with you and Dane," he said glancing down then up again.

"What did Drake do? Is my mother OK?" Marc asked, angry.

"It's Donalt, not Drake. Apparently, he doesn't feel his time is over. Marc, you don't have to come to Delen with me, but you have to at least go to Pelhan – for your safety."

"Oh, I'm going with you – and don't try and talk me out of it," Marc said, opening the door to gather his things. Landen reached for his shoulder and looked past him. Stella had come to see who was there.

"You need more time. I'll be fine," Landen promised.

"I'm going," Marc said, closing the door.

Landen sighed and pulled my hand for us to leave. As we drove to get Nyla, I tried to prepare myself for her reaction when we told her that she wasn't going to see August for three days. I couldn't envision her without her overwhelming calm.

When we got to her house, Nyla was standing on the front porch with two travel bags at her feet and two large books in her arms. As Landen pulled up to the porch, I stepped out and took the books from her arms. Both of them were no less than six inches thick, the pages were yellow, and the leather on the covers had worn on every edge. Landen walked around and loaded the bags.

"Where are you supposed to take me?" she asked, feeling somewhat excited.

"To Pelhan. Who told you to pack?" Landen asked, opening the backdoor for her to get in.

"I knew when you left here with that scroll that the influence of Venus was sure to begin."

After making sure Nyla was safely in the Jeep, Landen pulled the note August had given him out of his pocket. He looked at the titles, then walked to me, took the top book and checked the title. He did the same with the second. "These are the ones," he whispered, shaking his head. I could feel a sense of betrayal coming from Landen. He felt like this when we'd first met: that his family had him on a need-to-know basis.

"Best intentions," I thought.

"I hope so," he thought, opening my door. I climbed in and he set the books gently on my lap then closed the door.

Nyla slid to the center of the backseat and leaned forward so she could see me. I looked to my side at her, then down to the books in my lap.

"What are these?" I asked timidly.

Nyla stretched her arm forward and let her fingertips trace over the worn leather corners. Landen climbed in and began to drive us to the passage. "This one is of my ancestors. The one on the bottom is Karsten's ancestors," she answered. I glanced at Landen. Karsten was my grandfather, which meant that in my lap I held the history of both Landen and my bloodlines.

"You're both from Analess?" Landen said, confused by Nyla's answer.

"Yes, but we're from two opposite sides of the dimension. We're only connected by the Odiona."

"Odiona?" Landen questioned. I knew he'd never heard this before – that infuriated him.

"Our bloodline begins with twin sisters, Jayda and Samilya. I'm a descendant of Jayda and Karsten is a descendant of Samilya."

"Go on," Landen said, looking at her in the rearview

mirror.

"Samilya was given to the ruler of the East, Oba, as a wife. It is said that Samilya did love her husband at first, but years later she ran away from him, taking their children with her. She ran to her sister Jayda, in the West and told her that Oba was possessed by darkness. Jayda hid her sister away, but Oba sent guards to retrieve his wife and children. They took Jayda by mistake. When Jayda stood in front of Oba, he looked into her eyes, his body tensed and he fell to the floor and screamed in pain. As he did, darkness came from his eyes, ears, and mouth. When it had all escaped him, a bitter taste surfaced in his mouth. The darkness could not reside in a body that feels only pure love. "

I replayed her story in my mind, trying to place the names in the right place. I couldn't help feeling an utter confusion. "I don't understand. His wife was Samilya, not Jayda. Was the darkness confused – or was Oba?" I asked.

"No one was confused. If Jayda had been given as his wife, then the darkness never would have been able to invade Oba. It didn't matter that they were identical. Real love is beyond the surface."

"So where did the darkness go?" Landen asked as we approached the passage.

"It hasn't returned to Analess since then," Nyla said, sliding back to climb out of the Jeep.

Dane opened my door for me, then reached in and took the books. Clarissa was standing behind him. As I felt their solid intent on separating for my benefit, my stomach turned and dropped. I felt like I was leading an innocent lamb to sacrifice. "Dane, I think maybe you and Marc should stay with the others – that you need to shield them, not us. Perodine was not her normal calm. She could have been speaking irrationally," I said, stepping out avoiding their eyes. I was a horrible liar – and everyone knew it.

"Well, if she was irrational, then there's no reason for you to worry about me being at your side," Dane said, trying to catch my eyes.

I gave in and stared up at him. "You don't have to do this," I whispered.

"I know," he said, reaching back for Clarissa's hand. I walked past them to Landen's side. He was with Stella and Marc. I knew he was trying once more to dissuade Marc.

Stella smiled at me as I approached. I felt her calm and shook my head slowly from side to side. "You should be angry," I whispered as I pulled her aside. I was hoping that if I convinced her to get Marc to go with her, then Dane would follow as well.

"Why should I be angry?" Stella asked in an astonished, childlike manner as her eyes searched over my face.

"This has nothing to do with any of you. It's unfair that you're asked to endure it with us," I said in a low tone, looking deep in her dark eyes.

Stella stepped forward and hugged me. "We're all connected. You taught me that," she said quietly as she let me go and walked to Marc's side.

Landen reached his hand out for mine and both of us looked behind us to our home, then to our family that stood in front of us. We struggled to fight the emotion of grief. It felt like we were saying goodbye to Chara, to all the ones we loved. Rose caught my stare and I saw her move her head from side to side, telling us to remain calm, that we would return.

"Landen, do you want to lead? We'll stay in the back," Ashten asked casually. Landen nodded, then took my hand and led us all in the string.

"Willow," I heard Brady say. I looked back to see him

and Felicity walking in behind us. "Will you carry Allie?" he asked me as he reached his arm around Felicity to guide her through the darkness she was seeing. I smiled and reached to take Allie gently from her arms.

"Thank you," Felicity said, gripping Brady now. "I'm not a big fan of the dark," she said, smiling at herself.

"I'm sorry. It's to keep you safe. I promise," I said, cradling Allie.

"And we will be," Felicity said, smiling in the direction of my voice. I wished I could bottle her optimism. I looked down at Allie to see her eyes studying the hazes around us. I took in her calm, knowing I'd need to remember it soon.

"I want to go, too, Landen," Brady said in a muffled tone, not wanting Chrispin or the others to hear him.

"Brady, I need you to make sure our family is safe, to protect your daughter. Please do that for me. I need to know that you will," Landen answered in a low tone.

Brady looked at me then to his daughter and nodded once.

We walked swiftly through the flowing current. Without the storms to concern us, paths that would take hours now took only minutes. Before long, the string began to turn a beautiful shade of yellow. Stunning sparkles danced in thin air.

Landen stood at the passage. I stood opposite him and gently handed Allie to Felicity. They passed through first. Landen and I waited as each of the people we held dear to us passed through, then we stepped in.

Perodine was right: Pelhan must have know we'd be coming. Even though it was the dead of night, three women waited to meet us. Above, the stars seemed to flow like diamonds. A stunning white glow of energy lingered around everything. The women waited for Landen and I to lead our family, which we did as they gestured and led them through the streets to Pelhan's.

Pelhan was on the porch with Aora at his side, waiting. Behind them were four more women dressed all in white. They walked forward and guided everyone in – with the exception of Landen and me.

"Can you help us? What have the stars told you?" Landen asked him.

Pelhan stepped off the front porch and walked slowly to Landen, smiling. Aora mirrored his steps. "My friends, I cannot read the stars above. I never have been blessed with that understanding," he said.

"Then how do you know what you know?" I asked, confused.

Pelhan looked at me and smiled. "I listen to my higher self. In the silence, I find the answers I seek," he answered.

"Can you ask how to defeat him?" Landen said as respectfully as he could, but the sarcasm in his tone was apparent.

Pelhan nodded. "I have already…light is the balance of darkness," he answered.

I let my shoulders fall, then looked up at Landen. We were both hoping for an insight beyond that. We wanted to know how to avoid it, to endure it. Pelhan smiled and began to walk to the large garden to the left of his home. He glanced over his shoulder, assuring himself that we were following him.

He and Aora led us through the weaving paths of the garden. In the center of it were red rose bushes that towered over me. The thorns looked like steel razor blades. I pulled my arms close to me, wanting to avoid them. The rose bushes encircled a small area where the grass was short, which was where Pelhan sat slowly down and crossed his legs in front of him. Aora sat at his side. Landen glanced at me and sighed -- neither of us felt we had time for these slow, revealing lessons.

We sat in front of them and pulled forth as much patience as we could. With a small grin across his face, Pelhan looked at Aora and nodded. She then reached her hand for the closest bush. I squinted my eyes as her hand gripped the thorns and blood slowly drizzled down her wrist. When she released the stem, she showed us her palm: I could see four deep lacerations. My mouth dropped and I felt a cold sweat come across my forehead. I'd never been one who could endure the sight of blood. Landen reached his arm around me giving me as much calm as he could. I knew he was bothered by the display as well.

Aora stretched her hand toward Pelhan, who took her hand. With his touch, the glow around them grew brighter. When it dimmed, he released Aora's hand and she showed us her palm: the lacerations were gone, all the blood was gone from her wrist…it was as if it had never happened.

"How?" Landen asked quietly.

"This is a gift you taught me long ago. I've never been able to teach another – but I hope that changes tonight," Pelhan answered.

I swallowed and looked to the razor thorns, fearing that he was going to ask me to cut my hand so Landen could practice this new gift.

"You saw the light?" Pelhan asked. We nodded. "That was my energy, me wanting more than anything to take her pain away, to heal her body from its wounds." He paused and examined his own Aura. "You can see clearly that now, my energy – our energy – has been depleted," Pelhan said.

"Can you get it back?" Landen asked

"It will return when we join as one," Pelhan answered.

"You just wanted to heal her...just a focused thought?" Landen summarized.

Pelhan raised his eyebrows and smiled slightly. I could tell he was amused by Landen's eager interpretation.

"A much focused thought. No doubt or care for my own well being...willing to give her my energy, my life force," Pelhan said.

"At least I can heal you," Landen said, looking to his side at me.

"You can heal anyone," Pelhan said. Landen curiously looked to him. "It's an amazing gift, but you must be careful with it. When you take your energy and give it to another, you are depleting yourself, taking away your ability to shield yourself from others. I'm afraid that in your path you will find a need for both. Therefore, a balance must be enforced."

"But you said you could get it back by joining," Landen said as he tried to understand Pelhan's warning.

"Yes, but you would have to fully release yourself inside one another, losing touch with time and reality. During that time, your bodies are at their weakest point. Joining inside any dimension beyond here and Chara is not advisable for the two of you."

Aora reached her hand for the same stem her hand was on before. Blood was still dripping from the thorns. I closed my eyes and buried my head in Landen's shoulder, not wanting to see the display again. I could feel how nervous and unsure Landen was, so I put my hand on his leg, imagined the emotion of victory and gave it to him. A second later, I felt a warm hum rush through the both of us -- the sensation was amazing. I opened my eyes to see Landen releasing Aora's hand. He'd healed her completely. I could feel utter astonishment coming from Landen. Aora grasped the stem again and again and each time Landen seemed to heal her faster. The white glow around us dimmed more and more as he healed her. Landen finally released Aora's hand and said, "I feel weaker."

Pelhan nodded. "I feel that you have mastered this. We will leave you alone to join your energy," he said, standing.

"Wait – we don't have time for this. August and Perodine are waiting for us," I said, rising to my knees.

"You can return in a few hours. We will get your family settled and wake you then. It is important that you are strong," Pelhan said, helping Aora up.

We watched them walk into the darkness, leaving us alone in the rose garden. I let myself fall back on my legs then glanced to my side at Landen who was staring at the bloodstained thorns. "I don't think I can be calm enough to meditate," I said, trying to get his attention.

His eyes moved to mine then he reached his arms out for me to lean into him. I could feel a calm coming from his embrace. "I don't want you to worry. I can feel your grief. We'll come back for them and go home to Chara," he whispered.

"I can feel your grief," I whispered back.

He leaned his shoulder back so I'd have to look at him. "It's a grief for a life we'll never have, a life uninterrupted by anyone or anything in Esterious."

I reached up and let my lips rest on his neck, then thought, *"That day will come."*

We drifted into calm. As we left our bodies, we merged our energy, taking in the tantalizing, addictive rush.

Chapter Three

It seemed like only moments before we felt Aora and Pelhan gently touch our bodies. We took in a sharp breath it was agonizing to go from such bliss to the weight of a body. Once we focused we stood and noticed that the beautiful white line that connected Landen and me was brighter and wider. We were as strong as we could be at that point.

"It is time to return to Delen," Pelhan said, extending his hand to guide us out of the garden.

"We need to say goodbye," Landen said, wrapping his arm around me.

"Yes, they are waiting at the passage," Pelhan assured as he turned to lead us.

We followed Pelhan out of the garden and down the street to the passage. In the distance, I could sense our family. Overall, they were at peace. I began to focus on each of them as individuals, committing what I loved about their emotions to memory. Landen smiled down at me as he felt each one with me.

Pelhan stopped when our family came into view. "We will send our good thoughts to each of you," he said as he and Aora bowed their heads. I smiled slightly, then Landen nodded his head and we continued forward to our family.

In the center, our parents and grandparents stood with Libby and Preston at their side. Libby was staring up at me. I stepped forward and knelt before her to see her eye-to-eye. "Will you be able to tell me that all of you are alright when I'm in Delen?" I asked her.

She shook her head no. "I don't know how," she whispered.

"How did Perodine talk to you? How did you know I needed to go there tonight?" I asked, tucking a stray hair behind her ear.

"I felt it," Libby said.

I could feel frustration begin to emerge in her. Landen put his hand on my shoulder, urging me not to push her. I looked up at him, then back to Libby. "It's alright," I whispered.

"We'll try," Preston promised, looking up at Landen and me.

I forced a smile then rose from my knees. The others had encircled us. Landen reached down and picked up Libby, hugging her as tight as he could then he sat her down and reached for Preston to come to him. As he hugged him, Preston whispered something to Landen. Whatever it was Landen didn't understand it. Confusion was dominating his emotions. Landen nodded then stepped back, sighing.

"What did he say?" I asked

"I'll tell you later," Landen thought.

He crossed his arms and stared at our fathers, prepared to judge every word they spoke. "Is there anything that any of you know that may help us?" he asked.

Ashten and my father turned to Nyla and Karsten, waiting for one of them to explain. Karsten, my grandfather, cleared his throat. "The books we've given you are written in the first language, a language of symbols. August has spent decades with the scholars of Analess; he will serve as a great ally to the both of you," he said, showing us the emotion of confidence. "Nyla and I can tell you that the descendants of the Odiona have always been divided by one trait. It is said that Samilya lost her husband and never found another love. Her tribulation has been passed down from generation to generation. I am the only person in recorded history that has found a home in Chara, yet thousands from Jayda's decedents have," he explained.

"It shouldn't matter if someone before you couldn't find love," I argued, not understanding how half of a world could honestly believe that.

Karsten stepped forward and wrapped his arms around me. "I know. I never believed it either. Perhaps that's why your grandmother found me," he whispered proudly. I leaned out of his embrace and smiled at him.

Rose stepped forward and hugged Landen and me. She then whispered in my ear, "They're just stories. Only those who were there know the truth." I knew she meant to comfort me, but it made me more nervous. I wanted to know what those twins had to do with any of this.

Landen looked at his father and asked, "How come I was never told of this division?"

Ashten held in a breath and looked over Landen. He

wanted to stop us, to tell us we were foolish, but he feared it would only push us further away from him. "No one in Chara really knows of this. Our family is already seen in a rare light for being direct ancestors of Aliyanna and Guardian. Divulging information about being connected to other admired ancestors seemed to encourage a division between our family and the rest of Chara – something none of us want. Honestly, it didn't seem to pertain to the two of you, or Esterious," Ashten answered. His words echoed the truth.

Aubrey hugged Landen, then me. My mother did the same. "You make sure you're home for your birthday," my mother said in a cracked voice as she let go of me. She hid her face in my father's shoulder. I could feel her trying to call forth positive thoughts, trying to take herself two days in the future.

"Landen," my father said in a low tone, "you take care of my little girl." He pulled me to him and I wrapped my arms around my parents as I thought of how much I loved them. The emotion didn't comfort them as I intended. Instead, it only brought them more grief. They didn't want me to go.

Landen felt their emotion and placed his hand on my father's shoulder. "I will," Landen answered in a low tone.

My father slowly let me go and passed by us, taking my mother with him. Aubrey shielded herself behind Ashten and followed my parents. Nyla put her hand on Aubrey's back and walked with them. She was becoming a source of strength that August had served as before.

Rose stared at me then moved her eyes to Landen. "I wish I had wise words to give the two of you," she said, looking back at me. "Just know that there's no sacrifice worth the two of you being apart – for any amount of time." She kissed my cheek then hugged Landen. With Karsten at her side she followed our parents.

Landen looked at Dane, who was holding tightly to Clarissa, then at Marc, who was holding Stella. "You can stay. We'll be fine," Landen said in the most confident tone he could manage.

They both shook their heads no, then pulled Stella and Clarissa away to say their private goodbyes. We could feel the intent of Brady and Chrispin. They were trying to think of a way to convince us to allow them to come.

"I need the two of you to protect them. Don't allow anyone in the string until we return," Landen said, looking from Brady to Chrispin. They nodded, clearly not in agreement with Landen.

Olivia was standing to my left. Feeling her sorrow intensify, I slowly turned to see her. All around her, I could see the shade of light pink, a shade that meant high dream activity. Her dreams had forecasted Delen's redemption in the trial of Mercury. I knew then that she'd already seen my future in her mind's eye. I let out a jagged breath and asked, "Are the dreams bad or good?"

"I don't know," she said, stepping closer to me. She grasped my arm and pulled me away from the others. "Willow, you have to let me go with you," she whispered with pleading eyes.

"No way. I don't even want Dane and Marc to go," I answered, bewildered by her request.

"Why Dane?" she asked, looking in his direction.

"Perodine said to return with the Cancers that we've always known," I answered.

Olivia patted her hands quietly on her chest. "I'm a Cancer. You've known me your whole life – longer than you've known Dane," she said, pushing us farther away from the crowd.

I hesitated, recalling Perodine's emotion and intent when she told us to return with the Cancers; she was thinking of someone strong. Olivia was brave, but I wouldn't call her strong. "Olivia, I'm sure she meant Dane. You've been through so much. Stay here, where you're safe."

"Willow, you don't understand. Every part of me is telling me that I need to be with you. If you don't take me, no one else will."

"Tell me what the dream is," I said, knowing she was horrified.

"A wall," she said, crossing her arms.

"What do you mean 'wall?' The one they're building in Delen?"

"I don't know. I've seen a stonewall. I've seen a massive gray cloud that screams. I've seen what look like rain clouds gliding feet above the ground. I don't understand it – which is all the more reason I need to be near you."

"If you stay here, Pelhan will help you unlock your dreams. If you find an answer, tell Chrispin to bring you to me."

"He won't," she argued. "He'll go and leave me behind."

"You'll still be helping me," I argued, agreeing that Chrispin would choose to keep her safe there.

"Willow, please," she said, hugging me.

She was grieving for me and I couldn't understand why. I heard truth in everything she said. She believed she should be with me. It broke my heart to tell her no. I slowly let go of her. "I'll see you in a few days – K?" I said, looking away and catching a stray tear that had escaped my eye.

Olivia let her head fall. I walked away before my guilt would allow me to change my mind.

Felicity was waiting for me to say goodbye to her. Allie was in her arms and Libby and Preston were at her side. "Is Olivia OK?" she whispered.

"She wanted to go, but I told her no."

"Really?" Felicity said, bewildered. "I wonder why?"

Preston and Libby looked at each other, then up at me. I could feel their confusion.

"What?" I asked, looking back and forth between them.

They hesitated. Preston's eyes found Landen he looked him over carefully, then back to me. "It doesn't matter," Preston said.

Before I could question him, he and Libby ran to Olivia's side. It didn't take Chrispin long to realize Olivia was upset. He said his goodbye to Landen then went to meet her and the children.

"Don't worry, Willow," Felicity said to get my attention. "It's just a few days." She hugged me then walked past me to catch up with Olivia.

I looked over my shoulder and saw Brady and Landen whispering to one another. I then stepped closer to the passage. Stella and Clarissa blew a kiss in my direction and followed the others. Dane then came to my side, carrying the books with which we were to return. Marc had joined Landen and Brady's private conversation. I glanced up at Dane and shook my head -- his calm was too out of place.

"Do you know something I don't?" I asked under my breath.

"I just know how I feel and that's relieved to be able to protect you," he answered with a crooked smile on his face.

"You're insane. Anyone else would have run away – like you almost did when we were kids," I said, finding a little humor in the memory of Dane's young face so many years ago.

"Um, yeah…you zapped us to another place – freezing, if I remember correctly – then expected us to resume our game of hide-and-seek like nothing happened. I thought I was crazy," he said, laughing.

"You thought you were crazy? And what did you think I thought?" I said, laughing quietly.

"You didn't look crazy. You looked like you were doing what you were born to do, like you do now," he said, looking proudly down at me.

"Maybe so, but that doesn't mean you should be dragged into it…stay," I said, knowing his answer would be no.

"It's just three days – well, two now," he said, looking at Landen and Marc as they approached us.

"Promise," I said in a whisper.

Landen picked up our bags, which were by the passage, then took my hand and led us inside the string. I could feel him struggling to suppress his anxieties. *"What were you and Brady talking about?"* I asked.

He looked down at me, then back to Marc and Dane, then forward again. *"Did Olivia tell you about her dream?"* he asked. I nodded *"Brady thinks we should have taken her. I knew if we did, Chrispin would have come. And if Chrispin came, Brady would have come – they all would have come. It's bad enough that Marc and Dane are coming."*

"I'm sure Perodine meant Dane. It just makes sense that he would be more of a protector," I thought. I knew it was true that both Olivia and Dane had played that part throughout my childhood, but Dane had seen more; he'd traveled through dimensions with me. He was just stronger.

"I hope so. I told Brady if Perodine said we were

wrong about Dane, we'd come back for Olivia," Landen thought.

"Did that calm him down?" I asked.

"No. He thinks the dream is a warning, telling us that we'll be divided forever. In his opinion, I just left the key to finding them again there," Landen thought.

"Preston told me it didn't matter that Olivia wasn't coming. Brady is wrong," I thought, trying to convince the both of us. *"Do you agree?"*

"I know there's nothing that will keep us from finding them again," he answered.

"Brady said something else," I thought, feeling Landen suppressing his anxieties.

He sighed and nodded. *"Brady thinks that one of our past lives was in Analess. He has a theory that I was Oba and you were Jayda,"* he thought.

I looked forward and took in his words. It wouldn't be such a farfetched idea; apparently, we'd lived several lives oblivious to us. *"Well, it seems we defeated this darkness before,"* I thought.

"Yes, but only after the darkness had consumed me and I learned that I'd loved another woman and had children with her, leaving half of the ancestors believing that they could never find someone. I just don't want to settle for anything in this life. I want to defeat this curse and I don't want anyone who comes after us to pay for the choices we make. It overwhelms me when I think of it in that light," Landen thought, wrapping his arm around me tighter.

"You're being too hard on yourself. You don't even know if that's true – and if it is, we can't change what's already happened."

"That's what Marc said. I just have to work through it," Landen thought.

"Well, don't waste your energy trying to hide your emotions from me; I know them as well as my own," I thought, glancing up at him.

He smiled down at me. *"I'd imagine that you do,"* he thought, smiling and bringing his perfect dimples to life.

"What did Preston whisper to you when he hugged you goodbye?" I asked.

Landen tilted his head and I felt curiosity grow in him. *"He said everyone deserves to be healed – why would he say that? I mean, who would I not heal?"* he thought, looking down at me.

I raised my eyebrows as the memory of one person came to mind.

An understanding came across Landen's face. *"He was telling me to heal Drake,"* Landen thought as his jaw tightened.

"So we will see him," I thought, feeling plagued.

Landen pulled me closer to him. *"I'm not concerned if we do. I would heal him – even if I was the cause,"* Landen thought, a little offended by Preston's words.

I held him tight. *"Let it go. You have no way of knowing why he said that. He's just a little boy,"* I thought.

"In this life," Landen thought, smiling at the memory of Preston and Libby.

The gray, ashy passages of Esterious came into view.

"Landen," Marc said. "There has to be a passage inside the palace. I can't imagine Drake using the ones that we use."

Landen stopped and stared at the passages along the wall. "I think when I fought with Drake that first time, I threw him in this one," he said in a confident tone.

"Let me go first," Marc said, stepping in front of Landen. Dane came to my side. Marc stepped through then we followed him.

The passage did lead inside the palace, to a stone room. An enormous bed draped in black silk centered one wall. The ceiling opened above us. The night sky was clear. Around the bed on the floor stood tall ivory candles. Paintings reflecting my image hung on every wall. At the foot of the bed was a podium and you could see the outline of a book in the dust.

"This must be where they invoked the nightmares," Marc said.

I could feel the anger and tension building in the room, but my emotion – one of sorrow – was the strongest one among us. I imagined Drake as a little boy, being asked to lie in this bed with lit candles all around him and Alamos speaking words over him; seeing the demons, hearing them. Though it was obvious that Drake had grown used to his monkey friends, I couldn't imagine that was always the case.

Landen looked at me curiously. I answered his emotion and thought, "*When they started, he would have been too young to stop them. He was just a little boy.*"

Landen tilted his head and looked at me. "*It's not the child he was that I have an issue with. It's the man he is now, the one that chose to invoke them after eight months of peace,*" he thought.

"*The childhood makes the man,*" I thought, defending my point of view.

"*I don't want to debate now, Willow,*" Landen thought, smiling sardonically. He took my hand then turned to follow Marc and Dane to the lit hallway.

From the ceiling in the room, we knew we were on the top floor, the same floor that held the observatory. Landen tilted his head to the left, letting Marc know that we could feel August and Perodine in that direction. The hallway was wide, like the estate I'd stayed in just days ago; it had large paintings on the walls and narrow couches between the doorways. We walked past at least twenty doorways before the walls ended. The floor continued and over the banister we could see more than eight stories down. In the distance, we could see the walls begin again.

"How would you debate it?" I thought when I couldn't contain my curiosity anymore.

Landen looked down at me and shook his head side to side. I could see a sparkle in his blue eyes, which took my breath away. *"I just think that people who hide behind their childhoods are foolish. Just because your parents were great doesn't mean that you are and just because they're bad, it doesn't mean that you are. All the time people spend using their past as a crutch could be spent living a life they want to have. We control our thoughts – no one else,"* he thought.

I stared forward at the hallway that was approaching, going over every word he just said.

"Waiting for your comeback," Landen said aloud in an amused tone. Marc looked curiously over his shoulder at me.

I blushed slightly and smiled. "Well, don't faint: I don't have one. I agree," I answered, looking up at Landen. He laughed under his breath.

"If you've managed to leave her speechless, you have to tell us how," Dane said.

I playfully glared at him -- he shrugged his shoulders. "I'm just saying," Dane said, avoiding my eyes and adjusting the books he was carrying. Shaking my head, I reached for one of the books.

"From the outside, it doesn't seem as big as this," Marc

complained as he continued to walk forward.

"Go to your left up here," Landen said, still smiling at me.

We passed five more doorways before we turned left into another hallway. From there, we could see August and Perodine at the end of the long hall. We entered the room through one of the doorways that framed the fireplace. August looked up, startled to see us come from that direction. Perodine never lost her gaze with the scroll. Marc looked back at Dane and us when he saw her; it was clear they weren't expecting to see her so dressed down: she'd pulled her silver hair back into a ponytail, her pant legs were rolled up and she was still barefoot. Landen set our bags beside the couch and took the book from me. Marc let his and Dane's bag fall next to ours.

"Is Nyla safe?" August asked. Landen nodded. "Did you bring the right books?" he continued.

Landen and Dane set the books on the table. "The ones about Samilya and Jayda, yes," Landen answered.

Perodine looked up at us, then to August. "Who are they?" she asked, puzzled.

"They're from another dimension. Long ago, Jayda managed to defeat the darkness inside of her sister Samilya's husband."

Marc pulled out a chair at the table and took a seat. Landen leaned over the table, looking at the notes August had made. Dane and I leaned against the back of the couch.

"How?" Perodine asked, tucking a loose lock of hair behind her ear.

"Well, love, I guess they were twins. Samilya was given to a ruler; years later, she ran to her sister Jayda, telling her that darkness had consumed the man she loved. Jayda was taken by mistake by the ruler's guards. When she stood before him for punishment, the darkness left. Jayda and the ruler lived a very long life completely in love," August explained.

I could feel astonishment come over Perodine. Her face lost all of its color. She slid into the chair in front of which she was standing.

"Are you alright?" Landen asked.

"I just…I just remembered Donalt from long ago…he wasn't always…cold," Perodine said in a quiet voice. She looked at me. "I told you that at one time I did love him. I…I lost our first two children. The grief changed me. I went months without even seeing him. I just don't remember when he changed. I mean, I remember coming to him, wanting to try again and…he felt empty. He made me feel like a nuisance," she said. She sighed and looked to the shadows of the room, then to the scroll. "I just want to know what I'm fighting: the man I gave my life to, or a darkness that took him from me." Perodine reached for the books and turned the pages, then looked up at August. "Can you read this? Tell me more so I'll know." she said.

"I'll show you what I know," August said, placing his hand on hers.

"Have you learned anything else about the scroll?" Landen asked, stepping closer to the table.

August broke his stare with Perodine and looked up at him. "Perodine has assured me it's not the orbit that brings the trials," he answered.

I looked at her. "Then what is it?" I asked.

She looked up into my eyes and I could feel her grief. "After Donalt saw you for the first time, he was furious – he knew that you would end his dark reign. I had him watched. My spy witnessed the chant that envisioned the battle you're in."

"Chant? Like a curse? You're saying I'm cursed?" I said, grasping for a clear mind as hopelessness consumed me.

"No," she said, rising to come to my side. "No one can 'curse' us; our thoughts control our lives. Even if it were possible to be cursed, I'd already protected you at that point."

"What was the purpose of the chant then?" I asked, growing too tired to understand half-spoken myths.

"Its purpose was for him to see each time you'd be strong enough to strike him, to cause his reign to crumble. In his mind, he thought if he could see when you were coming, he could cause you to fail."

"I'm not coming for him. I wouldn't even know he existed if it weren't for Drake coming after me with the Blue Moon. Why would I chase a devil?"

"You're seeing this from the moment you're in now. Try to imagine a grand scheme stretching across a multitude of lifetimes. In reality, a million different circumstances could have led you there on that night. The point is there are ten moments in this lifetime that you will be strong enough to bring the devil to his knees. These moments are reflected by the universe above – eight planets beyond the sun and moon will be your power to come full circle and defeat the dark ruler," she answered.

"Can you see the moments? Can you tell me when the next one will be?" I asked with pleading eyes, shaking in fear of what was to come.

Landen came to my side and tried to push peace into my body. The numbing feeling was chasing away my fears, but I still trembled.

Perodine fought back tears before turning to walk back to the table to look at the scroll. "Each moment was traced by the stargazers of that time and recorded here. Some will be easily seen, like the Blue Moon; others will be more obscure. The only thing I know for sure is that the influences will come in order of the orbit. To find the time, we'll have to watch the skies above and the prediction of the scroll. When they match, we'll know that the trial is upon us."

As we all felt the weight of helplessness, the room grew still – and at that moment, I wasn't sure that I wanted to know. It was like having someone tell you that your life would end on this day at this time…who would want to know that?

August leaned closer to the scrolls and began to study them more ambitiously than ever before.

"The skies almost completely match what the scroll reflects around Venus. Now, to make you as strong as possible, we must find out how he plans to defeat you, understand what you'll face so you'll be prepared physically and mentally for anything he can use against you," Perodine said, pulling her notepad closer to her.

"Have you found any answers so far?" Marc asked.

Perodine took in a deep breath as she read her notes over. "We're pulling out the symbols now. Landen, have you tried to heal anyone on your own?" she asked.

"Pelhan just taught me. Does it say that there?" he asked her.

"We think this symbol of a fish and a hand means a Pisces healer. We just didn't know if it was you or Drake," Perodine answered.

I felt the tension rise in the room. It was exhausting me. "*I need to sit down,*" I thought.

"*Are you alright?*" Landen thought.

"*Just tired,*" I thought as I slowly walked around the couch in front of the fireplace and fell into it. Dane took a seat on the opposite couch and protectively watched my every breath.

"So who are we fighting here – Drake, Donalt, or both?" Marc asked.

"I don't know," Perodine answered, still puzzled. As I gazed at the raging flames in the fireplace, Drake's perfect image surfaced in my mind; all I could see was the pain I left in his eyes.

"Tell me about what Venus will bring, the characteristics. Is it not the planet of love?" Landen asked.

Silence filled the room and the tension continued to climb. I could feel August and Perodine struggling with the emotions they feared the worst, but they didn't want to show them to us.

"Just say it," Landen said in a low tone.

I heard August clear his throat before he began to speak. "Well, yes, it does influence love – most of the time. But Venus is entering retrograde in the sign of Scorpio," he said.

"Go on," Landen said.

I turned in my seat to see them behind me. Marc and Landen had their arms crossed. Perodine and August were staring at each other as if they were trying to give one another some kind of hidden communication. Perodine looked past them at me, then back to Landen. "Your decisions will be made with a clarity that does not know the emotion of guilt. There will be nothing that can be held back. Every truth that can be told will be. Past relations will surface," she said.

"What do you mean? Relationships in past lives? We already had to deal with that," Landen argued.

"Son, that is not the part we're worried about," August said, sighing deeply. "You've had the privilege of making decisions with your heart. The heart often has no clear reason. This time, Venus will influence you to make a rational decision based on what you see – not what you feel. Throughout history, it has been known as the heartless, the opposite of the love Venus normally gives us," August said.

Landen looked back at me, then to August. "Does this affect only me and Willow, or all of you?" he asked.

"Everyone," Perodine answered. "We must realize that now, because as the hours move forward and truths are revealed, we have to hinder our anger. This darkness feeds off the negative – and right now it's being fueled by the workers on the other side of that wall."

"What truths? Willow and I have held nothing back, have we?" Landen asked, confused.

"If you remove the emotion of love and look at things from a rational point of view, you will find a truth that has escaped you before," Perodine answered.

"Why did you think Drake was a healer? Is he not on the same side as Donalt?" Marc asked, trying to comprehend what he was hearing.

August looked at Marc and a sense of grief came over him. He understood Marc's anger, but he wanted him to move past it, to see Drake as the brother he was to Marc – not the enemy.

"For all we know, Drake is just an innocent bystander – someone Donalt planned all along to use as a vessel. His and Landen's charts are weaved so closely together, you can barely see the defining line; at this moment, I fear his life is the one in danger – not Landen's," August said, looking down, prepared to block himself from the arguments he thought would come his way.

August believed what he said. As Landen heard the truth in his words I felt the emotion of grief and sorrow fill him. I was too tired to try and understand if the sorrow was for August or Drake. Instead, I turned forward and resumed my stare at the raging flames in the fireplace.

"Does that say nineteen?" I heard Marc ask.

"Nineteen is represented all over Venus," August said.

"It's Willow's nineteenth birthday," Landen said.

"It's more than that. The symbol of the hand and fish also has nineteen embedded in it," August answered.

I heard the shuffling of papers, then felt an astonishment coming from Perodine. I turned in my seat and watched her recording symbols from my birth chart and the scroll we'd brought.

"What is it?" Landen asked.

"Willow was born in the nineteenth second, hour, and minute, on the nineteenth day," Perodine answered.

"Yes, and this is her nineteenth year," August said.

"That may be the time we will face the climax of Venus, the window Donalt will use. The universe is a sea of perfect numbers. Donalt would had to have found a way to weave himself into the equation, into the place of Landen or Drake. If this is right, he will have the chance on Willow's birthday, the nineteenth hour, minute, second," Perodine answered.

I felt August's fear. "A number that can only be divided by one and itself," August whispered.

"What are you saying – Donalt is going to try and become me?" Landen asked, feeling just as scared and confused as I was.

"Maybe…maybe you, maybe Drake, but one of you," Perodine said, leaning in to look closer at the scroll. Landen felt my uneasiness and came to sit by my side. I curled up in his arms and watched the fire.

"How close do I need to be to him?" I heard Marc ask.

"You're in the room. That should be enough," Perodine answered.

"If I can shield Willow and me, what can they do – add to it?" Landen asked, moving us sideways so he could see the table behind him.

Perodine looked up. "Water is powerful. If he moves through their energy, he will grow weaker – and if I know him, he will wait for the nineteenth hour to use his force. They will not be able to protect you from that moment – but they should keep you safe until then," Perodine said, looking to the shadows of the room.

"So in theory, any water sign would be able to protect us?" Landen asked. I knew he was looking for clarity that leaving Olivia behind was the right decision to make.

"Yes, but the ones who have been at your side your entire lives are old souls who have lived before, fought at your side," Perodine clarified.

I looked over my shoulder at Dane. He was so calm. If I were him I'd be nervous – and it wouldn't matter if I'd been here before in another life. I turned back and looked up at Landen. Perodine's answer didn't give him any peace. I laid my head against his chest then closed my eyes and let the memory of my family come to me. I was ready for this to be over…for me to be home again.

"Landen," I heard Dane say. Feeling Landen's lips on my forehead, I opened my eyes and looked at him.

"Come on, we'll find a place to rest," he thought as he stood and pulled me up with him.

While Dane stretched out on the couch he was sitting on, Marc continued to try and help August and Perodine. Landen and I walked to the doorway next to the fireplace; as we walked down the hall, he peeked in the first two doorways before deciding to enter the third. The room was vast: a full sitting room was on one side, a large bed with a canopy was to the other. Windows made up the back wall with beautiful ivory drapes framing them. In the distance, I could hear the workers building the wall. It was a dim reminder that we had more to worry about than Donalt. Before long, a war would erupt and the newfound innocence of Delen would be lost.

I walked to the bed and slid off my shoes. Landen followed. Once by my side, he hooked his arm around my waist and pulled me to him so our eyes were just inches apart. He then reached up and gently outlined the frame of my cheek. His touch sent a peace through me that froze time and took away all my worries. We drifted and awoke next to our bodies.

Landen let his hand rest inside of mine. We knew that was as far as we could go here. I focused on the sensation there and let my thoughts leave me for the moment.

As the sun rose hours later, we woke and lay in silence for a while. We could feel the determination coming from Perodine and the peace of sleep coming from August, Marc, and Dane. We were sure Perodine was still devouring the information on the scroll. If she were right, then tomorrow at seven nineteen we would face Donalt. When we faced the moon and Mercury I remembered wishing that time would freeze, that I'd be able just to live in the bliss of Landen's love, but this time was different. We were away from our family and they were making sacrifices to keep us safe. I would never want anyone to be frozen the way we were now. I just wanted it over.

"What are you thinking?" I asked Landen.

He rolled on his side so he could see into my eyes. *"That this will be over before we know it and we'll be home in Chara with the ones we love the most,"* he thought.

"How can you be so confident?" I asked, tracing his eyes.

He smiled. *"I don't mean to be, at least not in a bad way. I don't want to do any of this, but I have to realize that we managed to bring back your friend's sight and hearing – that just a week ago, we relieved this city from the torment that they'd been under for millions of years...I just think we've come too far to lose now...we've been tested and we've passed."*

I sighed and nodded. He was right; it was hard to think that there was anything that was impossible. I looked to the dark shadows of the room, then back to Landen.

"I don't see how him consuming you will bring him power. I cannot – I will not – live without your soul on this earth," I thought. As tears came to the corners of my eyes, he pulled me closer and we both felt a grief – a grief we had to suppress before it consumed us both.

"I don't care what his plan is. He will not take me from you – I promise," Landen thought.

I knew he believed what he said and I took shelter behind his words. When he kissed my forehead and rose, I knew his intent was to find our bags and shower for the day. I lay in the bed and looked to the window. The sound of the workers building throughout the night had never halted. The wall was close to three feet high now and from where I lay it looked like it almost completely surrounded Delen. I could feel the sadness from a majority of the people in Delen. They weren't sad that they were being built in, they were sad that the rest of the world was still held by a darkness, a darkness that made them forget who they were. I shared in their sadness. It just didn't make any sense to suffer when there was so much life to live.

Landen came back into the room, with our bags, then

took out his clothes and made his way to the doorway next to our bed.

Chapter Four

While I waited for my turn to shower, I daydreamed that I was home, celebrating the passing of another year, hearing the stories of every minute of mother's labor, what she thought, how happy she was to have me as her own. I barely noticed when Landen opened the door, now fully clothed in his black slacks and button down black shirt. Though I'd grown weary of the all black attire months ago, I couldn't help but love the way his dark locks of hair and crystal blue eyes complemented the shade.

"I'll wait for you," he said, pulling back my covers. "I want to explore today," he said, handing me my bag.

I smiled and shook my head. I didn't really care to. It was too eerie. Even with every light burning on a sunny day, the shadows seemed to dominate the rooms.

The bathroom was very stunning. The tub, sinks, and shower were all made of beautiful marble. Three of the walls had mirrors that centered them and they were framed with drapes. I tilted my head, questioning why they would do that. I mean, it looked good, but it just didn't make any sense. I turned the water in the shower on as hot as it would go then pulled out everything I needed before undressing.

As the water came over me, I felt a numbing calm ease through me. I turned so the heat of the water would surround every part of my body. Then, suddenly my ring and necklace began to burn my skin. I turned the water down, but the heat in the metal intensified. I felt a rush of wind then the water that was falling all around me turned to blood. I could smell it. I felt it coursing over me. I screamed as loud as I could and charged out of the shower, noticing that the mirrors didn't reflect me. Instead, they showed Chara, my home, immersed in fire.

Landen busted through the door. "Willow – what? What's wrong?!"

"BLOOD! BLOOD! It's all over me!" I screamed, jumping in place and crying breathlessly.

"There is no blood Willow...Willow, look at me... there is no blood!" Landen yelled back at me, wrapping a large towel around me.

I opened my eyes and looked down; I was just wet; I looked in the shower: the water had no trace of blood. My eyes rushed back and forth. My heart pounded in my chest. I shook my head from side-to-side, then I looked to the mirror -- I could still see Chara burning...I could even feel the heat from the flames. Landen's eyes followed mine then I felt the horror come from him as well. People were rushing in every direction. We saw Libby. She was running with the crowd. She saw us and reached for us Landen didn't hesitate. He reached for her and I watched as her arm came from the mirror and Landen grasped it.

At that moment, Perodine charged in the door. "NO!" she yelled at us. "It's an illusion!" she said, pulling the drapes on all the mirrors.

"I can feel her," Landen screamed, pulling Libby to us.

"Marc! Dane!" Perodine screamed.

I looked into Libby's eyes I could see the fear and terror that I felt from her. I began to help Landen pull her by grabbing her other arm.

"It's an illusion!" Perodine yelled again.

Dane and Marc crashed into the door and the little girl we were pulling – the one we thought was Libby – turned demonic and began to pull us to her. Dane wrapped his arms around my waist, Marc did the same to Landen. It took all of their force to pull us free. We landed in a pile on the floor. With haste Perodine tied the drapes that surrounded the mirror closed.

I fell apart. I couldn't be strong anymore. I cried breathlessly, gripping my towel against my chest, trying to understand how, why. I pulled my knees to me and buried my head, trying to block the horror I'd just seen. Landen pulled himself free from Marc, scooped me up in his arms and rocked me back and forth.

A roar filled the room, then we heard breaking glass on the other side of the drapes. In a whisper, we heard Libby's voice say, "You left me," over and over again. Landen gripped me tighter, feeling the pain of the words.

"Come, let's leave this room," Perodine said, walking calmly to the door.

Landen picked me up and Dane grabbed my things. In the room where we'd slept, Marc and Dane turned, allowing me to dress. My hands trembled as I pulled my clothes together, so Perodine calmly helped Landen dress me. When I pulled my shirt over my head, I squinted with pain. The necklace had burned itself into my skin.

"Let me see," Landen said, examining my neck.

He gently pulled my hand away to see what was hurting me. It looked like they'd melted into my skin. Blood seeped from the sides of the metal. I closed my eyes and looked away, blocking out the thought of the pain. I felt Landen's hand on my chest, bringing with it a warm rush of energy, calming and peaceful. He reached for my hand and the rush intensified. I opened my eyes to see him staring at me. His eyes glowed as the healing energy left him. I looked down and saw that my wounds were gone. He'd healed me on his own. He wrapped his arms around me and held me as tight as he could.

"Look at me and tell me it was an illusion, that they're safe," I heard Landen say.

"It was an illusion. They're safe," Perodine repeated, we both heard the truth in her words.

I let go of Landen, then pulled my jeans up and put on my shoes. A shiver ran down my back as the smell of the blood came to my memory. Landen's hand was on my shoulder as soon as he felt the emotion. "I'll be fine. Don't use all of your energy," I whispered.

"We need to cover all the mirrors in the palace. We need help," Perodine said, walking to the door that led back to room where they'd been working. When I focused, I could feel someone beyond August in there. I assumed it was the woman that had been shadowing Perodine since her return.

Marc and Dane peeked to make sure I was dressed. When they saw that I was, they walked closer.

"What happened?" Dane asked, looking over me carefully.

"A cruel illusion," Landen said, wrapping his arm around my shoulder and guiding me to the study.

When we entered the large study, we saw August sleeping soundly on one of the couches. He had one of the books we'd brought open across his chest. Perodine was whispering to the young woman, she glanced up at us as we entered the room. "She's going to ask the old staff to return and help us cover them all. It will take us a week if we try to do it on our own," Perodine said, nodding for the silent girl to go.

I felt a rush of fear and looked to August. It was coming from him. He sat up straight, focused his eyes then stood. "We have to cover the paintings," he said into the room.

"You mean the mirrors," Perodine corrected.

"That, too, yes – but the paintings, the paintings must be covered," August said, walking to one of the walls to turn the portraits.

"Where did you read that?" Perodine asked, walking to the table to look at the scroll.

"I didn't read it. I dreamed of Nyla. She said that Libby and Preston told her to tell me to cover the paintings," he said, turning the next painting. Marc and Dane began to help him.

"Were they OK?" I asked in a shaky voice.

August hesitated when he heard me, then looked in my direction and nodded yes. "Are you?" he asked. I shook my head no and gripped Landen tighter. August looked at Landen for an explanation.

"We've already seen the worst illusion imaginable," Landen answered.

I felt a shock come from Perodine. "They are right.

How did I not see that? Venus rules art; he can use that as a passage...Willow do not sketch anything," she said, still looking down at the scroll.

"I think you need to rest," Landen said to Perodine.

She shook her head no. "I stopped sleeping a million years ago – I am not going to start now," she answered, reaching for a pen to write down something she'd found.

I think that was the first time that I put into perspective just how long she'd lived in that form. I felt sorry for her. How awful it must be to stand still in time. I heard breaking glass and jumped, then turned to see that Marc had covered a mirror.

"They will all break when you cover them. It means you blocked him," Perodine said, not looking up from the scroll.

In the doorway, I felt the familiar emotion of Patrick and I turned to look at him. I could sense he was eager to help. "Ma'am, Sir, we are going to start with the floors below ground while it's daylight. I have close to a hundred people helping me," he said to us.

"The paintings have to be covered, too," Landen said to Patrick.

Patrick nodded and left the room. The young woman came into the room behind him with another girl, pushing a cart of food. They left it in the center of the room and nodded in our direction before they left.

"All of you need to eat. Each hour will grow more difficult. You need your strength," Perodine warned.

Dane and Marc didn't hesitate. They made their way to the cart and began to fix themselves a plate. Landen and I stood frozen. We weren't sure where to start. It was hard to imagine how many mirrors and paintings were in the enormous palace.

"Eat, Willow," Perodine said in a firm voice.

I shook my head in defiance. Dane nudged my shoulder then handed me an apple. I looked at him as if he were insane. "You'll be able to think more clearly if you have your strength," he whispered. I sighed and took the food from him.

Landen released me and went to the cart to find himself some food. August went to the table to look over what Perodine had found while he rested. "Have you disproven it yet?" August asked.

"Disproven what?" Landen asked over his shoulder as he fixed himself a plate.

Perodine looked at August and nodded, telling him to explain their discovery to us. "Have I ever told you of the pentagonal synodic series?" August asked, looking from Landen to Marc. They both shook their head no. "Come," August said, gesturing for us all to come closer. He turned his notebook to a blank page and we all encircled the table and leaned in to watch what he was drawing.

"Alright, here's the sun," August said, dotting the center of the page. "Here's Venus," he said, putting a dot parallel to the one in the center. "And here's earth," he said, putting the third dot parallel to the second. "This is what it looks like when the earth aligns with its sister planet, Venus. Now, Venus moves faster than earth. To align, it has to orbit the sun two point six times in the same time the earth will orbit one point six. In our solar system, this alignment will occur five times – seven signs between each." August drew a large circle to represent the solar system, then he began to draw the dots for Venus and Earth throughout their next alignments; as he connected the lines, I felt my stomach drop: he was drawing a perfect pentagon. I was beginning to hate stars. They'd brought me nothing but trouble through all of this.

"The pattern of a star in the sky – a few weeks ago, everyone was telling me a star in a looking glass," Landen said, frustrated.

I reached for the charm on my neck. Landen had placed the star behind the sun and moon just a few days ago. We had thought that the supremacy of man was behind the power of the universe – God – that is where it belonged. In my memory, I saw the rings of the looking glass falling apart. That victory was starting to look insignificant now. Perodine's eyes were on me, on my charm. I felt a grief in her, a sorrow for a life I couldn't remember.

"I cannot undo what was once said," she said in low tone, looking from the charm to my eyes.

"What did you say?" I asked in a voice that reflected the terror I was feeling.

Perodine looked around the room to Landen, then to me. "I did not understand what was happening to Donalt. Without his knowledge, I witnessed rituals, the priest with candles, snakes, speaking in tongues – I saw the upside down pentagrams drawn in chalk as he stood in the center. I assumed he was calling on dark magic to grow his power that he wanted to rule beyond our world, to bring a devastation that would blind us all. I had no choice but to counteract their words. I studied rituals from ancient times and spoke the words that limited his power. I wanted your innocent heart to restore our world. To anyone else, that is a simple charm, a sun, moon, and star – but to us, because Donalt and I believe it has power, because you believe it has power – it does."

"Are you saying that it's what I want it to be? I don't understand," I said, staring back at her.

"That would have been true in your first life. Now, after so many, you have given it a power that is more that all of us could imagine," Perodine said.

"How?"

"When you lost your friend," she looked at Marc, "when you lost your father," she looked back to me, "you grieved, you felt emptiness. What you do not realize is that you were grieving the absence of their energy. When you love someone, have them in your life, their energy becomes a part of you. It builds you. When they leave you, they take their energy with them. We feel a void, a loss. You believed that charm had a power in your first life. When you were taken into the string and found your world, your belief grew stronger. You left that life believing that it held an unimaginable power. In each life, you found it again and as you studied its history, heard the stories of what it could do, your belief grew stronger. All of the thoughts you had of love and redemption grew more intense with each life. Your signature, your energy, the love you and Landen have for each other and the universe around you was left in that charm. You have protected yourself from what lies ahead. You just have to trust the decisions you made then and now."

"This charm's power is me? My energy from before?" I asked.

She nodded. "Every woman you were is there," she said, glancing to my charm. "It is a part of this because you wanted it to be. It has always made you feel safe. If you ever surrender, you will not do it alone. Every woman that you have been will surrender as well," Perodine warned.

"An army of Scorpios," Marc said under his breath.

"So there's no connection between the star behind that charm and the pattern you're drawing?" Landen asked

Perodine shook her head no and looked at August for

help. He cleared his throat. "When Venus lies between the Earth and the sun, it is called an inferior conjunction. When an inferior conjunction is about to begin, Venus moves into what appears to be retrograde. A new pentagonal cycle will begin soon. Willow's first birth happened at a moment like this. It symbolized that she would be a power. If Donalt wanted to take her power, he could do so at this juncture," August said.

"So, you have a new time – what happened to the nineteenth?" I ask, flustered.

"Not a new time – a deeper connection, a clearer insight to the way this trial is orchestrated," Perodine said, looking down at August's sketch. "Many people throughout history have gained power at the synodic point. It was at that point that Jayda overtook the Darkness," Perodine said confidently.

"You're confident because I'm a descendant of Jayda," Landen said.

"Not as confident as I would like to be," Perodine said, pulling the scroll to her. "You see, these symbols are the same as the ones in the book of Samilya and Jayda. It seems that they are one of the ones who you sought council on with your original birth charts. On the last page of Jayda's book, it said that Jayda and Oba disappeared into a white glow late in their years, taking the scrolls with them. Their people believed that the couple was so great that death took mercy on them – taking them as a whole, body and soul," Perodine said.

"Now," August picked up from where Perodine left off, "we can reason that when Jayda released Oba from the darkness, they realized that there was something bigger than them. We read that they found deep mediation. I would guess that they – well the two of you – discovered who you were and began to try and unravel these charts. Pelhan himself said that the two of you found your final resting place in his dimension. I know for a fact that you found your way to Chara in my lifetime."

"So history repeats itself," I said, almost to myself.

"Unfortunately, never in the exact same way," Perodine said. "When you face an enemy, you learn their weakness first-hand. Whatever you learned then, you have forgotten. I assure you that he – it – has not forgotten yours."

"Well, was it recorded in detail here?" Marc said, reaching for Jayda's book.

"Nothing more than Jayda seeing Oba for the first time. It says here 'the past will not mirror itself. It shall consume the blood of Jayda and subdue the power,'" Perodine said, running her finger across three words written in a script I'd never seen before.

"A warning," Landen whispered.

August nodded. "We think it means that the darkness will consume either you or Drake then subdue Willow's heart," Perodine said, looking at Landen.

"Drake?" I questioned.

"He, too, is a descendant of Jayda – and is most definitely weaved into this fate," August said in a heavy tone.

It always escaped me that Drake was a part of Landen's family, that through their veins the same blood coursed.

"So it's Drake we're fighting," Marc said through his teeth.

"Marc," Landen said in a low tone.

"No, I'm right: the darkness is going to consume Drake, then fight for Willow's heart. Drake, with the darkness inside of him – would that make him stronger?" Marc said, looking back and forth between Perodine and August.

"Do you understand what the darkness is? What the purpose of Allie, Preston, and Libby is?" Perodine asked in an astonished tone.

"No. We don't." Landen said shortly.

Perodine looked from the sketch to Landen. I could feel her sympathy. She nodded and sighed. "This world, overall, has forgotten what they were made of, forgotten their power. We live in ignorance – a hell. If we were to learn and practice unconditional love on all levels then we as a planet would be connected to a higher plane, a celestial plane of knowing. Once we have reached that point, we will never return to the ignorance that bore us. You can imagine the glow the planet would reveal if each of us found that place," Perodine said. She paused and looked to the shadows then back to the scroll. "Light is the death of darkness. It is said that the darkness, the ignorance that we live in will fight for its existence. The children will bring the light. The darkness will fight to stop them. Right now, at this crucial point, you are their only line of defense – the darkness must defeat you before it can reach the ones that will bring its death," Perodine explained all too coolly.

"It's evil, fighting for its right to live," August added.

"This evil will dwindle itself inside a human body. It is a sacrifice it must make to keep the veil over all of our eyes," Perodine said.

"What do you mean 'dwindle'?" Dane asked.

"This evil is the opposite of the light. It opposes – but it is capable of – immense power, more than one body can possess. When it enters the body, it will be at its weakest point. Over time, the body will build a tolerance – and then an immorality will set in," Perodine answered.

"So we can't defeat it in the form it's in now?" Landen

asked.

"No more than you could outrun your own shadow," Perodine replied.

"I haven't heard a reason to be confident yet," I said, leaning closer to Landen and avoiding eye contact with everyone.

"Well, that depends on the body it chooses to consume – and if we find the weapon we need," Perodine said.

"What weapon?" Landen asked, wrapping his arm around me.

"There is a symbol that represents a weapon that's meant to bring harm to Donalt in the flesh – strong enough to defeat the spirit of the darkness as well," August answered.

"I'm almost certain it is the knife that cut the cord on Willow's first birth," Perodine said.

"How do you know?" Landen asked.

"Everything from conception to birth was planned perfectly. I only ate certain foods, wore certain clothes. At her birth we used the strongest, most beautiful stone, shaped into a blade – a blade made of diamonds. The handle was molded from a small meteor that crashed into the earth. It is the blade that separated us," Perodine answered.

"Does it show it here?" Marc questioned.

"No, but it says here that what was once coal will divide innocence from sin," Perodine answered.

"Do you know where the knife is?" Landen asked.

Perodine looked down and shook her head no. "I have searched for it for over four million years as well," she said bleakly.

"Which room was I born in? Maybe it's hidden in the walls or paintings?" I asked.

Perodine looked at me, then around the room. "Right

where you are standing, this has always been my personal parlor. My pregnancy was kept secret from everyone. I did not leave these two rooms for eight months. After your first breaths, I carried you to the water in the observatory and let the reflection of the stars bathe over you, giving you the strength and power you needed to stay alive, protected," Perodine said in a shaky voice.

I was almost certain she was holding something back from us, but it seemed foolish to push her any further at the moment.

"Which language does it say we need a weapon in?" Landen questioned, leaning forward.

"Here," Perodine said as she pointed to a Scorpion in the center of my chart. "Written in the symbols of Analess, next to Aliyanna's birth time, you see Jayda's name and blood and below that you see Willow's birthday," Perodine said.

"Aliyanna, Jayda, and Willow," August said. "And here it says that the three will be strong as the darkness overtakes the blood."

"I've already had enough of blood," I said in a low tone.

Silence filled the room. I could feel the swarm of emotions: anxieties, fears, tension, and remorse. It was almost too much to bear.

"I think we should send for Drake," August said into the room. We all looked at him as if he was a fool. "If his life is at risk, he deserves to know. If he's consumed, his life will be over," he explained.

"I assure you, Alamos watches the stars very closely on Drake's behalf. I would even say that they knew this day was coming," Perodine said as resentment rose in her.

"Listen to me, this darkness feeds on negativity. It's

counting on us being divided. It would be best if we all focused our anger in one direction," August said.

"I don't think we need the added stress of having him here," Landen said under his breath, pulling me closer to him.

August shook his head from side to side. We could feel his disappointment in us. It hurt us, but we couldn't help being human. Drake had been a source of turmoil – but according to all of this, he wasn't even the bad guy. Landen's reasoning was that everything that he'd done to us – the nightmares, taking my friends, Livingston's life and me just a few days ago – was done for Drake's own selfish reasons, for him to have the power of my heart – the power to rule.

"Promise me if he comes to you, you'll listen and work together. Both of you loving Willow may be the one thing that saves all of your lives," August said, looking at Landen.

Landen kissed the top of my head and wrapped his arms as tight as he could around me. I felt an anger rise inside of Marc and Dane. They couldn't believe August's request.

"I will *not* seek him – and I can't tell you what I'll do if he comes to us. I can only promise you that I'll make the decisions that I feel will keep Willow safe," Landen said.

August looked down at the table and nodded. He then tore the drawing that he'd made into shreds and began to arrange the birth charts and the books of Jayda and Samilya so he could study them for a deeper understanding.

Perodine moved her chair closer to August. "I would die in peace if we could just find a way for me to kill the evil bastard for you," she said under her breath.

Suddenly, a violent force pushed through the room, moving the couch in front of the fireplace, then plowing into Perodine – knocking her into the wall behind her. I screamed as I watched her body fly across the room. Marc and Dane ran to the large painting of Perodine that hung over the fireplace and pulled it down – breaking it into pieces and throwing it into the fire. Landen, August, and I then rushed to Perodine. The force had caused her to lose consciousness. Blood was pouring from the back of her head. I could feel a terror inside of her as she fought against submitting to the pain.

"Do something, Landen!" I screamed, pulling her body onto my lap.

Landen's hands were already on the back of her head. I watched as he focused his energy. A white glow came from beneath his hands. The blood vanished instantly. Perodine's eyes opened and she looked up at me and reached to wipe away the tears that were washing down my face. Landen focused his energy around me and Perodine shielding us from another blow. Marc and Dane were pulling every painting off the walls and throwing them into the fire. Suddenly, a roar filled the room and the glass windows shook from the sheer force.

"That's right, you bastard!" Perodine said, sitting up. "Waste your energy – we will send you back to hell where you belong!" she yelled into the room.

The table where the scrolls and books were sitting began to burn. As August rushed to protect them, he stopped when he reached the table.

"Grab them!" yelled Landen, helping me pull Perodine up.

"They're not burning – only the table," August said in an astonished tone.

The fire on the table dwindled and the smoke faded, taking the evidence of rage with it.

"I protected those scrolls long ago and last night I protected the books of Jayda and Samilya. He cannot destroy them," Perodine said, moving out of the shield that Landen had put around her.

"I don't think it's wise to mock him – it – whatever it is," Dane said as he walked over to me, satisfied that they'd burned every painting. Marc was starting to throw in pillows that had artwork stitched into them. He was determined to burn anything that even resembled an image.

"I'm not mocking him. I was just making sure we were right. He could be out causing torment and breeding anger, but instead he is lingering here. We are getting closer to the truth that will defeat him," Perodine said as she adjusted her ponytail and rolled her sleeves up farther.

"Landen, I think we need to start on this floor. We need to cover whatever passage he might have," Marc said, walking to Landen's side.

Landen nodded then pulled me to his side. As he walked past Perodine, he glanced over her to make sure she was healed.

"Are you staying with her?" he asked August.

"Yes. There's more that needs to be understood. Do not leave this floor," August said, running his hands through his hair.

Landen nodded and took my hand. As we followed Marc to the hallway, I tried to stop my body from trembling. I'd seen things that most others hadn't, but I'd never felt a force like that before. I felt defeated already. Landen pushed a peace through I glanced up at him and tried to hide my worries from him. He pulled my hand to his lips and kissed it gently. I smiled and breathed out. We looked at the long hall ahead of us, as well as the massive number of paintings. The doorways only led to more rooms, more paintings. The task of turning them all was beyond over-whelming.

Chapter Five

The four of us began to turn the paintings in the hallway. When we reached a room, we'd all enter and cover every mirror, then turn every painting. For the first hour, no one really said anything; we just worked aimlessly. It felt like we were plugging holes in a sinking ship. As Dane and Landen covered a mirror that was over six feet high, the breaking glass made us all jump.

"This is insane," Dane said, looking at Landen. "Do the two of you understand any of this?" he asked, moving on to another painting.

"I understand that we must unravel a broken message from our ancestors to find a way through Venus," Landen said, turning on the fireplace so he could toss in the pillows and throws that had artwork on them.

"I think that's where they lost me," Marc said, making a pile for Landen to destroy.

"Yeah, me, too," Dane said.

Landen looked up at them. "I'd think that all of you would understand that we've lived before," he answered.

"Yeah, I got that part," Dane said. "But you're a descendent of Jayda, right?" he asked. Landen nodded. "OK," Dane said, leaning in the doorway and waiting for us to finish burning the pillows. "But they're saying that Willow was Jayda back then."

I was handing Landen a pillow, but I froze when I heard Dane's response. Landen looked at Marc, then back to Dane. "Do you know that you were always a girl – always a boy – I mean, which one of you was Jayda?" Dane asked.

Marc threw the last pillow in the fire. "We're always in the same sun. We always have the same sex," he said, looking around the room to make sure we hadn't forgotten anything.

"How are you so sure?" Landen asked knowing Marc believed what he was saying.

"Well, I asked my father that day you took us to see him. I wanted to know everything about dying. I wanted to make sure he was not going to come back as a chicken or something," Marc said, almost amused by his words. "And that was the answer he gave me."

"When I first met her, Aora told me we always stay in the same sun," I added.

"I think Willow was Jayda and Landen was the ruler – and over time, through all the generations, Landen just happened to be born on Jayda's side and Willow on Samilya's," Marc said.

"Then what are you confused about? You seem to have

a better understanding than we do," Landen questioned Marc.

"I just think they're missing something. They're mixing Aliyanna, Jayda, and Willow," he said, looking at my charm. "I'm sure you've lived more than three times. There are at least four languages on that scroll. Last night, August admitted that there could be more – that some of the languages are so close, it's hard to distinguish them." Marc crossed his arms and stared at Landen then continued, "We just can't afford for them to have something wrong. Did you feel that power that knocked her across the room? I mean, it just moved above me and Dane and it almost knocked us down...this isn't a game of who gets the girl... it's bigger than that...bigger than we can *ever* imagine."

Dane was nodding along with Marc. They weren't afraid. They were resentful. They hated that we had to weave through Pelhan's slow lessons and Perodine's allusive truths.

"Right now, I'd rather unravel half truths than sit around and wait for the unknown," Landen said, putting his hand on my back and guiding me out of the room.

We all made our way back to the hallway. When we'd reached the point where it ended, we stood across a banister. Now that it was daylight, we could see out of the large windows. The workers along the wall were missing, but we could see them in the distance, gathered in large groups.

"They're anxious," Landen said, focusing on them.

"Well, as long as they're not angry, that's good – I suppose," I said.

Landen nodded in agreement. I envied that he could feel them all. I hated and loved that I had a barrier to almost half of this dimension. I loved the fact that I wouldn't be tormented by the depths of their darkness, but I hated that

Landen had to feel it. I couldn't even feel them through him; he had to bear it on his own. We'd had deep discussions on the matter over the past few days as we helped restore Delen. I'd ask countless times for him to tell me what the workers were feeling. I thought that if I knew, I could find a way to break through to them – to release them. Landen, though, seemed content with my barrier. He felt it was protecting me.

"Maybe the two of you should give a speech of something," Dane said.

"What are they going to say?" Marc argued. "Um… there's a devil that's trying to overtake us, so we have to take a break from defending you against the rest of the world – but don't worry, we have these books and this scroll…it'll be fine," he mocked.

"No," Dane said as he rolled his eyes at Marc. "But I think they're more than aware that our family didn't show up today and that the two of you are in here," Dane said shortly.

Landen reached for Marc's shoulder and I reached for Dane's arm. They were letting the pressure get to them and we wanted them to feel calm. They each let out a deep breath with our touch.

"Save that," Marc said. "I can see that your Aura is dimming," he warned.

Landen nodded and let go of Marc, then looked at Dane.

"I understand what you're saying, Dane – but we don't want to do anything that will give the people of Delen the impression that we're going to rule over them. And, if we told them what we were facing, the darkness would feed off their fear. We have just over thirty hours before this will all be over. We need them all to be calm," Landen explained.

Dane nodded, understanding Landen's point of view. We walked to where the hallway began and resumed the task of turning the paintings. The doorways led to small rooms with only simple beds and tables inside them; we assumed we were in a servant's wing. We felt like we were making faster progress. As the hallway expanded, the paintings grew larger. Little nooks led to short hallways with only sitting rooms in them. We were growing braver so we separated to gain more ground faster.

I wandered to the doorway on the left, where I could see small frames lining the walls. I looked back and saw Landen and Marc turning a large painting. Dane was covering the mirrors. The breaking of glass still made me jump. At the end of the hall was a bay window. The light from it and the dim lamps was the only light in the nook. I took in a deep breath and started turning the small paintings, deciding to walk down one way, then up the other.

I'd made it to the middle of the hall when I came across a painting too large for me to turn on my own. It was of who I assumed was Donalt in his younger years. He was sitting a golden chair. The back of it raised two feet above his head. The look in his eyes was surprisingly warm. I know from my own work that you can't paint what you can't see. It seemed Perodine was right: at least one time in Donalt's life, he had the warmth of a soul shining through his eyes. It was sad to think that it was possible for us to forget how to love one another.

Out of nowhere, a gust of wind blew my hair, the doors to the hall slammed shut and the dim lights fluttered with the vibration. I froze and let my eyes search over the shadows in the hall, then held my breath when a man's figure began to emerge. When the light came across his face, I saw that it was Drake. A sense of relief came over me because I knew he wouldn't hurt me, but my eyes questioned why he was there. As he stepped closer, I could see that he was hurt. There was a slash across the side of his neck. I looked from the wound to his eyes, which stared blankly at me. His face held no emotion. His eyes were cold.

In one swift step he reached for me and when his skin touched mine I felt paralyzed. His mesmerizing touch was stronger that it had ever been – so powerful that I could barely breathe. He pushed my back against the painting I was standing in front of. I fell limp in his arms as his hands slowly moved across my body. I wanted to stop him, to push him away, but I couldn't find the strength to move. My heart thundered with the terror that had seized my emotions. He leaned in and began to move his lips across my neck. I managed only the strength to whisper, "Drake, you're scaring me."

His lips hesitated. He leaned back, then looked at me like it was the first time he noticed me. I watched him try to focus on where he was, then he stepped back – releasing me. I watched his whole body tense then he fell to his knees and screamed a horrible roar. Suddenly, from deep within him – from his eyes, mouth, and ears – I saw darkness leave. It rushed to the shadows, vanishing from sight. Drake fell forward, coughing and spitting on the ground. The large doors then banged open. Landen, Dane, and Marc rushed toward me. I could feel August's urgency to find us in the distance. He must have heard the commotion.

"What are you doing here?" Dane yelled at Drake, who was trying to stand.

Landen wrapped his arms around me and tried to get me to look at him, but I was still, frozen in place. *"What did he do? Tell me,"* he thought.

"It wasn't him. Whatever it was is in the shadows," I

thought, replaying the image in my mind.

"You're bleeding, Willow," Landen thought as he frantically looked over me.

"No, it's him."

Drake stood just as August came to the hallway. He stared at me in absolute disbelief then looked around as if he was realizing where he was for the first time.

"How did you get here?" Landen asked Drake.

Drake focused on Landen, then tilted his head and reached for the wound on his neck. He pulled his hand away and looked at the blood, then back at Landen. "You brought me here," he said.

"He was with us," Marc argued, stepping closer to Landen.

"You would defend him – brother," Drake said shortly, making a face as if he had a horrible taste in his mouth.

Landen had an amused smirk across his face. "We may not agree with one another, but the likelihood of me locking you in a room with Willow is impossible," he said to Drake as he looked over his wound.

Drake looked down, then around the room again. He was confused, there was no doubt about it. August stepped forward and cautiously put his hand on Drake's shoulder, his eyes warily searching over him. Drake returned the stare. It was a seminal moment: August was saying hello to the grandson he never knew. I could feel a remorse coming from August. "Is your mouth bitter?" he asked. Drake nodded. "Marc, get him some water," August ordered.

"I'm not leaving Landen," Marc argued.

"Dane will be strong enough to keep him away for a few moments. Hurry," August said, looking over Drake.

Marc looked at Landen, who nodded for him to go. Dane stepped closer to us.

"What's the last thing you remember?" August asked.

Drake looked at me; I could see the familiar pain there. He sighed and looked back at August. "I was asleep, dreaming. Then I was awakened by a sharp pain in my neck." He looked at Landen and said, "You pulled me to the string." He then looked at me and said, "And then you whispered my name. I couldn't move. I felt so heavy, I had to push a weight away from me. It felt like it tore me in two as it left my body," he concluded, looking back at August.

Marc returned with a glass of water and handed it to Drake. As he stared into Marc's eyes, a crooked smile came across Drake's face. I felt anger surface inside of Marc. Landen reached his hand to Marc's shoulder to calm him before he lost control. Drake turned the glass of water up and drank every drop, but it didn't look like it brought him any relief. He made a face as he swallowed.

"It was Donalt, Drake. He's using you," August said.

Drake glanced at him and shook his head. With his jaw locked, the pain I saw in his eyes turned to anger. "I've heard that before; like father, like son – I suppose," he said with a smirk. The night he lost his life, Livingston had told Drake those same words.

"He's telling the truth," I said, stepping forward. Landen and Dane mirrored me. Marc blocked me completely from seeing Drake.

"Well, this is a little unfair – three against one," Drake said in a causal tone, tilting his head so I could see his dark eyes.

"No, it's all of us against Donalt," August corrected. "He's counting on all of you being divided. We cannot make this easy for him. You need to stay here with us."

At that moment, I felt a rush of panic consume me and I reached for Landen. He glanced back at me and I could tell that he felt it, too. It was too strong to come from one, or even a few – it was coming from a mass of people. Perodine swiftly came through the doorway; she didn't seem to be surprised to see Drake. In fact, she walked right up to him. "You must stop this," she said to him.

"I haven't done anything," Drake said coldly.

"Alamos just announced that Landen kidnapped you. They're charging the wall!" she yelled at him.

"Well, he did – so I guess this little redemption is over," Drake said, pulling back his shoulders.

"You fool, this is what he wants. You're playing into his web. He will consume you if you do not stop this...let us help you," Perodine said in a lower tone.

"He'll use the energy from the anger to make him stronger," August warned.

"Let me talk to him," I thought. Landen looked back at me before slowly stepping aside.

"Drake...make time stand still," I whispered.

I'd seen Drake stop time on the streets of New York. Landen and I had never quite figured out how he managed to do it. Drake looked at me as if the others in the room had vanished, then raised his hands and effortlessly stopped time. While the others stood frozen around us, Drake stepped closer to me, his eyes, full of pain, were searching somewhere deep in my soul. "Is it their life you fear for – or mine?" he asked in a low, deep, commanding tone.

"I told you I didn't want to hurt anyone," I responded timidly as I dared to hold his stare.

"Well, it's a little too late for that scenario," he said, looking away from me and crossing his arms.

"How can you be angry with me for something I can't control? My heart will love who it wants to," I whispered back.

"I just don't see how you can't remember…mine are vividly haunting," he said, looking back at me.

"I want to help you forget. I want you to forget so you'll find the one who's waiting on you; it's not fair to her," I said in a quivering voice, realizing for the first time that there had to be someone somewhere that completed Drake.

"I'm looking at her," Drake said, shaking his head in disbelief.

"Drake, stop them from charging the wall. Don't let the people in Delen pay for my mistakes," I pleaded with him, stepping cautiously forward. He stared at me; pain was held in every part of his expression. "I will not betray them," he whispered.

I felt my stomach turn. Just a few days ago, when I was lost inside of Evelyn, Drake had told me that this world thought that he and I had betrayed them.

He moved his hands, resuming time, then dropped his eyes and sighed. He then began to walk to the doorway, but Landen stepped in front of him to block him. They stared at each other. Then Landen cautiously reached for the wound on Drake's neck.

Marc reached for Landen's shoulder to stop him. "You need to save that. You don't know what's yet to come," he said in a harsh whisper.

Landen looked at Marc, then to Drake. "Everyone deserves to be healed," he said, staring at Drake – fully intent on healing him.

"Not everyone," Marc repeated sarcastically. "I'm sure that's the same opinion he had every time he tried to kill you."

Drake shook his head, staring at Marc. "Kill him? Really? Yeah, that would be the best way to win Willow's heart," he said in a slow sarcastic tone.

Marc's eyes shot to Drake. The stare they shared was nothing less than arctic. "We all know what you're capable of," he said through a locked jaw.

Out of nowhere, Drake charged Marc. Landen and August jumped in the middle of them. Landen held Drake back. August guarded Marc. Meanwhile, Dane pulled me behind him. Perodine put her arm around my waist with the intent of pulling me out of the room. I stood stiffly, though, not allowing her to move me. The tension in the room was a suffocating wall.

"You fool! Do you think I meant to do that?!" Drake yelled over Landen at Marc. Drake stopped pushing against Landen then stepped back. He looked into my eyes, then to Marc. "I lost everything...I had a beautiful woman, a family that loved me, a throne with my name on it – then out of nowhere I'm told that I'm a monster, a secret too dark to share...in the blink of an eye, everything and everyone I knew changed – and now I have to listen to perfect son 'Marc' tell me that I don't deserve to be healed."

As Marc took in Drake's words – seeing it all through his eyes for the first time – his anger suppressed itself. Struggling against feeling sympathy, he gave Drake one nod. Drake then let out a breath that he was holding and the wall of tension began to fall. Landen tilted his head to get Drake's attention, then carefully reached for Drake's neck. I felt a rush of energy and saw a white glow under Landen's hand. Landen pulled his hand away then Drake reached up and touched his healed skin. He nodded once and walked past Landen.

"If you want our mother to return with me then you need to come. I can't guide and defend both her and Alamos through the string," Drake said over his shoulder to

Marc.

"Alamos," Perodine repeated, stepping in front of me.

Drake stopped and turned around. "If you think I'm going to allow you to read my stars, you've lost your mind. He's the only one that's never lied to me," he said.

I could feel Perodine's emotions going out of control. She was scared, excited, dreadful, and blissful...it was if she had butterflies rushing through her.

Marc looked at Landen.

"Go," Landen said.

"What about you? He's protecting you," I thought.

Landen walked over to me and looked over Perodine, trying to judge her emotions. He then wrapped his arm around my shoulder and thought, *"Drake intends on returning within the hour. I'll be fine."*

I looked feverishly to Dane, who was looking at me. "It'll be fine. I'm not going anywhere," he said calmly.

I sighed and leaned into Landen; he felt my anxieties and pulled me closer as we followed Drake out of the room. He walked down the large hallway then led us to the room we'd entered last night, the room in which Drake had dreamed throughout his childhood. He stepped in and looked at the bed and candles. I saw him let out a deep breath then walk to the passage we'd entered. Marc looked cautiously back at us. Landen nodded forward, telling him to go. We could feel Marc's excitement about bringing his mother there. Since he'd discovered that she was alive he hadn't had a moment that wasn't rushed with her.

When they disappeared into the white glow, Dane and August began to turn over the paintings of me that were on every wall. Once August was sure all the paintings had been turned, he and Perodine rushed out of the room. I could feel the fear all around me. It sent a chill down my spine. Landen wrapped me in his arms and began to lead us out of the room. *"Come on, let's go watch the wall,"* he thought as he led us in the direction of the study. Dane followed us; I could feel his placid calm. I glanced back at him and he smiled slightly then looked to the shadows around us.

"Are you sure you're alright?" Landen thought.

"I think Donalt is more powerful than we've imagined," I answered.

"He can't hurt us, Willow. You have to believe that. I won't let anything happen to you," he promised, believing his every word.

We all but ran through the long hallways that led to the study. When we reached it, Landen stopped in the doorway and pulled me close to him so I'd have to look him in his eyes. Dane leaned against the wall, waiting for Landen to say to me whatever he needed to say.

"Listen to me: everyone may think that our love is tested with these planets, but I know that -like all soul mates – our love is tested every minute. With every breath we take, we make a choice, a choice to love one another. We endure because we know that love is the most powerful thing in the universe – the air our soul breathes," he thought, cradling my face.

"Landen, I don't care who or what tests me. I'll only love you," I thought, furrowing my eyebrows so he would see how serious I was.

"I can see…I can feel how his words cut through you… you haven't betrayed anyone. We'll release them."

"I know we will." I tilted my head, questioning how he'd heard what Drake had said.

"I don't think he can stop time for either of us…an odd flaw, I suppose," Landen thought, trying to hold back an

impish grin.

"You stood frozen," I thought.

"Your intent was to speak to him alone. I learned the hard way to let you do what you want to do," he thought in a more serious tone.

"I really do wish we could help him forget," I thought. Landen smiled and moved his head from side to side. *"What?"* I thought.

"It's just ironic that we want this whole world to remember – and one man to forget," he thought.

"I love you," I thought. Landen pulled me closer. I closed my eyes as I felt his tender lips on mine as our lips gently moved against each other I felt an undeniable passion. I pulled him as close as I could. In our embrace, I could feel the panic from the ones around us drift into a peaceful victory. I knew that on the other side of the world Drake was standing before them, telling them that he was fine and to back away from the wall that surrounded Delen. Within that second, the palace vibrated all around us and an angry roar rumbled through the hallways. Landen wrapped his arms as tight as he could around me, looking in every direction. Dane stepped closer to Landen and me -- the fear between the three of us was irrefutable.

Silence came. The stillness seemed just as eerie. I stretched out my senses. The emotions around us were still of victory and peace. Landen looked down at me and smiled.

"Looks like we hit a nerve," Dane said, looking from shadow to shadow.

Chapter Six

August and Patrick came to the doorway. I could feel their abundant relief; they were unshaken. August smiled at Landen and patted his shoulder.

"Is everyone OK?" Landen asked, intending to heal whoever needed it.

"No one's hurt. In fact, the ones that did come over the wall are staying here – almost a thousand more," Patrick answered, grinning from ear to ear.

"Amazing," I whispered. Landen looked down at me and smiled.

"We're going to get through this now that we're all working together," August said, sighing and feeling relieved. He was proud of Landen. His relief did bring us some comfort, but it couldn't hinder our anxieties of having

Drake there.

Dane shook his head from side to side in disapproval. I knew he wasn't looking forward to being in the same room with Drake for any length of time.

August sensed the tension between us and reached for Dane's shoulder, then looked back at Landen. "I know there's a lot to be resentful about. Forgiveness – or even a simple truce – is too much to ask of any of you, but you have to understand that Donalt is counting on that. We need to pull together to beat this monster. When this is over... well...then maybe we can find a way to resolve the past."

His tone was fully of sympathy and left Landen and me with a surge of guilt. Dane, however, held a different emotion. "I respect what you're saying, August," he said, leaning closer to me, "but I want you to see this through my eyes. When I was six, I saw terror in my best friend's eyes. It was so strong that I felt it. It went on, happening once a month like clockwork. She endured a fear that no one should have to. I couldn't protect her – no one could. It's going to take more than an angry ghost to get me to forgive Drake Blakeshire." Dane looked at Landen and said, "I know you have even more than me to disagree with – so if you tell me you want me to let it go for now, then I will."

August stared at Landen while holding the emotion of pride and confidence. In his subtle way, he demanded a peaceful compliance from us. Landen let his eyes fall to the floor. I could feel his emotions turning inside of him. He wasn't ready to forgive Drake either, but his desire to protect and help the people of Esterious outweighed the anger that wanted to surface.

"We'll treat Drake with as much respect as he gives us," he said, looking up at August.

August nodded. "That's all I need to hear," he said

with a sigh.

Perodine approached the doorway. Oddly, she'd changed her clothes. She was now in a black formal gown and her hair was set perfectly on her head. Jewels decorated her neck and wrist. She looked the same as she did the first time I saw her: like royalty. On the surface, she was calm and reserved, but inside I could still feel her emotions swarming in every direction.

"I fear your trial will begin when they return," she said.

She handed me a change of clothes. I'd forgotten that I still had Drake's blood all over my shirt. She then walked past us to the table and began searching over her notes. Landen walked to her side, studying her. She glanced up at him as he reached the table.

"Is it Alamos or Drake that's concerning you?" he asked.

Suddenly realizing that there was something odd about Perodine, August walked to Landen's side.

"Before retrieving Willow a few days ago, I hadn't been in a room with Alamos for close to four million years," Perodine answered quietly. Landen and August looked at one another, questioning the words she'd said. I knew she was telling the truth. I just didn't understand how it was possible.

Seeing our questioning eyes, she said, "Alamos was suspended with me and Donalt."

"But you both lived here, right?" August questioned.

"It's a big palace," Perodine said, looking down at her notes again.

"Why was he suspended?" Landen asked.

Perodine looked up at Landen, then across the room at me before looking down at her notes.

"I'm sure he'll be more than eager to tell you himself," she answered.

Patrick cleared his throat. "I'm going to get more people to help us with the mirrors and paintings. Do you need anything?" he asked, looking at me.

I shook my head no; I was still stunned, trying to figure out what Perodine was saying. I looked up at Dane, then down to my clothes. If changing them meant I'd have to leave his side, I'd rather wear the bloodstains I had on.

"Come on. I can turn my back," Dane said, tilting his head to the hallway.

Landen glanced back at us and Dane waved, telling him to come. Landen glanced at Perodine once more then walked over to us. Dane briskly crossed the hall to open the door for me. The room lacked the elegance of the palace. There was only a bed and a table consuming the small space. I assumed it had been a servant's room as well.

Dane closed the door and stared at it. I quickly began to change while Landen paced in front of the bed, tossing mixed emotions and intent back and forth inside him.

"I don't know about you guys, but I'm thinking this is all about to get real interesting," Dane said in a low tone.

"That's what I'm afraid of," Landen said, almost to himself.

I pulled my shirt over my head then Landen reached back and touched Dane's shoulder, letting him know that it was safe to turn around.

"How was that guy suspended? I thought this had to do with your first parents or something?" Dane asked.

"It wouldn't be the first time we've been told half-truths," Landen said through his teeth, trying to suppress unwanted anger.

"No one ever said why they were suspended. August

just said that the power Perodine found in the stars suspended her and Donalt's life. Alamos can read them just as
well as she can. She said so herself...maybe he found
power, too," I argued, defending our family.

Landen shook his head from side to side, staring at the
floor.

"I'm with Landen. There's more to it than that...she's
too nervous," Dane said.

I raised my eyebrows, questioning Dane. "Getting a
new insight?" I asked.

"No. Common sense. Ten minutes ago her hair was
down and she was in pants. She looked exhausted. Now,
she's dressed like she's going to a ball – and she won't give
a straight answer," Dane whispered harshly.

"You've met him. Do you think he has a bigger part in
this?" Landen asked me.

I let my eyes search over the time Alamos cared for
me. "I don't remember. I mean, Drake seemed to be the one
in control of the situation," I answered.

Dane looked back and forth between Landen and me.
"I don't trust any of them," he said under his breath. "I just
have a really bad feeling,"

I could feel Dane's placid calm cracking. It was making me uneasy. So far, he and Landen had been the very
thin string holding me together.

"Just stay calm," Landen said, looking between Dane
and me.

In the distance, I could feel Beth. She was near panic.
Landen pushed past Dane and opened the door. I rushed out
behind him. Dane followed us in a confused urgency. On
the other end of the hallway, we saw her running to us –
and Alamos was walking casually behind her. We began to
run in her direction. When we reached her we saw tears

pouring out of her eyes. She wrapped her arms around me and squeezed me as tight as she could.

"What happened?" I yelled over her sobs.

"The string…something's wrong…you can hear them screaming," she said between broken sobs.

"Who's screaming?" Landen asked, pulling Beth away from me so he could see her face.

"All of them…our family…Marc and Drake pushed us through here and went to find out why," Beth said, trembling.

Landen grabbed my hand and we raced down the hall with Dane right at our side. We almost knocked Alamos down as we ran by. Once at the passage, we pushed through – and we heard the screams immediately; they were blood curdling. I could hear Allie crying and Preston and Libby screaming our names. We ran in the direction of Pelhan's world. As the passages of Esterious ended, we saw Drake and Marc. The string was blocked by what looked like a gray wall, Olivia's dream was coming to life in front of me – and Brady's fears were confirmed. I glanced at Landen. His face was engulfed with the panic I felt coming from him.

"We can't push through, Landen," Marc said as Stella's voice yelled his name. "Do something, Landen!" he yelled as he pushed against the wall – only to get burned.

"Stop hurting yourself!" Landen yelled, pulling Marc back.

I paced in front of the wall, trying to read the emotions, to see what was hurting them. I couldn't tell one from another.

"I think it's an illusion," I thought. Landen looked at me for an explanation. *"I've felt Stella's terror before and that's not it,"* I thought, cringing at the sound of her voice

echoing in the string.

"Are you sure?" Landen thought.

I nodded and swallowed. As I focused on the emotions of the string, I was very sure. They didn't have the soul of the people I knew beneath them. I'd taught myself when I was only a girl that there's a signature in all of our emotions, something that can't be mocked or completely covered by another dominate emotion. I'd tried to teach this to Landen, but it was harder for him to perceive. His gift of intent seemed to overshadow the one of emotion.

As Landen's eyes moved back and forth from one emotion to the next, he realized I was right. "It's an illusion Marc. She's not hurt," Landen swore, grasping Marc's hands before he burned himself again.

"This wall is not an illusion," Drake said as Preston yelled his name.

"Tell me how you know," Marc said, putting his hands on Landen's shoulder. He was so angry and scared that his whole face was red.

"She doesn't feel the same...they all feel the same. There's nothing making them individuals," Landen explained, trying to calm Marc – but Marc pushed away, not allowing Landen to calm him.

"I told you to save that," Marc said, harshly covering his face and falling to his knees, trying to calm his own emotions.

I sat down in the center of the string and closed my eyes, blocking out the screams and dark images my mind wanted to create for me. I wanted to assure myself that they weren't there. I knew if they were in distress that I'd feel the pull of the string, that they'd appear before me as an image – and we'd find a way through the wall. I felt nothing. Emptiness. I could barely feel the people of Esterious.

I opened my eyes to find the four of them staring at me.

"Nothing," I said to them.

"Landen, can you find another path? Let's make sure they're alright," Dane bit out as he heard his name echoed by Clarissa's voice.

Landen nodded and reached for my hand to pull me up. We walked in the opposite direction and when the passages to Esterious ended, another gray wall was in front of us. The devastation coming from all of us was almost too much to bear in the vibration of string. This wall was silent. There was no emotion behind it. At that moment, it was as if the only dimension that existed was the dark one of Esterious.

"We're trapped in hell," Marc said in an angry tone.

Drake looked at him and shook his head. "Trust me – you'll get used to it," he said, running his hands through his dark hair.

"You're enjoying this, aren't you?" Marc said as his face turned to stone.

Drake pulled his shoulders back, ready to defend himself, but Dane stepped in front of Marc and Landen stepped in front of Drake.

"My little brother is trapped on the other side of that wall with people I don't even know – and you think I'm fine with that?" Drake said, looking over Landen's shoulder.

"Trust me – he's better off there than he ever was here," Marc yelled in Drake's direction.

The current in the string began to rush around us and the roar of the energy mocked an evil laugh. We all stood frozen, listening to it.

"This is what it wants," I whispered. "It wants us to be angry and scared. Divided. August was right: you guys have to call a truce for now," I said, looking from Drake to

Marc.

I felt their tension leave and calm come – and at that moment, the screams of our family grew louder. "See, when you grow calm – it gives you another reason to be angry," I said.

Landen stepped away from Drake and put his arm around me. "Come on, we need to leave here before some-one really gets hurt," he said over his shoulder as he guided us back to our passage.

Drake's eyes looked over the embrace in which Lan-den had me. His jaw locked. Whatever he wanted to say or do, he suppressed.

Landen and I led them back to the passage of Drake's room, but before we stepped through, our names were all screamed out from the voices of our family. A chill ran down my spine as Drake's dark room came into view. We walked quickly back to Perodine's study. We wanted her to assure us that we were right, that dark illusions were toying with us.

When we reached the study, we saw the silent girl that had shadowed Perodine comforting Beth on the couch. August was at her side, rubbing her back. Perodine was at the table, lost in her work. Alamos was nowhere to be seen.

"Are they safe? Tell me he's safe," Beth said, walking to Drake. Her eyes searched over his face, which held only sympathy for her. "Marc?" Beth said, moving to him – only to find Marc reflecting the same sympathy that Drake had. "Willow? Landen? Someone answer me," she said, walking to Landen and me.

"There's a wall, a gray wall. We can't reach them, but we're more than sure that the screams are an illusion," Landen said, looking across the room at Perodine. I fol-lowed his stare to see Perodine nodding in agreement.

Beth covered her mouth and held back a scream she wanted so desperately to let out. She then walked slowly to the couch, fell into it, and looked up at Marc. "Who did you leave him with? Is he with Chrispin?" she asked as grief for Preston overcame her.

"We left all of them with Pelhan," Marc said, walking to the cart of food that was in the room.

"So, he's with your father?" Beth said as relief came over her.

Drake looked at Beth, astonished by what he'd heard before he looked at Marc. Marc nodded and reached for a towel to make himself an ice pack for his burns. Drake looked at me for understanding.

"No one ever really dies," I said, quietly letting go of Landen and walking to sit on one of the couches. I looked deep in Drake's eyes as I passed him; some of the pain I always saw there seemed to melt away. I assumed he was forgiving himself for taking Livingston's life.

Landen went to Marc; he wanted to heal his burns. Marc, though, just turned his back as he saw Landen approaching. "Why won't you listen to me? You need to save that," he said, holding the ice pack in his hands.

"It's a small wound. Let me take the pain away," Landen argued.

"I don't care how big or small it is – what's going to happen when something big happens and you don't have the energy to heal it because you've wasted it on this small stuff?" Marc said.

Feeling Marc's solid intent of avoiding him, Landen abruptly turned Marc's shoulder and grasped his hands. The light was immediate. Marc didn't have the chance to pull away before Landen had healed him. "You being hurt makes you weak. If you're weak, how are you going to protect me?" Landen said as he released Marc's hand.

Marc looked down at his healed hand, then up to Landen. "I know I'm unbearable. I just didn't expect all of this," he muttered, glancing around the room.

I looked at August. His eyes were lost somewhere in the distance. I felt him struggling to calm himself. He hadn't really had the chance to say goodbye to Nyla, to any of them.

"Olivia dreamed of a wall, a stone wall, a gray wall of screams. Also gray clouds floating just above the ground." I said, regretfully wishing she were there now.

Landen glanced at me. I felt his regret. He not only wished we'd brought Olivia, he also wished Brady was with him. Brady always had a way of seeing through the chaos. Marc didn't have his patience. I tuned my head from side to side, letting him know that we were fine, hoping that I was right. Landen looked at Marc. I felt the two of them fighting the urge to find another passage to Pelhan's world.

Dane took a seat next to me and let his arm stretch out behind me, trying to guard me with as much of his energy as he could. Drake's eyes widened, then he looked across the room at Landen and shook his head in disbelief. He then sat down on the couch opposite Dane and me.

"Her dreams should bring you comfort," Perodine said, not looking up from her work.

Landen walked to her side. Marc followed closely.

"Why? Why should we have not taken them as a warning?" Landen asked Perodine.

"Whatever she dreams reflects a victory for the two of you – even if it shows the conflict," she answered.

"So that wall *will* fall?" Landen asked.

Perodine nodded. "I assume it is there so you will have

no choice but to face the synodic cycle. He now has the three of you in the same room. In just a matter of hours, he will consume either you," her eyes moved to Drake, "or you, then move to overtake Willow."

I saw Beth gasp, then her face turned white as a ghost. I moved in front of her to calm her. I knew she was near the point of fainting.

"Why?" she said in a cracked voice. "What did I do? Why are my children being served to the devil?" she said, putting her face in her hands.

No one had the nerve to try and answer her. Instead, Marc looked at Drake, waiting for him to do something.

Drake turned his head away and stared at the flames in the fireplace. "Where's Alamos?" he said in a low tone.

Out of the corner of my eye, I saw Perodine's body freeze. The butterflies I'd felt before were back. "You did bring him?" she said under her breath.

Drake looked at Beth. "He did come through the pas- sage with you – didn't he?" he questioned, leaning forward.

As Beth nodded and rubbed her hands across her face, I felt a calm come to her. I moved from in front of her back to Dane's side.

"He said he needed to gather things from his study," Beth said, falling back into the couch.

I felt the butterflies in Perodine all but consume her. Landen looked at me and I nodded. He then reached for Perodine's hand and sent calm through her.

"It is going to take more energy than the two of you possess," she whispered to Landen as she pulled her hand gently away from him.

Drake leaned back in his seat his elbow rested on the arm of the couch. His hand covered his flawless profile as his dark, mesmerizing eyes carefully studied Perodine. He tilted his head slightly then the corners of his perfect lips turned into a curious grin. "I can't recall ever seeing you and Alamos together," he said. Then his eyes moved to me and he said, "Well, once – but not beyond that."

Drake finished looking back to Perodine. Beth glanced at Drake then to me then she slowly turned to look at Perodine. You didn't need the insight of emotion to sense that Perodine was falling apart on the inside. Dane let his arm fall from around me and I leaned back into him, hiding from whatever was going to happen when Alamos joined us. Drake's eyes moved to us, his jaw tightened, then he then looked at Landen. "You're proving to have more will-power than me," he said. "I would have divided the two of them long ago," he finished, moving his eyes back to Dane.

Landen rolled his eyes, finding Drake's words childish. "I know without a doubt that Dane's soul belongs to my sister Clarissa – just as I know that Willow's belongs to me. Dane's sun is water. The closer he is to her, the better," he said in a casual tone.

As he heard Landen's words, Drake's eyes turned a shade darker. "You'd think that she'd only need you. That if you were her soul mate, you'd be able to satisfy her needs without the help of another man," he said as his eyes stared through Dane.

Marc began to rush at Drake, but Landen blocked his way. August stood, prepared to block Drake, but Drake didn't move – he just grinned impishly.

"Why are the two of you determined to give this darkness the anger it needs?" August said, looking back and forth between Marc and Drake.

"I'm not angry. It just doesn't make any sense to me," Drake said, moving his hand to cover his flawless grin.

Landen stood in front of Marc and stared at Drake. "I

don't care who I have to ask to protect her – I love her that much. If the time comes that I need you – if I have to watch her in your arms just to assure myself she's safe – then I'll endure it. In fact, I'd even beg you to do so…if you call that willpower, then I'd say that I do have more than you," he said.

I heard the truth in every single one of Landen's words. *"I love you,"* I thought.

Landen smiled as he heard my thoughts, then walked behind the couch I was sitting on and leaned over. I looked up and he kissed my lips softly and thought, *"I love you."* He then glanced at Drake and patted Dane on the shoulder and moved him closer to me before returning to the table where Perodine stood. I looked across the room at Drake to find him staring at me with eyes that were engulfed in pain.

"Why am I here again?" Drake said into the room. "All of you fear that there's something that could hurt me worse than this."

"Do you want that darkness to consume you again?" August asked Drake.

"I don't know which would be worse," Drake answered.

"The darkness – I promise," August said, moving to Drake and letting his hand rest on Drake's shoulder to comfort him.

Drake turned to stare at the flames. The silent girl at Beth's side stood; I could feel her intent of preparing dinner for us. I looked to the windows behind us; the sun was beginning to fall, signifying that the hour that Venus would test me was moving closer – faster than I thought.

"August, maybe you should sleep again to see if you dream of Nyla," Landen said.

August looked up from Drake and nodded. Beth stood,

making room for August to lie down. When he stretched out, I could feel his emotions of worry and anxiety hindering him from falling asleep. I moved away from Dane and sat on the floor beside August and he reached his hand out for mine. Landen started to make his way to us, but I shook my head no.

"Save your energy," I thought, *"I can do this."*

Landen nodded and walked back to Perodine's side, pushing Marc to follow him. They then took a seat at the table. I could feel Drake's eyes on me. I stared at him as I pushed a peace through August. At that moment, I wanted more than anything to bring a peace to Drake, but I knew that was impossible – and my intent was making Landen uneasy. I let my eyes fall to the floor and thought of Nyla and the rest of our family. I let everything I loved about them – particularly the peace I felt from having them in my life – come to me. August eventually submitted to my emotion and drifted off into a peaceful sleep.

Chapter Seven

I moved back to Dane's side and stared at August as he dreamed. I focused on his emotion, trying to prepare myself for what I'd do if I felt grief or fear. The minutes moved forward oddly August's peace relaxed me. I felt my eyes become heavy then the calm of sleep came to me. When Landen picked me up, I was startled awake.

"Shh…Sleep…I'll be there in a minute," he thought.

He carried me across the hall to the servant's room and Marc and Dane followed him. They leaned against the wall as Landen laid us across the small bed. A moment later, he calmed himself into a sleep. We rose next to our bodies. At the foot of our bed, we let our hands melt into one another. Marc was right: Landen's Aura had dimmed throughout the day. I knew he needed all the energy I could give him. It was just now dusk in Delen and we both thought this would be the last time we'd be able to rest until my birth hour the next day at seven nineteen at night.

I suppressed my fears about the safety of my family. In the back of my mind, I knew the only things I was relying on were my insight and the reassurance of Perodine's words. I knew I wouldn't find relief from my doubt until they all stood in front of me once again.

We let hours slip by. Marc and Dane had drifted into a peaceful sleep. They needed their rest to gain strength as well. When Landen's Aura had resumed its bright light and the line that connected us had grown stronger, he let his hands emerge from mine. As the sensation left me, I looked into his eyes -- the blue was so perfect. The eyes of his soul gleamed in the darkness. I could feel Landen's resolve. He felt stronger and was ready to face what was still before us.

"We'll be alright," he thought, smiling.

I nodded and woke and he opened his eyes next to me. I leaned up and let my lips rest on his, taking in his warmth and the emotion of being complete in his arms. He pulled me closer to him.

Suddenly, the silent room filled with a dark roar. Dane and Marc jerked awake and were standing in front of us before I could blink. Landen sat up slowly and let his eyes move across the darkness. I couldn't feel the emotion of anyone beyond us – but I could feel a presence. A chill ran down my spine, but Landen suppressed whatever fear he had and pulled me up to him. We moved cautiously to the door, not turning our back on the room. Marc opened the door and stood at the threshold, ushering us out. Once we all reached the hallway he slammed the door shut. Right then it began to rattle violently. Then just stopped.

Landen wrapped his arm around my shoulder and

moved us into the study. Perodine was still at the table, studying the scrolls. August was asleep where we left him. Beth and Drake were stretched out on the other two couches, sound asleep. In the center of the room were three carts full of untouched food. The aroma reminded us that we'd only eaten once that day – and that meal had been interrupted by an astronomy lesson.

As Landen and I stared in August's direction, Marc and Dane made themselves a plate. His emotion was calm. Near blissful. My gaze moved to Drake he looked so innocent as he slept. My eyes searched carefully over his perfect features. His lips were turned into a slight grin. I wondered what he was dreaming.

I felt Landen's eyes on me and turned to look at him. He looked to Drake, then back to me.

"It must be a good dream," he said, explaining Drake's emotion to me. I looked away, not wanting it to seem like I cared.

I could see Marc shaking his head in disapproval. He hated having Drake this close. He saw him as a threat. I looked at Dane, who was looking back and forth between Marc and Landen, waiting for one of them to say or do something.

"He won't hurt her – that's all that matters," Landen said to Marc.

I breathed out, pushing the tension I was feeling away from me. I walked to Landen's side and buried my face in his chest. Landen wrapped his arms as tight as he could around me and let his head rest on mine.

"He does love you – but it can't compare to what I feel for you," he thought.

I heard the truth in Landen's words. A single tear fell from my eye. I squeezed him tighter.

"It doesn't matter that he does. I can't love him back. You are the sole keeper of my heart," I thought.

He kissed the top of head and whispered, "I know."

The tension Marc was putting off fell and I felt Dane relax a little. August began to stir. The four of us walked to the couch he was on and leaned over. In our eagerness to hear what August had to say, we'd managed to stir Beth and Drake. As he turned in his sleep, August's eyes were still closed. Drake and Beth slowly sat up and waited with the rest of us for him to wake. August's eyelids fluttered, then opened. Startled to see us all leaning over him, he struggled to focus.

"Well...?" Landen said.

August sat up slowly and glanced around the room at all of us then to Perodine – who was lost in her own world, looking over the scroll. "I didn't dream of Nyla," he said. "I did have a vivid dream of Preston and Libby standing in a white glow – as bright as the string. Before them, I saw a dark wall. Then Willow appeared. At her side were two others that looked just like her – and then they merged," he hesitated, then looked at me, "then everything turned red, like blood."

I swallowed, imagining his dream. I looked over my shoulder to Perodine. She was staring at me. Once I noticed her stare she let her eyes fall back to her notes. I turned back to August.

"Were the children alright?" Beth asked, sliding down the couch she was on to get closer to August. He nodded.

Drake stood up and stared at the ground. Landen leaned against the back of the couch and stared into the distance. "We have to find that knife," he said under his breath.

Drake looked up quickly. "What knife?"

Suddenly, I could feel Perodine's emotions elevate out of control. I turned to look at her and saw that she'd stood abruptly and was staring at the doorway. My gaze followed hers; Alamos stood in the threshold of the door. His hands were full of books and behind him a young man was standing with more books. Alamos and Perodine were locked in a stare as if they were in a world of their own. I looked up at Landen, trying to judge Alamos's emotion through him – but he was a void to me as well. As his eyes searched over Alamos, Landen tilted his head curiously. I knew that whatever he was feeling – he was having a hard time believing it.

"The one that cut the cord separating the woman I love from our daughter," Alamos said, answering Drake's question.

The entire room froze. It was as if Perodine's butterflies were consuming us all. A truth was being told to us for the first time: Alamos was my first father – not Donalt.

Alamos moved his eyes to me and searched carefully over my face. Dane leaned protectively in my direction and Landen just stared forward. Drake walked slowly around the couch, looking from Alamos to me. "You wait until now to tell me this?" he said, crossing his arms.

Alamos looked back at Perodine, who was still frozen in place. He then walked slowly to the table she was standing behind and laid down the books he was carrying. The young man behind him walked swiftly to the table and set the books down that he was carrying then nervously glanced up at Alamos. Alamos nodded and the young man left the room.

"I take it you haven't spent the remainder of the day divulging your secrets," Alamos said, staring at Perodine.

She took in a deep breath, then broke her stare with

Alamos and looked across the room at me. I knew the stunned look on my face tore into her. She looked back at Alamos. "Why should I have wasted my time, my dear? I knew you would find great pleasure in divulging them yourself," she said in a placid tone.

"There's more?" Drake questioned.

Alamos looked at Drake, then to me. "Your mother and I have been fighting this demon for longer than any of your lives," he said.

Drake shook his head from side to side then looked at Landen to see how he was taking all of this. Landen was calm. It was as if he were relieved to know that in my first life I wasn't connected to the demon inside of Donalt. Landen pulled me to him and I leaned into his body, shielding myself in his energy. I knew from Perodine's swarming emotions that I wouldn't be prepared for what she'd kept from me.

"Why don't we start from the beginning?" Landen said, tightening his arms around me.

August and Beth stood and walked around the couch. Dane stood on one side of me and Landen and Marc stood on the other. We all were staring at Alamos, who sighed and looked back at Perodine. She nodded and looked away; it was easy to feel she now found it difficult to look into Alamos' eyes.

"When Esterious was an infant, it was much like it is today," Alamos began. "The only difference was that until adulthood, there wasn't a division of class. At the age of eighteen, your position for the rest of your life was chosen for you. It could be anything from a farmer to a member of the court. Like most young adults, we didn't always wait for a role to be given before we fell in love with someone," As his eyes moved to Perodine, she turned her back, hiding her face from all of us. Alamos stared at her for a second before looking back at all of us.

"Not waiting was a foolish thing to do. There was no way of knowing if you'd be separated from the one you found. We just didn't care. We couldn't control the way we felt about one another. We kept it a secret from everyone. We feared that if any of the elders knew we'd fallen in love with each other before our fate was decided, they'd separate us on purpose as a form of punishment." Alamos stopped, then pulled out a chair at the table and sat down before he began again.

"When the day came that our fate would be decided, my worst fears were confirmed. Because Perodine was the most beautiful woman of her age, she was given to Donalt, a young ruler who'd just assumed the throne – and I...I was assigned to be his priest. I had to stand before them and join the woman I loved with Donalt. I had to listen to him tell me how much he loved her. That the stars above had given him a precious gift."

Alamos looked over his shoulder at Perodine. I could see her trembling. Beth walked to her side and let her hand rest on her back.

"I was prepared to continue our love affair, not caring if it meant death if we were ever caught – but somehow Donalt reached her and convinced her that he loved her. Perodine asked me to leave her alone. Of course, loving her, I did as I was asked and served at Donalt's side, advising him on his every move. Years passed, then Perodine was with child. She carried the baby boy to full term, but he never took a first breath. She waited a year before she tried again. This time, the baby didn't reach its second trimester. The grief almost killed her. Donalt blamed himself. The two of them divided. Perodine moved to this side of the palace and Donalt to the other." Alamos looked to the shadows of the room, then at each of us before he began again.

"I remember leaving Donalt alone for a few weeks…I thought he needed time to himself. When I approached him again, he wasn't the man I knew before. The look in his eyes was cold, dark. I feared the grief had taken him over. I tried to counsel him. When I said Perodine's name, he looked at me as if he had no idea who I was talking about; all he wanted to talk about was his followers. He thought they weren't giving him enough. He complained that they were too happy. He began to take their privileges away. The positions from that point on were never appointed to the court; they were all of manual labor. I sent word through another priest to Perodine, telling her that Donalt needed her – but I knew I wouldn't be able to send her into his arms again." He looked back at Perodine, who had laid her head on Beth's shoulder. He then looked at the ground and continued.

"She listened to me and went to him. Months went by and nothing changed. Donalt just grew darker and more determined to bring devastation to his kingdom. When I couldn't bear it any longer, I came to Perodine one night." Alamos looked around the room, taking in the memory. "I found her here, crying, lonely. She wanted more than anything to be a mother, to feel an unconditional love. She'd tried over and over again with the man Donalt was, only to leave his arms feeling cold and used. In my time as a priest, I'd been taught the beauty of the stars above. I knew that there were influences in the stars that could protect any child Perodine wanted to conceive. I had the observatory built next to her room," he said, looking to the doorway that led to it.

"As I taught her the magic of the stars, the passion between us was reignited – and she asked me to father her child. At that moment, I felt like my life did have a purpose. I submitted to her request and we planned everything perfectly – even the time that Perodine would go to Donalt. We knew that in order to protect our lives, he must think the child was his. We couldn't have imagined, though, that we'd conceive a child as great as Aliyanna," he said, moving his eyes to me. I felt my stomach turning and my heart racing. Landen tightened his hold on me, sending a peaceful emotion through me.

"Perodine waited until Aliyanna was three months old before she presented her to Donalt. I was standing at his side. To say the least, he was shocked; he had his doubts. Perodine took our daughter back to her wing, only emerging when she was forced to for social occasions. Donalt turned to me; he said he didn't trust the child that its purpose was to destroy him. He had me and three other priests construct her birth chart then move them forward in time throughout her life. I led the project and carefully omitted anything that would allude to the fact that Perodine and I had conceived Aliyanna." Alamos let his eyes fall to the table to the scroll before him. He then folded his hands. His dark eyes seemed to echo a pain he was feeling.

"As I moved my daughter's chart forward, I saw not one amazing life – but several. I saw her moving people. Not only restoring Esterious to the way it was – but better than it could ever have hoped to be. I simply told Donalt that she'd have a good life, that the man she loved would rule his throne well after his final days. I'd hoped that would be enough to calm him – but it wasn't. He was enraged. He sealed the wing that Perodine was in and said that his daughter was the most valuable thing in the kingdom and that every man that would seek her – would seek to kill him. His resolution was to choose the man for her. He found a young boy, Alazar. The child was an evil little person. He found pleasure in not only tormenting other children, but anything that had a heartbeat. I tried to steer Donalt in another direction, but he said, 'A man such as he will be will keep my daughter in the place she needs to be.'"

Regaining her composure, Perodine looked over her shoulder at me. I stared back, feeling an overwhelming sympathy – not only for her, but also for Alamos.

"There was a servant woman who'd cared for Perodine since she was a child, a sickness took her daughter from this world. By law, children must be raised by a woman, so the servant's grandson, Guardian, was sent to live in the wing with Perodine and Aliyanna."

Alamos looked at Drake, then to Landen. "I was there when Guardian and Aliyanna saw each other for the first time. They were barely six years old – yet they stared at each other with a magnitude beyond anything I'd ever seen before."

I felt Drake's eyes on me. Landen tightened his arms around me. Dane leaned in closer.

"I knew…I knew then that she'd never submit to Donalt's request to be given to Alazar. She was too stubborn to hide the way her mother and I had. I did what I could do to conceal this love for the next twelve years. I had Guardian's name removed from the book of residence. Perodine and I never allowed them out of this wing. With each day that passed, our heart broke. We knew that our daughter would have to endure what we'd already lived through: she'd have no choice but to be given to the evil man Alazar had grown into."

As Alamos leaned forward his eyes found August then fell back to the scroll.

"Just before Aliyanna's eighteenth birthday, she decided to explore. She found her way to Donalt's chambers and heard him with the other priest, speaking over Alazar. She ran terrified to Guardian then they went to Perodine for help. They called for me and I told my daughter to submit – that I would find a way for her to still see Guardian…I'm sure that was the moment she decided to hate me." Alamos' eyes found mine. I could see an agonizing pain in him.

"Perodine sent me away. A few days later, rumors surfaced in the palace – and then in the kingdom – that Donalt's daughter would be joined with a servant boy. The world was elated. They thought it was Donalt's way of joining the classes again. Celebrations were on every street in every town – and you can only imagine how Donalt took this news: he was enraged that there was happiness in his kingdom."

Alamos' eyes moved to Drake then to Landen. He cleared his throat.

"Guardian proved to be a brave man. He came to me and asked me for the scroll, the birth charts; he feared that Donalt could use them to bring harm to Aliyanna. I told him where they were and that night they sought to retrieve them. I stayed in the shadows, prepared to give my life to protect them. Somehow Donalt knew; he knew everything. There were priest waiting for them. Donalt stood before them and told Aliyanna to give him the necklace her mother had made for her and submit to Alazar – or she would take Guardian's life with her own hand. Like her mother, Aliyanna didn't respond well to threats. She took the scrolls and Guardian's hand and turned to leave. The priest then forced their energy to her. I was on the other side of the room and

I sent mine to them. When our energy collided, a passage opened. The force pulled both Guardian and Aliyanna in – never to be seen again."

Silence seized the room. We were all taking in the wealth of information that Alamos had given us. I'd tried to imagine the person I was in my first life; the conflicts I'd faced, the choices I'd made. It had never occurred to me that sacrifices were made on my behalf – that I was conceived out of love.

"I'm sure it's not hard for all of you to imagine Perodine's response to the news of the vanishing of Aliyanna: her grief was mirrored by the world around us. The skies turned gray and silence came to the voices of the people. I assumed we'd all die a sad, lonely death – to pay for the mistakes we'd made; but death never came. Twenty years later, Perodine, Donalt, and I looked the same. Others in the court died off one by one. I surfaced from my grief and began to study the stars again, looking for the hour of my death. Instead, I found every reason to believe that my daughter was still alive, happy, and in a world so beautiful that my imagination couldn't even take me there. I went to Perodine, overjoyed with what I'd found."

Perodine had turned and was staring at Alamos; her expression was calm, but her emotion was a deep grief.

"She already knew. I'd taught her the stars so well, she'd discovered Aliyanna's fate long ago. She also knew that we wouldn't die until our seed had filled its purpose, that we'd have to wait the course of time for the universe to move back to the same as it was the first time Aliyanna took a breath. Perodine has never forgiven me for asking Aliyanna to submit; she believes that if we'd stood up to Donalt back then, this world wouldn't have had to wait for time to move forward."

Alamos' eyes moved to the shadows. "I think I was almost two hundred before Donalt confronted me about the love I had for Perodine, the child we had together. He took mercy on me. He thought that by me not allowing Aliyanna to disappear with Guardian when they were children that I'd proclaimed my soul to him. I became his most trusted and admired priest and stood at his side as the chapters of time moved forward."

Beth walked around the table and stood before Alamos with tears in her eyes. She then slapped him as hard as she could across the face. Drake and Marc dove across the room to stop her from hitting him again, Drake grabbing her arms and Marc her waist.

"You bastard!" she screamed. " You and your stars... you knew...you knew all along that it was not my son... that it was not Livingston and my price to pay...not our boys...you have ruined him," Beth said in broken voice.

Drake moved his arms around her and held her as tight as he could. Marc looked down at the ground before returning to Landen's side. With grief consuming the room, I stood frozen, unsure of what to do.

The presence I'd felt before in the darkness came again – and I wasn't the only one who felt it. Marc and Dane stood at attention and Landen shielded his energy around us. Drake slowly let go of Beth and pushed her in Marc's direction -- she ran to his open arms. The ceiling above us turned black and began to circle. Suddenly, it moved in Alamos' direction. Drake threw a shield that looked like clear water in front of him. As the darkness collided with it, the sound was as loud as thunder. The entire room vibrated from the force of energy – and then the darkness...vanished.

Chapter Eight

We all stood still, waiting for it to come again; but it was gone – at least for now. Landen didn't release me, but he let his shield fall, saving his energy. Alamos reached for his face to cover the red marks of Beth's fingers. He then stood slowly, looking at Perodine, then to Beth.

"I did know. I knew that fate had dealt him a cruel card, that he'd have to fight for every chance, through every life, just to hold her for a moment. That he'd be seen – just as I was – as the bad soul mate," Alamos said in a tone that reflected resentment toward Perodine.

Perodine walked around the table and stood in front of us all. I could feel anger coursing through her. She stared at Alamos. He stood up straight and stared back.

"Stop now – you have said enough," Perodine said

through her teeth.

"I don't think he has," Drake said, moving to Alamos' side. "I heard the word 'soul mate'…I heard 'every life'… is that not what I've been saying all along?" he asked, looking at me.

Beth hid her head in Marc's shoulder and began to cry. Dane moved his head from side to side and smiled an impish grin. "It seems your hearing omitted a few words – like 'bad,' 'fight,' 'moment,'" he said.

Drake's eyes peered through Dane. He then sighed and looked at Alamos.

August raised his hands. "There's no such thing as a bad soul mate," he argued.

"According to Perodine, there is," mocked Alamos. He then stepped closer to August and said, "You see, she has this theory: every soul has two souls that belong to it. One is perfect in every way; the two share a love that is flawless, sustaining. The other…well…the other is love as well, but this love changes with time and circumstance; she feels its only purpose is to make us feel alive until we find the perfect love."

"That's foolishness," August argued. "That goes against everything Chara believes in. There is a soul mate for everyone. To even think that there are souls that have no purpose – that's insane."

"My friend, you have misunderstood me," Alamos said, smiling slightly. "She has no doubt that we are meant for someone. In her mind, we all have the role of both; we complete one and entice the other."

Perodine stepped closer to Alamos. "You mock me," she said, glaring at him, "but my theory was proven right as we watched Aliyanna's lives. She only loved two souls – and each of them loved another."

Alamos looked at Perodine. "You only see what you want to see. Reading it and living are two different things; only they know how they felt."

"I said that was enough," Perodine said to him.

As he looked at Perodine, Alamos shook his head from side to side. "I will admit my deeds, just as you will admit yours," he said, moving away from her. He walked to me and his eyes looked carefully into mine. "Your mother seems to believe that passion, desire, and infatuation are not included in the job description of soul mates." He looked over his shoulder at Perodine. "It seems that those are the elements of lust and lust can only belong to a bad soul mate. The soul that makes us feel alive, human, evoking every emotion – including anger – is just not enough. I was not enough for her. She believed that because I was born just moments outside of a chart that would have linked us together for eternity that we weren't meant to be. She let the study of the stars – a perfect math that can never be fully understood by the human mind – dictate who I would be in her life."

Alamos glanced over his shoulder at Drake, his eyes searching him over carefully before returning to mine. "I find that…unfair. Are we not human? Do we not have only the emotions we feel to go by?" He looked at Beth, who was still crying in Marc's arms. "I had no way of knowing which boy would be born here – the 'good' soul mate or the 'bad' soul mate. Drake's fate came down to moments, just as mine had. I did find it ironic that the child that needed my counsel the most was born in my care," Alamos said, staring at Beth.

She looked up from Marc and wiped her face dry. Anger was coursing through her. Marc must have sensed it -- he held her arms against him. "You're trying to live your life through him – to find a selfish victory – and you don't care who you hurt in the process," Beth said.

Alamos looked away from her accusing eyes, walked to the table, and opened one of the books he'd brought.

"I am not selfish. I traced his life. I knew that he'd paid the price enough times – that he deserved to finally get the girl. That passion would move this universe for the first time," he said, turning the pages in his book.

Perodine walked to the table and slammed her hands down. Alamos casually looked up, unshaken by her display of anger. "Passion is for the body," Perodine said, leaning dominantly toward Alamos. "It dies when the body does. Love, the love of a soul mate, is carried to the place between; it is felt from the first breath."

"If it can be dismissed so easily by you – why are you afraid of it?" Alamos asked.

"I have no fear of it," Perodine said, glaring at him.

He broke his stare with her and looked at me, then to Drake, who was completely captivated by what he was hearing.

"Then why did you take the privilege of allowing her to choose away from her?" Alamos asked.

I stood up straight; he was starting to make me angry. "I choose – I have chosen – twice," I bit out, glaring at him.

He closed the book he was looking though and walked over to me. Drake stepped closer. Everyone grew tense.

"You chose with a blind eye," Alamos said, taking in a deep breath. "You can't feel me, can you?" I shook my head no. He looked to his side at Drake, then back to me. "Have you ever asked your mother why? Why she spoke the words that would keep you from ever knowing that I love you," he looked at Drake, "that he loves you?"

I felt my stomach turn. My eyes moved to Perodine, but she refused to look at me. I looked back to Alamos; his dark eyes had softened. He wasn't looking at me; he was looking at the person I was millions of years ago.

"Why?" I whispered just loud enough for Perodine to hear me.

She looked up and I could see she was fighting back tears. "I had no choice. Alamos had evoked Drake's dreams...you would have felt his love and the love of Landen...it would have been too much for you to understand," she said in a low tone.

I felt my cheeks flush with anger and Landen's hands on my arm, sending a calm through me.

"He deserved to dream, to see her as Landen did... don't blame this on me," Alamos said, turning to look at Perodine.

"What was your plan?" Perodine asked him. "For her to be terrified – and then for some evil angel to come to her and show her the emotion of love?"

"He's not evil," Alamos said in a firm tone.

"No, but the demons you taught him to play with are – the ones that found her in her peaceful sleep," Perodine argued.

"If you hadn't suppressed his emotions – his energy – he would have been able to release her from the pressure they applied," Alamos argued back.

Perodine shook her head from side to side, glaring at Alamos. "And I suppose that is your excuse for giving him a seductive touch?" Perodine said, looking from Alamos to Drake.

Alamos tilted his head and looked at Perodine. "Is that not what 'bad' soul mates are known for – our seductive touch? I only enhanced what was natural to him," he said.

"You are an evil bastard," Perodine said in a low tone. "If I was your soul mate – as you have proclaimed over the years – you would have never had the stomach to hold another woman; you have proved my point more than once," she said coldly.

"Soul mate or not, I am human and I have had a very long life; forgive me if I wanted the illusion of love – even if I knew it would only be for a moment."

"How cruel can you be? You have plotted and planned to take the soul of our child and put it into the body of a daughter you conceived with another woman…you cannot even see how sick you really are," Perodine said.

I knew what Perodine was talking about. Landen's body and my body couldn't be divided and Drake's solution to this was for my soul to merge into Adonia. Adonia and her soul mate, Justus, were close friends of my fathers. Their story was the first story I'd ever heard of Chara and Esterious.

"After all these years, having my two daughters as one seems to be nothing more than a small reward for my pain," Alamos said, walking back to the table.

I stood up straight and took in a deep breath. Everyone was looking at me, waiting for what I had to say. I looked at Perodine, then to Alamos. "Undo it all. I want to feel everyone. I want Drake to forget every life beyond this one. Take everything you've done to us and undo it," I said in a calm tone. The room remained silent. "Did you hear me?" I said louder, my eyes staring at Alamos. "I will feel and he will forget and you all will see for the final time that nothing you do will take me from Landen. I have sympathy for the both of you – but neither of you had any right to toy with our lives. I am not you," I said, looking at Perodine, "and Drake is not you," I said, looking at Alamos. "You should have just left us all alone. Adonia would be alive and Drake would have had a blissful childhood." I looked behind me at Dane, Landen, and Marc, then continued, "He would have found unconditional love long before he ever searched for his soul mate. You have not counseled him; Beth is right: you ruined him – sentencing him to a lonely life, just as you have lived."

I felt Landen stand behind me then his lips on the back of my head.

"Those words cut into Drake and Alamos," he thought.

I knew he was telling me their emotion because he thought I was bringing more harm than good to the situation.

"I can't help it. I'm sorry," I said, looking at Drake. I stepped forward and reached for his hand. His touch was just as seductive as it always has been. He looked up slowly into my eyes and I saw the pain that Landen had said I inflicted. "If you forget, it won't hurt anymore," I whispered.

He moved his hand to my face, cradling it with his seductive touch. "If you remembered, you'd change your mind. You'd see that we've been fooled by our emotions before," Drake said.

I moved my head side to side. "If we were meant to remember our past lives, it would come to us naturally. The universe has its reasons for that barrier," I said, moving Drake's hand from my face and letting go of him. I looked back at Landen and saw the confidence in his eyes that I felt coming from him.

"The universe is cruel," Alamos said quietly.

"Undo it all," I repeated.

Looking at her, I felt Perodine's grief. "We cannot do as you ask, my precious daughter," she answered.

I looked down, then walked slowly to the couch and

fell into it. Dane was at my side. Beth followed. She wrapped her arms around me as I cried quietly on her shoulder.

"Why not?" I heard Landen ask. "Let her feel him. I assure you, it will change nothing."

"It is not that we do not want to," Perodine answered. "It is because time moves forward. We cannot change what we have done. It is not a magic spell. It was a choice we made. If it were possible, I would not only do as Willow has asked – but I would take her memories of the night-mares away. All that you have lived through is now a part of you."

Beth's arms tightened around me. We were both griev-ing – grieving for a life that was taken from Drake. I heard August clear his throat and I looked up from Beth's shoul-der to see him walking to the center of the room; I felt clar-ity inside of him. His wise eyes looked over Perodine, then Alamos, before looking across the room.

"This has been a very revealing evening," August said into the room. "I think that now that all of our secrets are out in the open – we'll be able to move forward." He walked to the table where the scrolls were laid and looked down at them, then back to the room. "Forgive me if what I'm about to say offends you," he said, looking from Ala-mos to Perodine, "but I think you've both been played as a fool."

He'd offended Perodine. She crossed her arms and waited for him to go on.

"We're fighting darkness – not a man. A darkness that does not know the limits of time. Looking back over your lives it is easy for me to see how it weaved itself into you. It never had a doubt that Aliyanna belonged to the two of you, or what her purpose was: to kill it. I would even guess that it helped you find the passage to the string – knowing it would take four million three hundred and thirty two years before she would return." August paused as his eyes moved across the room.

"A lot of damage can be done in that amount of time. It was just too perfect that Drake was born here," August said, looking looked at Alamos. "A boy that had the path you'd lived in front of him. Both of you were so consumed by your own past that you didn't see it moving closer, closer and closer to the children – and now it's upon us, the moment of truth. We need to put the anger and resentment behind us and find a way to beat this demon."

Drake walked slowly over and sat on the couch across from me. As he stared deep into my eyes, his emotion was strong enough to cause Landen to turn and look at him. Inside Landen, I felt a remorse for Drake that I'd never felt before. Landen turned around and walked to the table and Marc followed. I felt Perodine move all of her emotions down deep into her soul. Alamos followed the others.

"What are these books of?" Landen asked Alamos.

"Once I discovered your kind – the travelers – I asked them to bring me any knowledge of darkness, of a dark person living in immortality. These are the ones I've collected over time." Alamos opened one of the books and flipped through the pages.

"You find a common story, a leader of many who turned dark. In most cases, it was moved out of the body it possessed with simple words," Alamos said.

As I looked in his direction, I could feel hope building in all of us. Alamos must have sensed it, too. He glanced around at all of us and shook his head no. "Every word I found, I said over Donalt. I thought if he died then I'd be released from this life. None of them worked. In fact, one time he caught me speaking them. His laugh bellowed through the wings of the palace. He said, 'Those words are for my children. They cannot hurt the father.' I assumed he'd gone mad at that point and resumed my role at his side, counting the days down."

"Do you know where the knife is?" Perodine asked.

Alamos nodded yes. "You'll need both Landen and Drake to retrieve it. The stone will not move unless the hands of the good and bad soul mate touch it at the same time." We all looked at him, full of astonishment. "I said the words when I discovered that they were both in this life. My intention was to give reason to spare Drake's life throughout the course of all the planets," he said, defending himself.

"Did you read somewhere that I was a killer?" Landen asked bleakly.

"I can't see everything in your chart. I also can't put limits on a man who's defending the woman he loves." Alamos looked across the room at Drake. "I find it hard to believe that you're both still standing."

As he heard those words, Drake closed his eyes. I imagined that Alamos had encouraged him to make a final division between Landen and me. Drake had declined. The new respect for Drake that I felt inside Landen told me that, more than likely, I was right.

"Where is it?" Landen asked, looking back at Alamos.

Alamos nodded his head in the direction of the observatory. "In the center of the pool, you will find a stone that is set deeper than the others. Beneath it, you will find a stone box. The knife is inside there.'

Drake looked across to Landen. "Let's go," he said, standing.

Landen nodded and looked at me and I stood to follow

them. Beth stood and went to the doorway that led in the other direction. I felt her intent of finding them dry clothes. Landen and Drake walked side-by-side. Standing behind them, I felt divided. I loved Landen with every ounce of energy that I possessed, but I couldn't help feeling a deep sympathy for Drake.

I could feel how uneasy Marc was. Dane let his hand rest on the small of my back. As we entered the observatory, I felt the chill of a November night in the air. I could only imagine how cold that water must be.

Alamos came in behind us and walked to the edge of the pool then pointed to the center that was over fifteen feet away. "The water will get deeper. That's how you'll know you're close," he said, looking at Drake.

Landen and Drake slid out of their shoes and pulled their shirts over their heads. Chills ran across both of their perfect bodies. As Drake rubbed his arms together to stay warm, I saw his tattoo. In my nightmares, it was of a dragon – but now it had been altered. The dragon now curled around a majestic willow tree. It didn't matter that it shielded the dragon – I knew it was there. It was a grim reminder of the horror I'd always felt.

I moved my hand to cover my tattoo, my ankh, which Drake had marked with a star. My fear caused Landen to look in my direction and when he saw me covering my wrist, he glanced to Drake's arm. Landen's attention didn't go unnoticed. Everyone – including Drake – was watching me. Drake moved his hand to cover his arm from my view, then walked to edge of the pool and moved his legs over to wade in.

Chapter Nine

Landen walked to Drake's side and moved his legs over the edge. As they waded forward, the water grew deeper. It was just over their waist when they reached the middle. I saw them look at the water as they moved their feet across the bottom of the pool.

"The water will get deeper than that when you get to it," Alamos said across the pool. Drake waded to his left and the water rose to midway on his chest. "Here," he said to get Landen's attention.

Landen waded in Drake's direction. When he reached him, Landen nodded and the two of them merged in the water. Seconds moved by. The water suddenly grew still. I felt my heart begin to race. I could feel Landen's frustration and anger. They both emerged at the same time.

"Move it to the left and I'll pick it up from the bottom," Landen said to Drake.

Drake nodded and they fell into the water again. In that instant, the water turned white. It was glowing, lighting the entire room. Landen and Drake came from the water at the same time and Landen was holding the box. They were both taken aback by the glow around them. The water began to dim. Images of our family appeared on the surface. You could hear their cries as watery images of hands stretched out of the water. The room began to roar. Dane wrapped his arms as tight as he could around me and Marc dove into the water to Landen's side. A dark shadow appeared over them. Drake raised his hand and pushed a force at it. When his energy reached the darkness, the sound was as it was before: as loud as thunder. It vanished into the night sky. The water returned to darkness. The cries of our family echoed along the stone walls.

I went limp in Dane's arms. The fear had knocked the wind out of me. The voices had torn my soul in half. Drake, Marc, and Landen waded carefully in our direction. When Landen reached the side of the pool, he handed the box to August, whose hands trembled as he took it from him.

Landen walked over to me. Dane slowly let go of me as Landen's cold, wet arms surrounded me. In his embrace, I felt a calm come over me. He kissed my forehead. *"They're only illusions,"* he thought, moving my chin up so I'd have to look at him.

"It still hurts," I thought back.

"Don't let them make you weak – I need you to be strong for me now. This is almost over," he thought.

I nodded, then reached up and moved one of his dark locks out of his eyes. "Let's get you warm," I said, letting my hand fall into his.

We led the others back to the study, where Beth had summoned the silent girl that had followed Perodine since her return. They had towels and changes of clothes laid out on the back of the couch. The girl was pouring steaming tea into cups. August, Alamos, and Perodine walked to the table. August set the box gently in the center of the table. Landen, Drake, and Marc began to dry themselves off before they changed. I turned my back, giving them privacy. When the young girl had filled all the cups, she handed Dane and me one, then smiled at me and turned and left the room.

"What's the deal with that tattoo anyway?" I heard Marc ask.

I looked up at Dane and he nodded, letting me know that it was safe to turn around. Drake was pulling a long sleeve shirt over his T-shirt. His eyes caught mine before he answered Marc. "Part of it represents my name. The other part represents what makes all of this hell worth it: Willow." Drake finished buttoning up his shirt as he stared at his mother. "I was named after a constellation in the northern sky that never rests: a protector," he said, sighing.

"The dragon in the sky," Landen said, looking at Drake. Drake nodded.

"I've heard it called more than a protector," Marc said in a teasing manner.

Drake looked at Marc, un-amused. "I've heard every mythology there is about that constellation and I find it foolish. It's not me and I'm not it…nothing more than stars," he said to Marc.

I sat my cup down on the tray and picked up two more cups of tea, then walked over to Drake and handed him one. As he took it from my hand, he stared deep into my eyes. I held back the emotions that wanted to move through me. I walked to Landen's side and handed him his cup. He took it, then protectively put his arm around my waist, pulling me to him. I took in his calm and leaned closer.

Dane offered Marc a cup of tea, but he refused it.

"We still need the two of you to open this," Alamos said to get Drake and Landen's attention.

We all gathered around the table. Alamos was carefully drying off the small stone black box they'd recovered. In the center of the box, there was a scorpion along the edges and there were stars made of metal nailed to the black stone. On the side of the box was a latch that divided into two separate parts, each lining the side of the box. Drake reached for one handle and Landen reached for the other; they then looked at each other, then to the box. They raised their handles slowly and pushed them away from one another. The metal cried out as it was turned. The levers clicked into place and the lid rose slightly. Alamos reached his hands vigilantly to the sides of the box and gently lifted the stone lid. A burst of energy escaped as it was removed.

Inside the box, lying on a dark purple cloth was the most beautiful knife I'd ever seen in my life. The handle was black with silver shimmers. It was round and thin. The blade was five inches long. It was so clear, you could see the purple cloth beneath it. The light of the room danced off the sharp edges. Perodine slowly reached her hand in the box. She let her finger barely graze the side of the blade before she pulled away. I could see the blood surfacing where her finger had touched.

"Now, that's a sharp knife," Dane said under his breath.

Perodine raised her eyebrows, confirming Dane's quiet remark. Alamos reached carefully for the lid and set it back on the stone box. He then looked at Perodine, then to

August. "Now that we have it, we must discover how to use it," Alamos said.

"Did you not create the scroll? Why can you not just tell us?" Marc asked as he pulled out a chair at the table.

"All I did was map the heavens. I didn't interpret them," Alamos answered.

"But you will now," Drake said quietly, looking blankly at Alamos.

"I will do my best, son," Alamos answered. His response disgusted Beth. She turned abruptly and walked to the couch.

I followed her. I thought if I helped her emotion, I would somehow calm myself. We sat on one of the side couches so we could see the conversation around the table. I felt a sympathy rise inside of Landen. I glanced across the room and saw him staring at Drake. He felt my gaze and looked back at me, then took a deep breath and gave his attention to Alamos.

Drake walked to the cart. He had his back turned to us, but I could see him reaching for the pot of warm tea. When he turned around, he had a full cup. His eyes caught mine. They were darker than before and looked so sad. He came to Beth's side and gave it to her. She smiled slightly as she took it.

"You need your rest," he said to her. She nodded and brought the warm cup to her lips. Drake watched as she sipped the tea. When she was done, he took the cup from her and leaned down and kissed her forehead. "I love you," he whispered to her. She smiled and said, "I love you."

Her eyes questioned his display of affection, but he looked away from her and made his way back to the table. Beth gave me a curious look. I shrugged my shoulders. I'd never understood the calm he always seemed to have.

Dane came to my side, sitting as close as he could get. I put Beth's hand in mine and thought of Preston playing, Chrispin laughing, and Marc and Stella's celebration. I felt her eyes on me and glanced at her. "I wish I could have been there," she whispered to me.

I looked curiously at her. "You could see that?" I asked quietly.

She nodded. "Is that uncommon?" she asked.

I glanced to my side at Dane -- he shrugged his shoulders. "I've never seen anything," he said as he stretched his legs out and closed his eyes.

My eyes moved to Beth's hand and I let more memories come to me: the first time I'd seen Chara, my celebration, meeting my beautiful family for the first time...as my eyes moved across the crowd that stood in front of me, I heard Beth gasp and I looked up at her. "Was that your mother standing next to Jason?" she asked. I called the memory back of my parents, how happy my mother was that night. She almost glowed. I nodded.

"She's beautiful," Beth said, gripping my hand.

"This is Libby," I said as I thought of Libby and Preston playing in the field of flowers by my house. "And Olivia, the one for Chrispin," I said, thinking of Olivia walking across the field with Clarissa.

Beth nodded. "I remember her," she said. I'd forgotten until then that Olivia had been held here and that her sight had been taken from her by this horrible place. As I looked across the room at Drake, my face turned red with anger. He and Landen had taken a seat at one end of the table and were watching August, Alamos, and Perodine work on the other end.

Beth followed my gaze. "Drake told me when he pulled her from the ocean that he felt connected to her."

She smiled slightly, "I didn't feel her in his heart – but I was more than sure she belonged to one of my sons."

The heat in my cheeks left as I remembered that Drake did save her life. She'd fallen overboard with my friend Monica, but they didn't reach her in time.

"You said you felt Stella in Marc's," I said, remembering the night Beth had watched over me. She nodded as she looked across the room at him. "You could help me find who's meant for Drake – couldn't you?" I whispered, sitting up a little.

Her eyes found mine and she squeezed my hand. "He's going to have to learn to forget you first," she answered.

I let my shoulders fall and leaned back into the couch.

"One day, when all this nonsense is over…he will," she said to me, but I knew she didn't believe the words she said. I reached my hand to my charm on my neck and let my fingers run across the sun and the moon. I hated that it – who I was – had caused so much trouble that day.

"When that wall falls – I want you to take me to visit Chara," Beth said.

"Why don't you just come home, live there?" I asked quietly. Her eyes found Drake. He glanced over his shoulder, catching her gaze.

"He needs someone," she said quietly.

I felt a horrible guilt rise inside of me. It was so strong that Landen glanced over his shoulder. He pushed away from the table and walked over to us. Beth stood, allowing him to sit at my side. "I'll sit over here," he said, pointing to the other couch that faced the fireplace. She shook her head no and stretched out on couch opposite us.

"It's almost dawn," Landen said, sitting down beside me. Dane had drifted to sleep next to me.

I leaned into Landen. "Did they say anything?" I

asked.

"August and Perodine are showing him what they found before," Landen said, sighing.

Marc found his distance from Landen uncomfortable and made his way to the couch beside ours. "You look horrible. You need to sleep," Landen said to him as he sat down.

"I'm fine – thanks for the compliment," Marc said, rolling his eyes. "Why don't the two of you sleep and do that thing you do and go check on our family?"

"No!" Perodine and August said in unison. Perodine walked up behind the couch where Marc was sitting and August came to our side. "It will follow you there," Perodine warned. "We have to make sure the children are protected."

"I don't think it's wise for you to even rise outside of your bodies," August added.

"We slept hours ago. It didn't appear until we had awoken," Landen said to calm August's fears.

"Yes, but as the hour grows closer, he becomes stronger," August said to Landen.

"Perfect. They'll be so exhausted by tomorrow, tonight – whenever – that they won't be able to think clearly," Marc said, folding his arms across his chest.

"We aren't tired. We'll be fine," Landen said to Marc.

Drake stood from the table and walked to the doorway that led to the hallway. I looked at Landen.

"He's going to get a blanket for Beth," Landen thought, answering my unasked question.

"You have sympathy for him," I thought.

Landen smiled slightly and looked deep in my eyes before he answered. *"I know what it's like to watch my mother struggle with the decisions that I've made, that were made on my behalf. We're all victims, but Beth – Beth has had to endure more than all of us,"* he thought.

I let my eyes fall from his and squeezed his hand. I'd seen the pain in Beth when she'd cared for me. She was a woman that had lost so much and had never been repaid. *"I want her to go home with us, but she says Drake needs her,"* I thought.

"Until this is all over – Drake has found his place – she won't be at peace. We just need to do what we can to make her comfortable with the path in front of us all," Landen thought, moving his arm around me as he stared at Beth's sleeping body.

My thoughts took me to my own mother, my father; I could only imagine how worried they were right now. I knew that Pelhan himself would find it a challenge to keep them all balanced in our absence. I hated it. I hated that I somehow always seemed to cause so much trouble for the people who loved me.

Drake returned with a warm quilt. He covered Beth's body and adjusted her sleeping head on the pillow. I felt a jealousy rise inside of Marc as he watched Drake care for his mother. I don't think Marc would ever get over not having her throughout his childhood, fearing that she was dead for so long. Drake took a seat on the opposite end of the couch where Marc sat.

"The wall will fall, right? We will see them again?" I thought.

"One way or another, we will find them again," Landen promised.

Drake stretched his legs out in front of him and sighed deeply, closing his eyes for a moment.

"It wouldn't be wise for you to sleep either," Alamos said across the room to Drake. Drake opened his eyes as he heard Alamos' voice.

Landen tilted his head curiously and looked at Drake. "You leave your body, too?" he asked.

"I can, but I don't prefer to. I'd rather dream," Drake said, looking into my eyes.

"Another gift from your dear Alamos," Perodine said under her breath.

My eyes questioned Drake, but he just smiled slightly and rested his elbow on the arm of the couch. "It's not that I remember my past lives. I relive them each night. To me... well, this is just a nightmare," he said, looking around the room.

"Ironic choice of words," Marc said, turning his head to the side to see Drake.

Drake looked coldly at Marc, his eyes softening as they moved to me. "I didn't see them through your eyes. To me, you were helping the people here – and I was bringing the light," Drake said quietly.

"Where are your demon friends anyway?" Marc asked casually, closing his eyes.

"They weren't mine, you fool. Their keeper lurks in the shadows," Drake said, looking to the dark corners of the room.

I saw a chill run down Perodine's back; she shook it off and returned to the table. August sat on the arm of the couch next to Landen and stared at Drake. I could feel his curiosity; he wanted to know everything about Drake, what he had seen and learned. "Who taught you to use your energy to protect yourself?" August asked Drake.

Drake took in a deep breath and looked into the flames of the fire in front of him. "I've had Donalt's attention all my life," he answered.

"Did he ever tell you where he received his power

from? Or what he wanted you to do once you found Willow?" August asked.

Drake's eyes moved to me and he shook his head no. "I never asked, he never said. I just knew that I was to love her and rule this world and beyond," he answered.

"Is he the one that taught you to make time stand still?" Landen asked, moving himself in front of me so Drake would have to look at him.

Drake sighed and smiled slightly. "No, my father taught me to do that," he answered.

"Livingston?" Landen questioned, leaning back in his seat.

Drake nodded, then looked to the flames in the fireplace. "He said he always wanted me have a way to stop and think before I made choices that would change my life," he answered.

August grinned and glanced down. I could feel the pride for his son, Livingston, come over him. Landen and I both felt envious. That was one lesson we'd never been taught.

"Is it hard?" Landen asked.

Drake stared forward and relaxed into the couch, then smiled slightly. "You just have to want more than anything to make things right. You have to have the best intentions," he said. Raising his eyebrows, he tilted his head and glanced at me. "Once you have that intention, you send it out through your energy. It has to be strong enough that all the energy around you is shocked into stillness as yours passes by. When you lose your focus, time begins again."

"How are you forcing your energy at that darkness over and over again and not getting weaker? How do you build yourself again?" Landen asked Drake.

Drake laughed under his breath and winked at Landen

before answering him. "My friend, I fear it is from the same place you find yours – only from another time. My dreams...I remember them so vividly that my imagination can take me back to the moment...to feel...feel they way you do when you're complete."

I felt like the wind was knocked out of me. Landen's perfect blue eyes found me. He was jealous, but he didn't show it to the others. He reached his arm around me and pulled me to his side.

August looked at Drake, to Alamos and then to Landen. "The dreams were unlocked to protect him, to give him the ability to withstand the darkness for so long."

"Is that true?" Landen asked Drake.

Drake shrugged his shoulders. "It would be impossible for me to tell you if there was any truth in what I hear or see," he said, catching my gaze.

I let my eyes fall from his; I could barely manage the pain I saw there. Landen sat at attention and looked at Alamos. Perodine was pointing to the scroll and the look on Alamos' face was absolute disbelief. August followed Landen's stare.

"Are we all on the same page now?" August questioned.

Alamos looked up from the scroll in our direction. "You intend to kill him – you've lured us here as a sacrifice," he said, standing to walk in our direction.

My face turned white as a ghost and my stomach turned. Drake looked slowly behind him at Alamos, then to his mother, Beth, who had drifted into a deep sleep.

"Kill who? What are you talking about?" I asked, sitting forward and looking back at Landen.

Perodine's face was full of grief as she followed Alamos to the couches where we were sitting. Alamos stood in front of the fireplace and stared at Drake.

"This family has betrayed you once again," Alamos said to Drake as he looked at Beth and Marc's sleeping bodies.

Drake looked unshaken by Alamos' words. My eyes raced between Perodine and Alamos. Landen let his hand rest on my knee. I knew he was trying to calm me, but it wasn't working.

"Answer me – who is killing who?" I said louder. Beth stirred but did not wake.

Perodine looked sympathetically at Drake, then to me. "'The darkness shall consume the blood of Jayda and subdue the power'...it cannot live in Landen...you are his soul mate. Jayda and Oba proved that point once before. It will consume Drake, kill Landen then overpower you at the moment Venus and Earth align," Perodine said carefully as she knelt before me.

I expected Drake to protest against Perodine calling Landen my soul mate, against the idea of his murder, but he didn't. Instead, he looked calmly at Landen, then to me.

August stood abruptly. I was more than sure that he hadn't realized the details before now. "It said 'three would stand strong'...we thought it was Jayda, Aliyanna, and Willow...it could be the three of them...dying is not an option here," he argued.

Perodine squeezed my hand to get my attention. I looked into her green eyes and found the sympathy that I felt coming from her. "Your only defense is to move the knife through Drake's heart at the moment the darkness consumes him. That's the only way to protect your life, Landen's life, the life of the children."

I shook my head from side to side. Tears gushed from my eyes. I then looked at Drake and saw that he was looking at me; his dark eyes reached in my soul and pulled at my heart. I glanced at Landen, who wrapped his arms around me and pulled me to his shoulder. I squeezed him as tight as I could and tried to find relief from the grief that was consuming me.

"This is not the answer. You saw what happened yesterday when Drake was taken from these people: war will erupt if he's slain – and everyone in Delen will pay the price for this decision," August said into the room.

"There is no other way. Donalt has been preparing Drake's body for this moment. He will be capable of immense power the moment he joins him," Perodine said, standing.

"He's already consumed him once. He didn't look any more powerful to me," Landen said.

As I heard his words, I took in a breath a released my hold on him. I then leaned back and glanced at Landen then at Drake. Hope was starting to come back to me.

"What was it like?" Alamos asked Drake.

As he answered Alamos, Drake's eyes never left me. "I cannot recall the moment he entered me – but I can recall the time he was inside of me. It was as if my dreams had come to reality. What I wanted was mine. Life was perfect," he said.

"It kept you calm so it could control your body," Alamos said.

"I suppose, but I don't want to live a fantasy. If I can't have what I want in this life – then I'm ready for the next," Drake said bleakly.

August stood and began to pace, then stopped abruptly in front of Landen. "The looking glass," he said, looking at Landen. He turned to look at Drake. "Is there another one?"

Drake's eyes moved to Alamos and August followed

his gaze.

"Do you honestly think that we've had time to reconstruct another looking glass?" Alamos asked. "It took Donalt over a year to build the original."

"Is it possible for us to reconstruct it if we all worked together?" August asked.

"No," Alamos said.

"Even if it was, you're assuming that I'll look into it," Landen said, looking bleakly at August.

August knelt in front of Landen. "Whatever your intent is – it'll be better than war…better than murder," he said.

Landen looked down. I felt him struggle with his intent. He'd told me that he'd never look into the glass. I knew right now that he'd do anything to protect me from the demon that was chasing me. Landen nodded, but he refused to look August in the eyes. He didn't want to promise anything to him.

August stood. "Are you certain that it can't be rebuilt in time?" he asked Alamos.

"Not in time for Venus. Not in time to save Drake's life," Alamos said. I could see the grief in every part of him.

Drake was staring at me. I let my eyes meet his. "I am not killing you – or anyone else," I said, staring back at him.

Perodine looked down. I knew I was letting her down. She felt after all this time – all of these lives – I was submitting to the darkness. She tried her best to hide the frustration she felt.

"I'll heal him," Landen said, standing. "Willow will strike him and I'll heal him – and all of this will be over," he said, looking at me.

"This is not a cut," Alamos argued. "She has to strike

his heart – that's the first place a soul connects with the body. Have you healed a wound of that degree?" Alamos asked sarcastically. Landen looked at Drake and shook his head no, but he still held the same confidence.

"She strikes him and as you begin to heal him, the darkness overtakes Willow…what's your priority – his life or hers?" Alamos continued. "His fate is sealed. Once again, the bad soul mate pays the price for loving the one he desires."

Sunlight peered into the room. I felt the astonishment and fear coming from Perodine and August. When Landen felt it, his eyes looked to the rising sun and a fear rose in him. At that moment he felt overpowered.

"What is it? " I asked as I watched them walk to the window.

"The sun is rising in the West," Landen said quietly. I stood and walked slowly to his side.

"Just as it does on the planet Venus. We're all trapped in an illusion now," Alamos said in a sullen tone.

I watched as the sun rose. I'd seen so many sunrises since I'd found Landen. I knew that it rose gracefully, that you could barely see it climb through the sky. This sun was different, though. Within a moment it was suspended in the middle of the sky. A purple haze reflected below it and darkness above it. The city of Delen, the wall that always had workers surrounding it, was abandoned. We were alone in this dark world.

Chapter Ten

Perodine turned and crossed the room to the doorway that led to the long hall. Drake hadn't moved from his seat. He seemed unsurprised by the sun rising in the West (as it did on Venus). That right now, in theory, the world was trapped in a prison – and the guard that held the key was the devil himself.

I walked slowly back to Dane's sleeping body. Alamos leaned against the back of the couch and let his hand rest on Drake's shoulder. Landen and August stared at the sun, which refused to rise any higher in the sky.

Perodine returned with a large hourglass. The top and the bottom of it were made of gold the bars that framed the glass bowls were made of emeralds. The sand was black. She sat it on the wide base of the fireplace.

"We will have to watch this and turn it twelve times. Can we reason that that is how much time we have?" Perodine said to us.

"For all we know, we have only minutes," Alamos argued. "This illusion could have begun days ago."

I felt her frustration. I knew that she had her doubts about the time of day as well. Suddenly, chills spread across my skin and the hair on the back of my neck rose. I felt something. Drake was staring at me. His eyes widened as he leaned slowly forward. His emotion caused Landen to turn to look at me.

"Wake him," Drake said quietly, keeping his eyes locked on mine.

My trembling hand reached for Dane's knee and I squeezed it as hard as I could. Perodine, August, and Alamos were now frozen in place staring at me and Dane -- who sat forward abruptly. I didn't look at him. My eyes were locked with Drake. I felt safe in his gaze. A look of terror, though, was across my face.

"Calm...be calm...hide the emotion of fear...think of something else," Landen thought.

I tried to, but I could feel the cold of the darkness all around me. Every muscle in my body tensed and began to tremble. The beat of my heart was as loud as drums in my head. I held my breath for so long, I felt dizzy.

"Stand and walk her to me," Drake said quietly to Dane, who was still staring at me as he stood.

Dane put his arm around my waist. As we stood, from the corner of my eye I could see a dark shadow on the edge of Dane's Aura. As we moved to Drake, we woke Marc. The darkness hovering around Dane and me was the first thing he saw. He jolted up and searched the room for Landen. Finding him, he climbed over the back of the couch and walked backwards to Landen's side. Landen had been slowly stepping closer to me, wanting to take me away from there. August and Perodine were behind him, searching for an idea to save me. I felt them suppressing their fears, struggling to make their energy as strong as they could. When we reached Drake, he reached for my hand. His warm, mesmerizing touch brought a calm that I wasn't capable of finding on my own. When he saw the relief in my eyes, he moved his eyes above me and pushed me behind him into Landen's arms. I turned and saw a dark wall floating in mid-air. It moved from side to side, teasing us. A low growl came from the shadow. Drake raised his hand – sending a force of energy at the wall. Landen shielded us with his energy. Drake's energy was repelled by the wall, which sent back at us the shields of energy that we were all hiding behind to protect ourselves from the blow. The cloud then evaporated, taking its chill with it.

Suddenly, I felt the tension in the room release. Marc pushed through us and leaned over the couch where Beth was sleeping. "Mom, are you alright? Wake up," he said as he reached for her shoulder.

Drake turned to look at Marc. "She won't wake for at least twelve hours," he said in a low tone.

As Marc's eyes moved to Drake, anger engulfed him. "You drugged her," he accused.

Landen let go of me and walked to Marc's side, reaching for his shoulder to give him a sense of calm – but Marc brushed him away. "No, this is uncalled for! How dare you? What else have you done to her?!" he yelled.

Drake's expression was placid. "I wasn't going to allow her to listen to all of you debate my execution. She's endured enough," he answered.

I glanced at Landen. *"You knew that's what he was doing,"* I thought, offended that he hadn't told me.

Landen looked at me. *"I knew he wanted to protect her from what was to come. I didn't know he already knew what they were going to ask you to do,"* he answered. His eyes reflected the truth I heard in his thoughts.

I stepped forward furious at Drake. He refused to look me in the eye. "You knew...you knew what they were going to say. If you knew, then you know a different way out of this – and if you don't, you better find one because I refuse to touch that knife to take anyone's life."

Dane and Marc were staring at each other, realizing what they'd missed as they slept.

"Love, it's either you or me – we have no choice," Drake said, letting his eyes rise to meet mine.

As I stared back at him, I felt the intent of the room. They were going to convince me, show me that there was no other way to break through this illusion in which we were all trapped. I felt so outnumbered, overpowered, and angry. I pushed by Drake and began to run from the room. I felt Dane behind me. The others stood still. I reached the hallway. I was going to go to the string, to find a way around the wall, an image, anything – just a way out. I knew if Rose were there, if my parents were there, they'd defend me, tell me that murder was never an answer.

I'd made it to the fourth doorway before I felt Dane's arms around my waist. I pulled against him, but his strength was overpowering and he turned me in his arms. I struggled against his body until the anger surfaced in breathless tears. My body finally numb, I reached my arms around Dane's shoulders and his arms tightened around me. He let me cry, holding me as tight as he could.

"I can't kill him," I said over and over again.

"Calm down. You can't think like this," he said, rocking us back and forth.

I breathed in and let the tension in my body diminish, then my tears stopped. I stepped away from Dane and wiped my face dry, then leaned against the wall and stared at him.

"They're insane – all of them. It's like Alamos and Perodine have been playing a game of chess. Drake, Landen, and I are the pieces…neither of them realized it was the devil's board, that in the end he'd find a victory," I said, tucking a strand of my hair behind my ear.

Dane's eyes held sympathy for me. "He's not going to win," he said.

"Taking a life before its time is a victory for him. Letting this dimension suffer to the degree that it has is a win for him. They'll always remember Donalt's reign. They'll never release themselves from the fear of his presence."

"Willow, they *will* forget. This is only the beginning. You have to have faith that all that you've done will be worth it," Dane said.

"Worth it? There is *nothing* worth the destruction I bring," I argued.

"You haven't done anything but dodge what those insane people have put in your path," Dane said, reaching for my shoulders. "And for the record, I'm not a fan of any of them."

"Well, I'm going to dodge another one because I'm not killing anyone," I said, crossing my arms.

Dane let his arms drop from my shoulders and stepped back. He then ran his hands through his hair and sighed. "Are they sure they're reading it right – that you have to do that?" he asked.

I nodded. "All of them agree – and apparently that doesn't happen often," I said in a low tone.

"August agrees?" Dane asked.

"He didn't argue once he heard that when the darkness consumed Drake, it would kill Landen, then overtake me," I said, a sick feeling rising in my throat.

An understanding came across Dane's face. "Listen to what you just said: even if you allowed it to take over you – would you want to watch Drake's body kill Landen? They're asking you to take the lesser of two evils. Everything you've lived through so far will be in vein if you don't stop it from ending your life too soon," he said sympathetically to me.

"The lesser of two – would you be referring to Drake, someone you hate?" I said.

"I may not like him, but that doesn't mean I want him to die. After hearing everything I've heard over the past few days, I'm surprised he's as stable as he is," Dane said, defending himself.

"If that bad soul mate stuff they were talking about has any weight at all, then that means there's someone for him. Chances are, she looks just like me...what I am going to do if I find my 'twin' and she's lonely? Am I supposed to tell her, 'Oh sorry, he found the bad soul mate first and he got in my way – so I had to just kill him?" I said sarcastically.

"Your twin?" Dane questioned.

"They say we all have one," I said, raising my eyebrows and considering the possibility for the first time. "I've been one before. That's the only way I can understand the dreams Drake is having. He said he strengthens himself with the memories of them – but it's impossible for it to have been me. Landen is the only one I can complete."

"How long was I asleep?" Dane asked, confused on

how he'd missed so much.

"Not long," I said, looking down the hallway to the study.

"What if she's not here? What if she's waiting for him in his next life?" Dane asked.

"You're *not* going to convince me to kill him," I said, glaring up at him.

"I'm just saying, Willow. You don't know. No one knows. All you can do is take what's in front of you and make a choice. That choice will lead to another and then another," Dane said as fast as he could.

I looked down. He was making sense – they all were – but I was the one that would hold the knife…I was the one that would have to live with this for the rest of my life.

"You know that no one ever really dies. You saw that in Pelhan's world when Livingston stood in front of you," Dane said.

"Livingston lingers because he feels his life isn't complete. He wants to see us all in this life. Drake's life isn't over. He'll linger too, a lost soul."

"Willow, this is just one guy's opinion, so don't hate me for it, but if he loves you half as much as he says he does, his life was over when he saw you choose Landen – twice," Dane added.

"So you're saying, 'He's suicidal – so it's fair?'" I said, holding back my temper.

"No," Dane said, rolling his eyes. "If he was suicidal, he would have found an easier way to die. I'm saying that he's struggling to find a purpose now and that he wants to lay his life down for you. Telling him that he can't is just as painful as losing you for a third time. All of you will die in vain."

I slid down the wall and pulled my legs to me. I

wanted it all to go away; I wanted to feel the way I did when I was one with Landen, to live in that bliss and hide from the pain in which the body lingered. Dane leaned against the opposite wall and watched me struggle with my thoughts; he felt helpless. I was surprised that he hadn't been more forceful with me. I knew my decision not to kill Drake would sentence us all to death.

I felt Landen, then looked up and saw him and Marc walking my way. Halfway to me, Marc halted. Dane understood the wordless direction and walked further down the hall. They were giving Landen and me a barrier, which was as much privacy as we'd be allowed to have. Landen reached me and sat down at my side. He then wrapped his arm around me and I hid my face in his neck. I felt the beat of his heart against my cheek and watched as his chest rose and fell. My imagination took me to watching Drake kill him in a dim future. I held him tighter as I pushed the thoughts away.

"Willow, I love you. I don't want you to have to do this alone, but I can't help you," he thought.

"I would never ask you to kill for me," I thought quietly.

Landen moved his shoulder so I'd have to look at him; his blue eyes looked deep in my soul. *"I would, Willow, but that's not why I can't help you now,"* he thought.

"What are you not saying?" I thought as my eyes raced over his face.

"August demanded that they show us why they were so certain. When they read the scroll again, Alamos argued the theory that it would simply kill Drake and enter me, that because you loved me it would have your heart, your power instantly."

"They said it couldn't live in a soul mate," I argued.

"They thought that because of Oba. Alamos argued that Donalt told him the words he used against him were for his sons – not him. He could be stronger; we have to prepare ourselves for that scenario."

"No," I thought. As the reality of losing Landen came to me tears pooled in my eyes. He pulled me into his lap and held me as tight as he could.

"I'm going to fight to stay alive; promise me that you'll do the same," Landen thought.

I nodded and kissed his neck softly, then let my face rest against his warm skin. *"I feel blind. I can't feel Alamos or Drake, and Perodine seems to hide her emotions from me at will...I don't know who to believe or if what I'm being asked to do is right."*

Landen let his hand run across my back. *"Everyone in that room's sole intent is to keep you alive, for you to be the person you've fought to be for so long,"* he thought, kissing the top of my head.

"How can Drake be so content with dying?"

"He doesn't want to die. He thinks he's saving your life by surrendering his."

"He told you that?"

"No. I can feel it. He did tell me not to look at you when it begins. That if it manages to enter me – one look into your soul would be all it needed," he thought.

"He's helping you."

"He's protecting you. I'm just his source."

"It's not fair, Landen. What are we going to say to Beth when she wakes up?"

His arms tightened around me, and I felt his grief for Beth for everything she'd endured. *"I don't know. I'd hope that she would focus her attention on Preston and help us defeat this monster."*

"I can't imagine them facing this one day."

As I felt the defeat in front of me, tears burned in my eyes. I didn't ever want my sister to feel the emotions that were coursing through me right then. A fear came through Landen, but he quickly suppressed it and brought forth the emotion of hope. *"I'm more than sure that when their time comes, they'll be more prepared than you or I."*

"What if it's you? I can't bear the thought of doing this to Drake. I know I won't be able to do this to you," I thought, sitting forward on his lap and staring into his eyes. I put my hands on his face and traced the beautiful indents of his dimples, which were hiding from me. He took a jagged breath and leaned his forehead to mine; he was doing everything in his power to remain calm, to keep me calm.

"You have to and even if I lose this fight, I'll go to Pelhan's and wait for you to finish what we've started. We will never be apart. I promise you. I need you to see it that way."

"Landen."

"Willow, listen to me: no one ever really dies. This is just a passage. Don't let this monster kill you."

I felt Dane and Marc's frustration. They'd both turned at the sound of our voices and were staring at us. Landen waved his hands, urging them to turn away. He then cradled my face with his hands and forced me to look into his eyes.

"I know you hate me telling you that there's a reason for everything – but there is. I want you to think of Libby – our Libby – and think of Allie. I want Brady to know that we did everything in our power to keep her safe. Preston, his life has been tested already; he deserves a chance to fill his purpose. You have to put your thoughts there. This isn't about who you love or how much you love them – this about a way of life for more people then we could ever

imagine."

As his words consumed me, I let out a breath that I'd been holding in. I then nodded as I set my intent to protect them, to protect their purpose at any cost. As he felt it, Landen smiled and pulled my face to his; he then let his lips rest gently on mine before he kissed me. I felt myself growing stronger in his embrace; he sent a calm through me that was hypnotic.

As he released me, he stared in my eyes and I could see his Aura growing brighter, wider, and more powerful than it had been the entire time we'd been there.

"How are you doing that? " I thought, smiling slightly.

"Following Drake's lead. Calling on my memories of you and me," he thought.

My smile left; I was relieved that Landen was able to make himself stronger with a single thought, but I didn't want to give Drake's memories any reality.

"They're not of me," I thought quietly.

Landen tilted his head and looked at me curiously, then smiled slightly. *"You think you have a twin,"* he thought. I nodded. *"I do, too,"* he thought.

"You believe the 'bad soul mate' story?" I thought.

"I don't know. They believe it. There's no doubt there. It's just...that image you saw me with looked just like you," Landen thought.

"I didn't think so; I didn't recognize her," I thought as the dark memories of Landen holding another girl the day we destroyed the looking glass came to me with a surge of jealousy.

"To me, she did," Landen thought, sending a rush of his love through his arms, which were holding me close to him.

"I want to find her – if you think she's real," I thought.

"When that wall falls, I'll take you wherever you want to go," he thought.

I looked in Dane's direction. I thought about going to the string anyway, but the memory of the screaming voices of my family hindered my desire.

"I know they're alright," Landen thought, sensing my uneasiness. *"And I know I can heal Drake – or myself. We're going home. We will beat this demon."*

"I hear the truth in your words and I feel your confidence, but I know that there's still a chance…this is not a game…someone could lose their life." I let my fear show itself in my eyes.

"Trust me, Willow."

"I want to talk to him. I want to see where they're reading this," I thought.

Landen grinned warily and nodded. I climbed out of his arms and stood. Dane and Marc turned when they heard us move. Landen then took my hand and led me back to the study, with Dane and Marc following silently behind us.

Chapter Eleven

In the study, they were all standing around the table. Drake was in the center. His arms were stretched out in front of the scroll. He looked like a king sending his army to battle. August and Alamos were at his side. Perodine was pacing in front of them. As we walked in, Drake looked up. His eyes met Landen's then locked with mine. He was trying to read me, to see if they'd convinced me to kill him.

As I came to her side, Perodine halted and watched, I looked into her beautiful green eyes and felt the sympathy she had for me. She wanted to bear the burden. She blamed herself for all my troubles.

I stood across the table mirroring Drake. Landen was at my side Dane and Marc flanked us. Perodine slowly walked to Alamos' side, trying to gauge my mood.

"Show me," I said, blankly looking down at the scrolls.

August cleared his throat and reached his hand for the center of the scroll, then pointed at the planet they thought was Venus. "This is Venus. The number nineteen is all over the image, a number that can be only divided by itself and one. This symbol," August said, pointing to a figure of two eights in the shape of a cross, "means 'inferior sister;' in broken translation, we can interpret earth and Venus, the alignment, and the number nineteen. Below this in the script, it says, 'It shall consume the blood of Jayda and subdue the power.'" August pointed above Venus; there, I could see the symbol of a fish with a hand and script. "This script says, 'Only in flesh shall it die, with the blade of diamonds.' I can't find a way to debate this."

"Does the nineteen mean more?" Dane asked.

August looked slowly up at Dane. "One and itself. Willow represents this number. Herself and one soul can only divide her. It will have no choice but to leave one standing before her – to consume the soul and overtake her."

"How do you know you're reading the script right? What if you're wrong? " I argued.

Perodine sighed and closed her eyes. "We are more than sure," she said, keeping her eyes closed, struggling to hide her frustration with me.

"You're out of time; we've made the choice for you," Alamos said sternly.

"You need to change your tone," Dane said, looking sharply at Alamos. He then looked at Drake and said, "You may want to rethink your alliances; this one seems all too eager to see you die." The sarcasm was heavy in his tone.

Alamos glared at Dane, then leaned forward and said, "Listen, child: you may think you're all that right now – but in a matter of minutes, your energy will have no purpose…you'll fall short just when you're needed the most."

Dane took a dominant step in Alamos' direction – only to be stopped by Landen.

"Stop," Landen said through his teeth, showing the room his frustration. He then pushed Dane back to my side and said, "All of you need to calm down; I'm going to heal us." His anger was apparent in his scarlet Aura. "It's not going to matter if they're right or wrong; we're all more than ready to get this over with."

The tension in the room was so heavy, I felt myself growing weak. Landen stepped protectively to me and wrapped his arms around me; he was having trouble finding the emotion to calm me simply because neither of us could see a way out of this hell in which we were trapped.

"I'm not going to let you heal me," Drake said into the silence. "I'm leaving this world tonight."

"You don't have a choice in the matter," Landen said, glaring over my head at Drake.

Alamos shook his head from side to side, slowly staring at Landen with a look of disbelief.

"You'd rather watch him suffer? How many times are you going to steal her away before you're satisfied?" Alamos asked.

"Are you blind or crazy, old man?" Marc yelled. "You're the guy who couldn't get over Perodine."

Alamos slammed his hands on the table. "If I had – Willow would not be here! I'm her father – did you forget that?" he asked.

"We didn't forget that you were too big of a chicken to defend her when she needed you to," Dane said, crossing to Marc's side.

Landen raised his hand and the chaos of the room was suspended. My eyes shifted between Landen and Drake, trying to conceive of the idea of Landen now having the power to stop time. He looked at me and smiled slightly, pushing down the thrill of the command he now had. Drake smiled and shook his head from side to side as he crossed his arms and stood up straight.

"Well done. You're a fast learner – but I must warn you that time will catch itself when you lose your focus." Drake turned to see Alamos frozen with his angry glare. "Alamos thinks we have the time wrong because I paused time yesterday; he's really going to be mad at you."

"It's not his emotion that I care about," Landen answered, looking into my eyes. He wanted to stop time forever, to stop the anguish that was suffocating me – but we both knew that the only way to defeat darkness was to face it. Landen looked at Drake; his anger told me that he was reading Drake's stubborn content. "Willow wants to talk to you alone. You look into her eyes and tell her that you want her to end your life."

Drake tightened his jaw and glared in my direction. He started to speak, but Landen reached out his hand to halt him. "You know what? It doesn't matter. She wants me to heal you. That's what I'm going to do. I'm letting this moment go – you take her out there and say your peace," he said, pointing to the observatory.

Drake hesitated, then pulled back his shoulders and nodded. As time resumed, Landen let out a deep breath. I blocked out the arguments and emotion around me and watched Drake walk around the table; I swear I could feel his hum before he ever touched me. As he gripped my arm and began to lead me to the observatory, I let a blissful breath escape. We'd reached the doorway before Dane had noticed; instinctively, he charged across the room at us.

"Where do you think you're going?" he said, reaching

for Drake's shoulder. Drake hesitated then looked across the room at Landen. Dane followed his gaze.

"He's more than capable of protecting her. Let them go," Landen said in a confident tone. Marc and Dane stood in shock.

Drake gripped my arm tighter; intensifying his mesmerizing touch, then guided me into the open observatory. The sun's haze had turned the room a deep purple. The placid pool of water sent a chill down my spine as the memory of images reaching from it came to me. Drake released my arm and stood in front of me forcing me to lean against the cold stone wall.

"Why is it when I need you to love me, you refuse – and when I need you to hate me, you act like you care?" he asked with a stern look across his face.

"Is that why you want to die – because I won't love you? That's weak," I said, offended by his words.

"Weak?" he gasped. "I've sat in that room with you for almost two days, watching you with him...I'd say that makes me the strongest man in the universe," he said with agony in his voice.

As I caught the gaze of his dark eyes, I lost my will to be angry. Tears pooled in my eyes. "I can't help it," I whispered.

He let out a jagged breath. "That's why I'm ready to move on. In a different life, you'll see things clearly," he whispered as his dark eyes softened.

"Dying is not moving on," I said, looking away and trying to hide the weakness of my tears.

"It's a way out of this hell. If I'm gone, then your challenge ends; I'm tired of putting you in harm's way," he said, turning my chin so I'd have to look at him.

"How do you know you're not meant to protect me?

That this is just the beginning?" I said, letting the tears wash down my face.

"According to you, my position has been filled," he said, looking away from me.

"I'm determined to make you see that you're wrong," I said, wiping my face dry.

"Don't waste your energy, love. If I survive, that will be my purpose – to make you see that you're wrong." He took a deep breath and stepped closer. His eyes slowly searched every feature of my face, then he reached his hand to me and gently reached to cradle my cheek; his touch felt so perfect – and for the first time, I leaned in to feel it more intensely. "We're nothing more than old souls, twisted in cruel fate – fighting for our right to heaven," he whispered.

"Heaven?"

"To be complete, one with another – that's my Heaven," he answered. He pulled me to his chest and held me as close to him as he could, rushing my body with his hum. I closed my eyes as I took it in.

"Willow, you take my breath away every time I see you…you're all I think about…it kills me that you'd rather believe a lie than me," he whispered.

I leaned back to look at him, to deny his words. He looked down at me and furrowed his eyebrows. "They told you I wanted the power…that seeing is all I cared about. You never gave me the chance to prove that all I wanted was to love you, to be the man you needed me to be. I spend my nights dreaming of our past and my days dreaming of our future; it's time for me to wake up and see things how they really are. I will *not* be the death of you; I love you too much – and my life is the price I'll pay to prove that. The moment you see the darkness enter me, you're going to strike my heart. You'll kill us all if you don't listen to me," he said carefully.

"People will still die, innocent people…war isn't the answer," I said, holding back another flood of tears. "You said you wouldn't betray them – but leaving them is a betrayal," I said, taking in the reality of war, that in an instant the wall around Delen could be charged and lives would be lost.

"I can't betray my brother. He has a purpose greater than mine; he and Libby need us to clear this path for them," Drake said with a sigh.

"Preston wouldn't want you to die. He wouldn't want anyone to die; his purpose is to show us how beautiful life is supposed to be. It's too precious. No one is dying tonight," I said, knowing that Landen would do as he promised and heal them if it was in his power.

"Love, I am afraid – without a doubt – that one life will be lost within the hour."

"He's going to heal you," I said, fighting against my anger.

"Landen can use any gift he wants on me – but it won't matter; to be healed, to want to live…that comes from the soul. If I don't accept it, he'll be wasting energy that should be used to protect you." He tilted his head to catch my eyes. "When this is over, you take my mother to Chara and never leave there again…we'll fight this demon in the next life."

"No. I won't rest until all the damage it's done is pure again. Hiding, giving up is *not* the answer."

"Willow, I lived with this demon for nineteen years. I've looked into his eyes and seen the cold greed that lies there. I don't trust anyone but myself to protect you from it. Let me pay this price. Live out your life in the sunshine of Chara. We'll meet again – and with you at my side, he will fall. I have no doubt," Drake said, stepping back to let me know that he'd said his peace.

"I don't believe you. You can't be OK with leaving this world," I said, trying to catch his gaze.

"If you could feel me, you'd know that I'm more than sure. Ask Landen; he has no trouble reading me," Drake said, looking to the doorway that led to the study.

I reached for his hand and wrapped my hands around his, feeling his mesmerizing touch consume me. "I can feel you...can you feel me?" I whispered. He nodded. As tears pooled in my eyes, I let the grief I was feeling flow through me. He raised his other hand to my face and I looked into his eyes and saw a sympathy that had never surfaced before. I watched as his eyes moved slowly across my face.

"We don't have a choice my love; our fate is sealed," he whispered.

As I closed my eyes and the tears streamed down my face, I shook my head from side to side in defiance. He leaned forward and gently kissed my forehead. "Another life, another time," he whispered as his fingers wiped away my tears.

I felt the air chill then the presence that I feared was all around me. Drake slowly turned -- the presence diminished before he had the need to protect me. He then reached his arm back and guided me in the direction of the study. I ran my hands across my face to dry my tears, but they kept flowing. I felt Drake's hand on my back as he urged me to walk faster.

Landen was waiting beside the door. He opened his arms and I let myself fall into his embrace. As I cried silently, he rocked us back and forth and let his head rest on mine. I knew my fears were shaking his confidence, but I couldn't control the way I felt; too much was at risk.

"I can't do this...what if it's you it enters...I won't...I

can't," I thought.

"I don't want you to see me, to see Drake...see the darkness – that's what you're killing...have faith in me," Landen thought, putting his hands on either side of my face.

I closed my eyes and felt the burn as more tears streamed silently down my face. I then nodded and took a deep breath. As he pulled me to his chest and held me as close as he could, I saw his Aura grow so bright that it was near blinding.

Drake walked to Marc, who pulled his shoulders back, prepared to defend himself if need be. "To prevent war," he said to Marc in a solemn tone, "you'll stand in the shadows of my balcony and speak to the people. Don't give them any reason to doubt that you're me; that will buy all of you enough time to find another solution." He then looked to Alamos and said, "My last request is that you help them in any manner they need. Don't let this city fall – or I'll haunt you myself." Finally, he looked in my direction and said in a tender tone, "Does that ease your fears, Love?"

I shook my head from side to side and buried my face in Landen's chest. I felt the sympathy and anxiety of the room. Landen pulled my chin up so I'd look at him, then he leaned in and kissed me.

"I love you; be strong for me," he thought.

"I love you."

He smiled slightly then stepped back from me. Perodine was at my side. She slowly slid the knife into my hand – but I refused to look at it. I stared at her, begging for a way out of this, but she just looked away as her tears began to fall.

"It could come at any moment," August said quietly.

I caught his sympathetic stare, then looked to Marc and

Dane. They felt helpless. Grief had already consumed them. Alamos walked to Perodine's side to console her. Landen and Drake were locked in a stare. I could feel Landen's frustration and assumed Drake's intent was still death.

"Are you ready to dance with the devil?" Drake asked Landen. Landen nodded. "Don't you dare look at her," Drake said firmly.

I could see the breath leaving my body. The room had turned cold – painfully cold – and the walls and windows began to tremble. All the light left. It was so dark that I felt blind.

I focused on the emotions around me. The only one I could feel was Landen. The only sound was my beating heart as it raced in my chest. Cracks of light began to emerge in the floor, then they slowly stretched out as far as I could see. It looked as if I were standing on a star-lit sky.

In the glow in front of me, I could see Landen and Drake. The others had vanished. I looked down in my trembling hand and assured myself that the knife was there. I had to tell myself to hold it tighter. My fear was paralyzing, I lost the emotion of Landen and trying to find it just scared me more.

I heard a low growl surround us. I stepped in Landen's direction, but he held his hands out, telling me to stay. His eyes looked away. I knew he was trying to protect me, but I felt so alone.

The space between Drake and Landen turned black. I felt the presence that had haunted us before. Suddenly, a light blue glow appeared around Drake and Landen. It gave me hope that Drake was at least attempting to protect himself. The dark shadow began to turn the color of ash, and the color brought forth the image of man with a perfectly sculpted body, a beautiful, flawless face, and eyes as dark as coal. Breathtaking wings stretched from its back, extending well over Landen and Drake. It was a vivid, evil, angel.

As it stared intently at me, it reached its arms out to touch Landen and Drake, its hands reaching through the blue glow as if it didn't exist. Their faces showed the agony that they were feeling. They were frozen, unable to move. I gripped the knife in my hand and stared back into its coal eyes, fighting back a flood of tears. Darkness came from its chest and moved inside of Drake – but before I could step forward, it crossed into Landen. The evil angel grinned deceitfully at me. I felt my body go numb when I realized that if I struck Drake and was wrong, it would have no choice but to enter Landen – and we'd all die that night.

Out of the silence, I heard beautiful laughter. As the laughter grew louder, the dark eyes I was staring into scowled. I knew the laughs. They belonged to Libby and Preston. Suddenly, an undeniable peace came to me and the air grew warmer. In front of Landen, an image of Libby appeared and Preston appeared before Drake. They smiled innocently up at me, unshaken by my appearance of terror. Libby looked beside me and I slowly turned my head and saw an image of myself. I was smiling and in my eyes I could see an adventurous spirit that I'd never seen before. The image reached for my shoulder and memories that didn't belong to me rushed through my mind: I felt a youth that I'd never felt before, full of curiosity and invincibility...I saw myself growing up in the Palace with Landen...our life once we reached Chara...the determination to redeem Esterious was more powerful than I'd felt in this lifetime.

The image gently released me and I looked back at Libby. She and Preston were looking to my other side. My eyes followed – only to find another image of myself. These eyes, they still had spirit – but they'd aged. This image reached for my shoulder and as she touched me a flash of another life came to me: I was standing in a beautiful garden, playing with my children. My sister, Samilya, rushed to me with her children at her side and she cried as she told me that something had taken over Oba. The memories flashed to a dining room: I was setting the food on the table when soldiers rushed in and carried me and Samilya's children back to Oba. I knew I loved Oba, but I still grieved. Oba's heirs would live with him and my children would be in the care of Samilya. I told myself I was protecting them, that if the darkness returned we'd all die. I spent the rest of my life trying to find a way to defeat the darkness that took me from my children.

The image of myself released my shoulder and looked remorsefully at me. I knew then that *I* was Jayda's descendant – not Landen and Drake. Their descendants never knew that the children weren't moved from their place of birth. The images of me moved before me, blocking the view of the children – and the pain the evil angel was giving to Landen and Drake. In my voice, I heard them say, "The darkness will consume the blood of Jayda and subdue their power."

I was the blood of Jayda -- it would take over my heart. The angel knew that neither Landen nor Drake would be able to end my life. In an instant, understanding came across my face and the images of me faded away – taking Preston and Libby with them. The darkness that was moving between Landen and Drake at the evil angel's request was growing larger and hesitating longer. I looked in its coal-dark eyes and smiled. My hand was steady as I raised the knife. As I turned the blade to my chest, my heartbeat slowed. I then took a deep breath and slowly, gently slid the blade into my chest. I felt the ground tremble beneath my feet and heard a horrified scream as I fell to my knees and gradually closed my eyes.

Chapter Twelve

I think everyone has heard the stories of what happens when you die: the white light, the tunnel. We're told it's painless, blissful. It must be different for everyone, though, because I didn't see a light or a tunnel. I felt pain.

As my last breath moved through me, my body seemed to scream out in protest. I felt cold, disoriented. Everything I'd ever done or said moved before me. I saw and felt the laughter of childhood, the fear of my nightmares, the joy of family and friends. I felt the impatience that's always surrounded me.

The moment I first saw Landen in the flesh came to me. I relived every second we'd shared together, feeling my emotions, his emotions, as if for the first time. The times I was alone with Drake came to me all the fear, anger, and sorrow I felt for him over the last few months rushed through my soul. My whole life as Willow Haywood was relived in just a few seconds.

Then my perspective changed. I saw my life through the eyes of the ones around me. I was standing in judgment. And I was the judge. As the images began with me being a little girl, I didn't fear them because I've always thought that I knew exactly how I affected the people around me. I could feel their emotions – what more could there be? I was wrong. We impact those around us on a level deeper than emotions. The emotions are just the end result – but before the emotions come forth, the soul, mind, and body take in all that they're given of the world around them. The three don't have to agree for an emotion to come to life. Often-times, the mind and body are at war and the soul plays the role of peacemaker.

I could see how in my childhood my distance to the ones around me made me seem cold. I could feel how nervous Dane and Olivia were when they tried to become my friend. Through their eyes, I saw them deciding not to be afraid of me, to take a chance. I felt the worry my parents have always shielded from me. My father, it seems, had mastered concealing his fear for my life years ago...I saw my distance cut him in two...I wanted to go back – to be a little girl again. I wanted to smile, I wanted to tell my parents that I loved them and that their decisions never brought me harm; their love was all I needed to get to Landen.

The first moment I saw Libby in my mother's arms came rushing to me. I'd forgotten the first emotion I'd felt: jealousy. It wasn't of Libby – it was of my mother; I felt that she was now in care of what was once mine. My soul cried; I was angry that I'd forgotten that. If I'd chosen to remember, I would have discovered long ago that she once belonged to me and Landen – and I would I have saved myself from the worry of not knowing if Landen was real, as well as from the fear of not finding him.

Landen…my perfect Landen…I saw him as infant, as a child, as the man he is today. I felt a perfect love; it didn't matter what I said or did – his love was unconditional, complete. I felt the joy he had each time we dreamed together before we met. I felt his anxiety as he searched for the beacon that would lead him to me, as well as the overwhelming relief he felt when he found me. Though he was bothered by the secrets that were kept from the both of us and the uncertainty of our past and future, he didn't care; all he knew was that with me he was complete, invincible. The emotion we felt when we joined as one couldn't compare to how it felt from this perspective. I knew then that it didn't matter if I had a body on earth or not; we would always be one, for all of eternity.

I lived through his family as they met me for the first time. They were overjoyed for Landen; they felt that he'd proven to them that, in this universe, love is a power that can't be hindered.

I've always thought that Landen's mother, Aubrey, was beautiful and strong, but I never realized how much she loved us until now. She wanted nothing more than to lead her son to me.

I saw Clarissa, his sister, willing to sacrifice everything to protect Landen, to send Dane to defend us; she thought that if Landen and I were ever taken from each other, soul mates throughout the world would mourn and have doubt for the first time.

Brady, Landen's brother – who was almost identical to him in every way – had always seemed brave to me. Willing to defend his baby brother at any cost, he proved to be even more loyal than I'd ever imagined. I heard conversations between him and Felicity; they'd decided to be the source of calm, balance, and protection we needed.

Ashten, a man who always seemed reserved and protective, had shielded who he truly was from both Landen and me. He was afraid, afraid that he'd not only lose Landen, but also everyone he loved. He didn't trust any decision he made. I wanted to tell him that we loved him and that we are all imperfect, that fear only has the power we give it.

Marc and Chrispin, they felt that they owed Landen and me their lives; without us, they felt that they wouldn't have found the one they loved, that Olivia and Stella would have escaped them somehow. It was foolishness that made me angry. I knew that – no matter what – they would have found them; at that moment, I even thought they would have been better off finding them on their own.

Rose…beautiful Rose…though she was my grandmother, she saw me through the eyes of her youth. She'd spent her life waiting for my return to Chara, to watch me and Landen move the universe; my soul grieved, for that dream was dying now. I could only hope that my grandfather, Karsten, would be able to comfort her as she heard the news of my death, that Rose would somehow be able to console our family.

August, a man that had always seemed to be one step in front of me and Landen, showed me his uncertainty for the first time. I could feel how he struggled to let us make our own decisions, that Nyla had been the one who'd held him back when he wanted to tell Landen what to do and how to do it. I could only hope that she could be the source of strength he needed now.

I saw them all standing at the passage in Pelhan's perfect world. The innocence of Preston, Libby, and little Allie called to me above the memory of the others. I wanted to know that Landen and I had led them far enough, that in a year's time they'd be able to finish what Landen and I had started.

I got colder. It became darker. The visions of my family started to fade. I saw Perodine come into view and the chill around my soul seem to lessen. She wiped a tear from her eye and moved her hand across thin air as if she were trying to undo it all, to let me make choices on my own. She was trying to let me know that she should have trusted me, that a heart can't be fooled for long. I don't know how she did it, but she took me back to where it all really began for me.

The day at the lake, the last day I spent in Franklin with my friends played out in slow motion as I lived it through them. They were overwhelmed with a mix of emotions; some of them felt betrayed because I was leaving, some felt jealous of the perfect life they'd imagined me having – but overall, they grieved. They felt like they'd taken my presence for granted; it made them realize that everything ends, that the people in our lives today may not be there tomorrow.

I heard conversations that had escaped me before, centered on them telling each other how much they meant to one another. A pain came through my soul as I listened to my friend Monica, the one who lost her life, telling Olivia and Jessica how much she admired me, how she was going to start living her life as I had – not worrying about what others thought; she said she was going to love herself and let life take its course. I felt a resolve in her, a peace. I was so involved with my own life, leaving them, discovering a new world, that I'd never noticed this emotion. If I had, I would have told her that I was proud of her, that it didn't matter how long your life was; it only mattered that you were happy.

The moment Drake arrived absorbed me: this time, as he stepped out of his Jeep, I felt him; it was like taking a first breath, seeing a new light. He was human for the first time. When his eyes saw mine, I felt his overwhelming relief of finding me, his faith that I wasn't lost forever – and yes, I did feel a love from him, a beautiful, imperfect love; it was for someone that looked just like me, someone he'd always known. Drake saw Dane as a devil taking me from him. In his mind, he thought if he took my friends, Dane would be willing to trade them for me, that I was being held prisoner by a web of lies.

Our time together on the night of the blue moon came: I could feel his anxiety, his fear of rejection. He was fighting for what he thought he loved, rescuing me from a life that didn't belong to me. I felt his desperation and his heart breaking as he showed me the dark images of the ones I loved in pain. In his mind, he was showing me that they were only temporary; his love for me was immortal.

The time I was trapped in Evelyn played out: I saw him standing in his study, Alamos telling him something was wrong, that over half of Chara was in Esterious looking for me. I felt his heart freeze; he demanded that they find out what had happened.

The scene shifted and I saw a man in a cloak hand him a sketch of Evelyn. When he discovered that Evelyn lived in a town that was almost completely destroyed, he guided over a hundred soldiers, his mother, and Alamos there. They searched through the night and at dawn when they found Evelyn and Stella's name recorded at the shelter, abundant relief overcame him. I felt how anxious he was as he waited for us to be called to the palace; it took everything he had to not run to me. I felt his rage when he learned that Damien had hurt me and his fear when Alamos told him that I couldn't have picked a worse body to be trapped in.

He struggled with himself; he thought that if he told me who I was, the shock would cause the body I was in to fail. He reasoned he only had two choices: either take me back to the web of lies he thought I lived in, or win my heart – which was something he thought should only belong to him.

When Landen came for me and I left without a word, I felt it tear Drake's soul in two. When I arrived with Landen to release the energy that Donalt had trapped, my presence took his breath away. He fought with the emotions of betrayal. He told himself that I only came back to give him a chance to show me how much he did love me, that when I saw our lives together and realized that Landen had held another, I'd melt into his arms and we'd have a fairy tale ending. When I told him that I couldn't give him what didn't belong to me, I all but took his will to live away. He'd stayed in his room, lost in lucid dreams, until the darkness had brought him to the palace. He awoke with me in his arms, which was the shock that gave him the power to push the darkness out him. He'd decided just moments ago that the only thing he could trust was the way he felt about me, that he'd love me even if I didn't love him; when the darkness began to move through him, he held that thought.

I knew then that if I submitted to the cold darkness that was pulling me, my last act would be a selfish one. Yes, I'd have Landen now and always, but my family would feel as if they'd failed, the path before Libby, Preston, and Allie would be too steep. And Drake...Drake would never find her, the one who looks just like me, the one who completes him. The darkness that had tormented all of our lives would win. Hell would make itself known on earth.

It took every ounce of energy that I possessed in my soul, but I fought against the weight that I was feeling. The pain that I felt intensified. I found myself above my body. As I looked down, I saw that I was lying in a pool of my own blood. Drake had pulled the knife from my chest and was holding my head in his lap. I felt a crushing grief from him. Landen was on his knees. I could see the darkness moving in and out of him – torturing him.

"Don't leave! I love you!" Drake said over and over again as he rocked me back and forth.

Something caused him to look up, to look into my soul, which was hovering over my body. A sensation of power came over him and he laid my head gently down and reached for Landen's hands, then put them over the wound on my heart.

A growl surfaced inside Landen's chest. The evil angel reached to pull him away – then I saw Landen's body pull forward.

"You've lost! You can't live in him. He loves her too much! You can't live in me. I love her too much!" Drake screamed at Landen's body.

Landen's body tensed -- sweat beaded across his brow. As he forced the darkness from within himself, his jaw locked and his soul screamed. The demon scowled then lunged its dark cloud at Landen again – but Drake instinctively shielded his energy around the three of us. Landen's energy was so depleted that I could barely see his Aura. He took a deep breath and focused on my open wound. A white glow hummed under his hands then pushed through my skin. I felt like I was being pulled through a tight vacuum. My soul screamed in pain as it took full ownership of the damage that I'd brought to my body. What Landen had left, he pushed through me. The pain was so unbearable that I tried desperately to escape the prison of my body – but my mind wouldn't submit. I breathed in and out as slowly as I could, feeling the healing power of Landen and the hum of Drake's touch. Somehow, I found calm and began to drift.

Somewhere, somehow, Landen's soul appeared before me. I could feel his exhaustion, his pain. He leaned in slowly, resting his lips gently on mine, then he pulled me into him – and we joined as one, submitting to one another. It was if we'd taken this amazing feeling for granted before; we'd never acknowledged the degree of separation that death could bring. That would never happen again; this was a perfect moment, a moment that easily could have escaped us.

I felt deep concern and someone squeezing my hand and I opened my eyes to see Beth on her knees at my side. I was lying in the center of the room between Drake and Landen. I looked slowly back and forth, assuring myself that they were only sleeping. I carefully pulled myself up and surveyed the room. Across the floor, I could see Alamos, Perodine, Marc, and Dane lying still, sleeping. I looked back at Beth, dazed and confused.

"What happened? Why was Drake holding the knife?" she asked, raising the diamond blade into my view.

I looked to my side and watched as Drake's chest rose and fell. My eyes moved to his perfect face; I felt the burn as tears welled in my eyes.

"He pulled it from me," I whispered, reaching to hold his hand, to feel his touch.

Beth's trembling hands covered her mouth, trying to hide the shock she was feeling. Everyone began to stir. Landen and Drake sat up at the same time. A terror came over Landen as he replayed his last memories. He laid me back down gently and pulled down my shirt to assure himself that I was healed. Drake leaned over me, searching with Landen for a wound that didn't exist. A simple white line was all that remained.

"You did it," Drake whispered.

"We both did," Landen said, pulling me up slowly and embracing me as tightly as he could.

Drake slid closer to me and took my hand to get my attention. "Why?" he asked in a cracked voice.

The others had surrounded us. "I'm the blood of Jayda. The children stayed. The twins changed places," I said, taking in a deep breath and feeling myself grow stronger.

I felt the astonishment and disbelief in the room. Everyone was realizing that they weren't as certain as they'd thought they were.

"How did you know?" Landen asked, leaning me back so he could see me.

"I saw them, Aliyanna, Jayda. They stood at my side and showed me the life I lived then."

Landen looked at Drake, who shook his head no.

"We didn't see them," Landen said.

"Did you see Libby and Preston?" I asked, bewildered.

They both looked blankly at each other. I knew then that they hadn't. The charm on my neck began to hum against my skin. I felt as light as a feather. All of a sudden, a light burst from it, then the room around us was filled with images of me. Drake moved protectively closer to Landen and me as the images floated through the room. Paintings that we'd burned came from the ash and hung in their place and the mirrors unveiled themselves, showing no sign of ever shattering. The shadows of the corners vanished. The room instantly lost any eerie feeling it may have once held. The images of me joined as one and flowed angelically back into my charm, and in their wake beside us was a small pile of gray ash. Drake carefully reached for the pile and let the ash slide through his fingers. Marc was kneeling at Landen's side.

"Is that all that remains?" Marc asked.

I slowly moved my head from side to side; I knew it was only a very small part of the demon I'd faced.

"The sun is setting in the West," I heard August say.

We turned to see him at the window. Dane stood in front of me and helped me up and Landen and Drake found their way to their feet. We made our way to August's side. Outside, we could see the people of Delen going about their day; the workers along the wall were moving forward with their task. I felt a new emotion and turned to see the silent servant girl standing in the doorway. She bowed her head then asked Perodine, "Shall I prepare dinner?"

Perodine looked to me, then to the girl. "What time is it now?" she asked.

"Almost seven-thirty, ma'am," she answered.

We all seemed to sigh at once in relief.

"No. Our guest will be leaving shortly," Perodine answered. The girl bowed her head and left.

Landen turned back and stared at the workers along the wall. He then sighed and looked at Drake. "They're anxious," he said, tilting his head in the direction of Drake's followers.

Drake nodded. "I need to appear before them before the sun sets," he answered, letting his eyes meet mine.

"Do you think the string's open?" Marc asked.

"There's only one way to find out," Landen said, looking down at me.

I was overjoyed to see my family, but my heart held sympathy for Drake and for Beth; I knew they'd stay there.

I stepped cautiously to Perodine and hugged her. "I'll be back as soon as I know they're safe," I said in her embrace.

She shook her head no. "Take a day to rest; enjoy the world you created so long ago."

I nodded and passed by her. August then walked to Alamos and Perodine's side.

"I'm going to help them escort my family home, then I'll be back to understand what happened here – and what will happen now," he said.

Perodine nodded. "Bring her," she said to August. His eyes questioned who she was referring to. "The one who's had your thoughts throughout this, your soul mate; you will be of sound mind if she is at your side," she said, smiling slightly.

August smiled and nodded.

Alamos looked at Perodine. "I must go with him to protect him from the court. I'll return when I'm sure they're not threatened," he said.

Perodine nodded as she looked at Drake. "Keep in rhythm of the man they think you are and you will be fine."

He nodded, took a deep breath, then looked at his mother; Beth looked down, fighting back the arguments she wanted to invoke. As he led us all to the passage in his room, Drake walked to her side and let his hand rest on her back. As we walked, he put his arm around Beth and began to whisper; I felt her fear and frustration as he spoke.

I looked up at Landen. *"He wants her to go with us, to see Livingston and Preston,"* he thought, pulling me as close to him as he could.

I saw Beth whispering in protest, then felt the two of them reach a resolve.

At the passage, Marc and Dane stepped in first. They weren't going to allow me or Beth to hear the screams if they remained. A moment later, Marc reached his hand through, telling us to enter.

August guided Alamos in the passage. Drake looked at Landen and me. "Guide her to your family and bring her back to me by day's end tomorrow. If she's missing too long, it'll cause a conflict in the court. I'll meet you at the palace; it's not safe for you to appear at my estate," he said to Landen.

I watched as Beth's shoulders relaxed. She was overwhelmed with relief. She hugged Drake, then came to my side and took my hand. Drake's eyes looked over me, then settled on my charm and slowly fell to where my wound was. He sighed and stepped in the passage. I gripped Beth's hand and forced a smile, then led her into the string. Drake had disappeared into the glow. When we reached the place where the wall had stood, we found Marc, Dane, and August waiting for us. When he saw Beth, Marc's elation was immediate; he immediately took possession of her and led the way. Landen pulled me closer and kissed my forehead.

"Are you alright? Did it hurt as badly as it seemed?" I asked.

We stopped and let the others walk on. He then turned to me and held my face in his hand. I stared into the beautiful blue that led to his soul.

"The only pain I remember is seeing you raise that knife to your chest. When I began to fight the darkness, I lost every insight I owned. Without them...not knowing

what you were seeing…feeling…I assumed that you'd found a love for him and couldn't bear to choose, that you were laying down your life instead," he thought.

As he said them, I felt the pain in his words – and every part of me ached.

"There's no choice. You're the only one…I saw that when I stood at death's doorstep," I thought, reaching for his face to pull it closer to mine.

"I think that's how I lost you before: I let my eyes tell me a story that was untrue. I let you go to him," Landen thought.

I moved my head from side to side, disagreeing with his thoughts. *"I refuse to give his memories life – and so should you,"* I thought.

He stared into me as he leaned in and kissed me so tenderly that I barely felt his warmth. I pulled him closer and let the love and passion I felt for him flow through me.

When we reached Pelhan's, the others had already passed through. I smiled up at Landen before we stepped in. Before us, only Pelhan and Aora stood. In the distance, we could feel the elation and excitement of our return. Pelhan smiled warmly and bowed his head; we bowed in return.

Pelhan's eyes moved to me. "You look well," he said, moving his eyes to where my wound was.

Landen reached his arms around me, pulling me to him and suppressing his anger. "Did you know? Were you trying to make us learn a lesson?" he asked as respectfully as he could.

Pelhan's eyes moved to Landen. "I cannot read the stars or the choices you make – we simply evaluated Olivia's dreams," he answered.

Landen released the anger he was feeling and nodded

in Pelhan's direction. "We should have taken her," he said, regretting his decision.

Pelhan pursed his lips. I felt him carefully choosing his words. "Nothing was harmed by leaving her here. We sent the dream to you; I know that August received it," he answered.

Landen and I looked at each other, then back to Pelhan.

"I knew that the two of you would not dream. That Marc and Dane would not rest deeply enough too. August was the only passage we had."

"That was Olivia's dream?" I asked, remembering the one August spoke of, the images of me, the children and the color of blood.

Pelhan nodded. "Your family feared this dream, but I knew it meant that the power of that charm was surfacing, that the spirit of Willow's soul would be a guiding light in the moment of choice," he answered.

"Her choice was death," Landen said, holding me tighter.

Pelhan looked at Aora. They smiled at each other then regarded me. "Her choice was life," Aora said. "She could have submitted, ending this battle with the darkness – but she made a choice: allowing you to heal her, to finish what you have begun."

Landen glanced at me. My choice had escaped him; we'd debated that the gift of emotion was pointless unless the person we were helping wanted our help. The same is true when you're being healed: you make your own choices. Others may guide you, but they can never live for you.

I broke my stare with Landen and looked back to Pelhan. "Did you know that I'm not Donalt's daughter? That Alamos and Perodine were my first parents?" I asked.

He smiled. "Only because you've told me before," he said, tilting his head. "You have brought a scroll here, seeking help. In your last life, you told me that you feared the day that all of the truths would come – for it would show you how clever the devil really was," Pelhan answered.

"They've been played as fools," I said, thinking of Alamos and Perodine.

"Living in one form for so long is their punishment and reward. The darkness knew the battles their heart fought. Your love story evokes emotions they have forgotten, clouding their guidance," Pelhan answered.

"Did you read the scroll?" Landen asked, filling with hope.

Pelhan shook his head from side to side.

"It's all foolishness to me. I know the stars may bring influence, but the soul leads the life. The answers you find there may prepare you for a possibility – but as you saw today, that possibility will cause you undue stress. A calm mind would have allowed you to see the likelihood of Willow being the descendant."

"Drake and I never would have put the blade through her; the stress would be the same – just a different degree," Landen said in a shaky voice. "I want to know the influence, the battles that have been fought already."

Pelhan's smile grew and his Aura seemed to brighten. "You always have. Seek what you wish – just remember to see every adversity through not only your eyes, but also the one you face," he answered.

Landen's eyes carefully gauged Pelhan. He was trying to read his intent, his emotion, and his energy all at once. I could feel Landen's frustration; like always, Pelhan revealed nothing beyond his vague words. Both of us felt unsatisfied with the resolution of that day's battle: a pile of ash that was all. Perodine and Alamos were still trapped in this life, forced to watch the battles I faced, Drake was still lost in the illusion that I belonged to him and the city of Delen remained demented in the eyes of Esterious. To us, it seemed the trials grew more difficult – and the rewards seemed smaller.

Pelhan stepped closer and hugged Landen, then me. "I've asked your family to come one by one to the passage; I know that, in your moment of death, you saw life through their eyes."

Landen glanced at me. I felt grief and anger surface in him. He hated that I'd been alone and unprepared for what came. I took his hand and sent a calm to him. I wasn't alone; everyone was with me. I let my memories of their perspective flow through me – and Landen found a peace and determination as if he could see them.

"You were given a gift, a marker in your life. You now know what you have done and what is left to be done," Aora said, stepping forward to hug me.

They turned to leave and in the distance I saw my mother and father approaching. I wanted to cry, but too many tears had already left me that day. As I saw them begin to walk faster to me, a smile filled my face. My father's eyes were green and his peace was relaxing. My mother was so beautiful, innocent, and vibrant in her emotions. I let go of Landen's hand and ran into their embrace. As she squeezed me as tight as she could, tears of joy came from my mother's eyes. My father wrapped his arms around us and held us as close as he could.

"I never thought I could be happier than the day you were born," my mother said, "but I was wrong."

Landen had slowly approached us and my mother released me and hugged him. My father's eyes searched over me carefully; he had Landen's full attention as he released my mother and caught my father's gaze.

"Is she healed all the way through?" Landen asked, afraid of my father's answer.

My father nodded and smiled at me. "I can see where you healed her. In time, I can imagine that the scar on the inside of her body will fade," he answered. "Both of you are showing signs of stress in your bodies. Rest; I can see shock is setting."

"Shock?" I repeated, not understanding what he was saying.

He let his hands rest on my shoulders then looked carefully at me. I could feel an immense amount of pride and grief in his emotion. I knew he was deeply concerned about the experience that I'd had that day.

"Right now, your minds cannot completely conceive everything you've been through. You need to calm your body, understand what you've experienced. If you don't rest, you'll jeopardize your judgment," he said.

I didn't want to understand; understanding meant remembering – and I didn't want to relive my agony in thought. I'd stared in the devil's eyes, met my past, and taken my own life. I wanted the forgotten details to remain forgotten. My moment of judgment came to me.

My eyes shifted between my parents. I'd always found it difficult to say how I felt. In my mind, I thought that the ones around me knew, but my new perspective had taught me that I was wrong.

"I don't want you to fear for my life," I said, looking at my father. "I don't want you to ever doubt the decisions you made for me. I always had Landen." My eyes moved to my mother. "I'm sorry I didn't smile or laugh when I was young," I said to her.

She reached for my face and pushed my hair back so she could see my eyes more clearly. She then smiled and said, "You did smile. When you woke from a peaceful night of dreams, when you helped an image, and when you painted. We wanted to help you understand, but we couldn't teach you what was a part of you."

My father stepped closer to me and looked into my eyes. "Smile," he said. I submitted to his request and let a smile come across my face. "Now, don't stop. You're a source of inspiration; if you want to help the people in Esterious, this world – then teach them to smile," he said, looking from me to Landen.

Landen let a smile come across his face, bringing to life his perfect dimples.

"The two of you guide Libby home; your mother is eager to get home and bake a cake," my father said, putting his hand in my mother's.

I hugged them goodbye and watched them pass into the string. Landen's parents, Ashten and Aubrey, were beside us when we turned. Aubrey reached for Landen and pulled him down to her. Ashten held his arms out for me to hug him. I smiled and reached my arms around his neck. "Don't fear that you'll lose anyone; we're a family that can't be divided," I whispered into his ear.

Ashten extended his arms and looked into my eyes. He nodded and smiled. I felt a relief overtake him. He released me and reached for Landen, and Aubrey let go of Landen and wrapped her arms around me. "So beautiful…so brave," she whispered as she squeezed me.

I smiled at her. "So are you," I said, letting her go.

Landen reached for me to come to his side.

"Do you need anything?" Ashten asked Landen.

"Just rest, according to Jason," Landen answered.

"How's Delen?" Ashten asked.

"The same. When we take Beth back, I'm going to talk to Drake to see what protection he can give them," Landen answered. Ashten raised his eyebrows, questioning Landen. "He was with us throughout most of this," he said, looking at me. "Since I wasn't angry, I was able to see the man he is; I know he doesn't want anyone to get hurt."

As understanding came over him, Ashten nodded. "Esterious is large. There are several priests who would seek to rule. I'm sure Drake has a very thin line to walk," he said.

As a confused look came across our faces, Ashten let his hand rest on Landen's shoulder. "The illusion of a power struggle between you and him would be better than the reality of facing all the priest Donalt has prepared for this day."

"Is he in danger?" I asked, prepared to make Drake come to Chara if he was.

"If he appears weak, then he could be overthrown. He has to play the part before him; whatever alliance you've formed should be held secret. Delen is outnumbered. A long road is in front of you," Ashten explained.

Landen nodded. Ashten then hugged him and he and Aubrey passed through the passage.

Landen looked down at me. "I don't know why we didn't see that," he said.

I sighed and pulled him closer. "My impatience is wearing off on you," I teased.

I heard him laugh under his breath. "So you admit that you're impatient?" he asked. I nodded, remembering that was one of the first things I saw when this life appeared before me.

Rose and Karsten approached us next. Rose hugged me as she smiled proudly. "You don't have to tell me what you learned. I can feel you," she said, extending her arms to look at me.

I smiled back and reached for Karsten. "You're going to have to tell your friends of the Odiona that they're wrong. Jayda's blood runs through them. She found love and so should they," I said to him.

Karsten reached his arms around me. "I stand witness to that, my dear," he said, letting me go.

Rose pulled Landen down to kiss his cheek before she and Karsten passed into the passage.

Clarissa and Dane approached next; they barely glanced up at us. I felt relieved to see her in Dane's arms again. Clarissa hugged Landen and me at the same time. "I told you everything would be fine," she said, looking over me.

"I don't want the two of you to part again. What Landen and I feel is no different from the two of you. The world would mourn if your love was lost," I said, looking back at her.

A stunned look came across her face and she looked up at Dane, then to Landen. "Well then, I take that as an invitation to face Mars – because Dane will always be there to protect you," she said.

Landen's eyes grew serious; she knew he'd oppose her conclusion and quickly pulled Dane into the passage before Landen could utter a word.

As he looked to where they'd vanished, Landen shook his head in disbelief. "She's always been too adventurous for my comfort," he said under his breath.

Chapter Thirteen

Brady and Felicity approached next. Libby was holding Felicity's hand and Brady was cradling Allie. Libby let go of Felicity and ran to us. Landen leaned down to scoop her up. She laughed as he raised her above his head. It was refreshing to hear it. She reached her arms out for me to come close to her.

"Were you really there?" I asked her. She didn't answer me; she just hugged us both as tight as she could, then let go as Brady and Felicity came to our side.

"The others are staying a while longer," Brady said to Landen.

I looked into the distance and felt the emotion of bliss; all of Livingston's family was with him – well, almost all of them.

"It took everything I had not to go through this passage; Marc said there was a wall," Brady said.

Landen nodded to confirm.

"He said he didn't know what happened, that they all fell asleep," Brady added.

Landen looked at me. We hadn't thought of what their perception of everything was; we were both just glad that they didn't see what we saw: the demon himself.

"We'll talk later," Brady said, putting his hand on Landen's shoulder.

I was sure that I wouldn't be a part of that conversation. Still, I hoped that Landen would open up to Brady and vent about what he'd seen, face it and then share it with me.

Brady gently handed me Allie, kissing my forehead as he let her go. "You're the bravest girl I've ever met," he whispered.

I blushed as I looked into Brady's blue eyes. He'd never shown any kind of affection toward me. I'd always imagined he saw me as Landen's soul mate, never just Willow.

"I'm only brave because he loves me," I said, looking into the blue eyes that belonged to me.

Landen picked Libby up and led us into the passage. As the darkness came to her, Felicity smiled at me. "You seem calmer with the passage," I said to her.

"I'm calm because I'm going home – and I know you'll be there," she said as she blindly looked in my direction.

Libby laid her head on Landen's shoulder and closed her eyes. I looked down to my arms; Allie was staring up at me with heavy eyes. I let calm flow through my arms then watched her drift to sleep. I felt relief and looked to see Brady staring at me.

"She hasn't slept in three days," he said.

Landen looked at Brady curiously.

"Libby, Preston, and Allie have sat in the center of Pelhan's front room, not sleeping, eating – nothing; we couldn't get them to say or do anything," Brady said.

Felicity blindly reached to let her hand rest on Allie. "If I took Allie from Libby and Preston, she'd cry endlessly," she said.

"We knew you had a victory when we heard their laughter. Preston and Libby were jumping in place, and Allie was waving her tiny hands and smiling," Brady added.

Landen looked back at me. Hearing that didn't make us feel any better; in fact, we were afraid – afraid that we were incapable of leading these children to any victory.

I let the calm I was feeling continue to flow through Allie. I felt Landen do the same with Libby. We knew how tired we were and it was hard to imagine that their little bodies had endured with us.

Inside Chara, I handed Allie's sleeping body to Felicity; I felt her relief when she saw how calm Allie was. Brady let me and Felicity in the back of Landen's Jeep, which was waiting by the passage. Landen sat in the passenger's seat, still holding Libby's sleeping body. I knew that Brady wouldn't rest until he had a moment alone with Landen; he wanted to assure himself he was fine.

I leaned between the front seats. "Can you guys take me home first? I want a hot shower," I said, looking from Brady to Landen. Landen looked back at me as fear suddenly came through him; his memory was sharper than mine: I'd almost forgotten the illusion of blood that I'd faced in the palace.

"We're home," I thought.

Landen smiled slightly then leaned back to kiss me.

Brady drove carefully across the field. I slid back into my seat and looked at Felicity, who leaned in and whispered, "Do you need to talk to someone?"

I shook my head from side to side. "I just need to rest," I said, smiling slightly.

She nodded. "I'll come by in the morning," she promised.

Brady stopped at my porch and I stepped out and leaned in to kiss Landen through his window.

"Will you tell everyone I said goodnight?" I asked him.

"I'm sure they're just as eager to rest as you and I," he thought, smiling.

I smiled at Brady and Felicity then turned to walk up my front steps. It was dark, but I could still see the glow of energy around the flowers of every color that decorated our house. The door was unlocked; it always was. As I climbed the stairs, I didn't turn on any lights. In a daze I walked to the bathroom in my bedroom.

I stared into the mirror at my refection: my eyes had dark circles beneath them; it seemed to enhance the emerald green that was staring back me. I did feel older – not one year, millions of years. I couldn't find the courage to turn on the shower; instead, I let the tub fill with steaming hot water. I pulled my shirt over my head and stared at the faint line that set above my heart. I could feel the scar beneath it, the pain I felt as the blade moved through me suddenly came to me…standing there now, I had no idea how I'd found the courage to do that.

Every moment from the time I saw Perodine wading in the water until now raced through my mind. I felt the emotions of every intense second as if it were happening at that moment. I started to breathe harder; it felt like my chest was closing in. I tried to focus on the mirror, my image, to tell myself that I was here now, that it was over. But in my reflection, I saw Aliyanna, Jayda, and all the images that I'd seen merge into my charm. I closed my eyes and took a deep breath – but calm still escaped me. I made my way to the tub and slowly slid into the steaming water, feeling it burn my skin. I then let my entire body submerge under the water.

Underneath the water, I found the silence and peace that I'd been grasping for. I felt my mind numb – finding peace for the first time in days. When my breath expired, I slowly rose. As my hands brushed the water from my face, I stared at my tattoo: the star Drake had placed in the center of the Ankh. His memory flooded my mind. I could have lost him; a few weeks ago I would have seen that as a victory, but that night I was selfishly glad that he was still in my life.

I felt Landen approaching the house and pushed my thoughts of Drake away. I then sensed Landen drifting through the house and heard water running; I assumed he was showering in one of the other bathrooms. As I moved the soap across my body, my mind began to play over the last few days. Now at peace I could see clearly. I'd wanted so badly to have a chance to know who I was in my past lives and that night that desire was granted. My hand settled on my charm. The visions of all I was moving back into it gave me strength. I let the memories that Aliyanna gave me dance through my mind: growing up with Landen at my side, coming to Chara, Libby – they were so beautiful.

My mind moved to Jayda's life. As the memory of her touch came to me, so did the grief she felt. I tried to call back the images of her children, to see if they even slightly resembled Libby, but she'd never clearly shown them to me. My charm hummed and her visions grew clearer to me. In my calm state, I felt every emotion she had as she traveled back to Oba. I heard the words she said to Samilya's children to comfort them.

Through her eyes, I watched as maids dressed me to stand before Oba for my punishment. I felt the fear as if the moment were occurring right then and there. Jayda had never laid eyes on him before. Through her eyes, I watched as she was escorted to his throne. When the doors opened before her, I expected to see the image of Landen as Oba, but I didn't. I moved slowly forward, gripping the sides of the tub as my memory played a lost past for me. Before me was a perfect face, the face of a king – the face of Drake. I watched as he fell and the darkness left him, just as I had days ago. My stomach turned and heat came to my face. I was struggling to remain calm, not to alert Landen. I didn't understand; how could he have been Oba? Oba was my soul mate; our love overcame the darkness.

Through Jayda's eyes, I searched every memory, looking for Landen – but he was nowhere to be seen; I realized that Jayda was not only grieving for her children, but also for not knowing Landen. As I took ownership of these thoughts, the charm on my neck warmed and disgust for myself emerged in my soul. His memories were of me. I'd given him every reason to believe that my soul was his. He was going to give his life for someone who never could have truly loved him.

My mood shifted to anger; if Drake could remember our lives together, then he knew all along who he was in that life. If he'd already had victory against the demon, it didn't make any sense to me that he'd ask me to take his life. My sympathy for him diminished. I felt betrayed; he was no different from the others that guided me and Landen

– they only tell us what they want us to know.

I grinded my teeth as the agony I lived through over-came me; I felt like I'd wasted three days of my life and put my family through torment – for nothing.

When the water turned cold, I pulled myself out, feeling more exhausted then when I'd began. I focused on how I'd feel in Landen's arms and pushed the anger and betrayal I felt for Drake deep inside of me. I pulled on my robe and opened the door, looking for Landen; he was sitting on the edge of our bed, holding a very small cake with one candle burning. A smile spread across my face as he walked slowly to me, humming "Happy Birthday." I blew out the candle and reached up to kiss him.

"Did you cook?" I thought, amused.

He slowly pulled away from me. "I may be able to heal and make time stand still, but cooking is a gift that still escapes me," he said, amused by his words.

I ran my finger along the side of the warm cake, gathering as much icing as I could.

"Your mother gave this to you. I told them that I didn't think you wanted a party," he said, tracing the other side of the cake with his finger.

I knew my mother wasn't surprised. I don't think I can recall a single birthday party when I was growing up; I hated the attention, the intensity of the emotions. I smiled, remembering that every year my mother had appeared in my room with a small cake, humming to me. Landen had assumed that role now.

"She gave you some inside tips to my birthday rituals, I gather," I said.

Landen nodded and set the small cake on the table, then reached his arms around my waist and pulled me to him. "Though, if I recall correctly, I all but had to drag you to our celebration; it wouldn't be hard for me to assume that you wouldn't have wanted any attention for a birthday."

"We were in the middle of major turmoil; a party didn't make sense," I said, brushing the dark, wet locks of hair from his perfect blue eyes.

"We still are," Landen said as he moved his hand to my face, "but we won't stop living to worry."

I laid my head on his chest, hiding in his energy. I felt his hand on the back of my head, as well as the calm he was giving me. "You can't hide your emotions from me, Willow. We are one; they belong to me as well – and pushing them down makes us weaker," he said gently to me.

I leaned back and looked into his perfect eyes and saw the seriousness there.

"What did Jayda show you?" he asked.

As a rush of adrenaline and panic soared through every part of me, Landen held me tighter, giving me all his love, his calm.

"Oba was Drake," he said, looking into my eyes.

I nodded and stared at him through the glass panes of tears that I refused to let fall. "How did you know?" I whispered.

Landen smiled slightly and let his fingers trace the dark circles under my eyes. "Anytime Drake is given the opportunity to proclaim that he's your soul mate, he takes it – except for when Perodine told you that the darkness couldn't live in me and that I was your soul mate. His intent was to save your life at any cost. His emotion was full of grief – a grief that he'd already passed through in another life." He sighed, then continued, "And when you told us that Jayda and Aliyanna showed you your lives, a rush of panic came to him. It was as though he was prepared for you to scold him."

"I don't understand," I said in a weak voice.

"Willow, I told you the day that Delen was redeemed that I didn't care who we may have loved before. We had each other now and that's all that matters. We can't change it," he said.

"I want to blame someone. I want to seek revenge on whoever caused Drake to live in his illusion, but these memories…they tell me it's me, that I did all of this to myself – and now you have to endure it with me," I said.

Landen let his hand fall in mine, then he pulled the covers back on my side of the bed; I gladly lay down. He was at my side and his eyes searched over me carefully; his emotions were balanced. I didn't understand…if I was him I'd be jealous, angry.

He began to trace my eyes and smiled slightly. "Why are you not angry?" I asked.

"If I was angry, that would mean that I doubted our love, that I thought there was a chance he could take you from me. You know that doubt doesn't live in me – not tonight, not in this life."

"When we find my 'twin' and she's your bad soul mate, I can't promise you that I won't be jealous – but that doesn't mean that I have any doubt that you belong to me," I said.

He smiled, bringing his dimples to life, then laughed under his breath. "There won't be any need to get angry because hopefully she and Drake will be so consumed with one another that they'll leave us alone," Landen said, amused by his words.

I rolled on my back and stared at the ceiling. "You don't think I'm wrong about the twin, do you? I mean, I had a twin then, Samiyla and she couldn't stop the darkness."

Landen pulled himself up on one arm and looked over me. "Let your thoughts rest. We have no way of knowing if it's love of soul mates or the power that rests in your heart that makes the darkness tremble," he said, smiling slightly.

"I'm going to ask him tomorrow. His memories must hold an image of her."

His smile lessened as he traced his fingers on my arm, trying to calm me. "I have the impression that his memories are only of the lives he had with you. He may not see her."

"We can thank Alamos for that," I said in a disgusted tone.

"Alamos only wanted to find a way to protect him," Landen promised.

I turned on my side and pulled him closer to me. "I'm not sure I like you defending them," I said in a teasing manner.

He laughed casually at me as his hand moved across my back. "I will never lie to you. I'll tell you what their intent is, what their emotion is; I only want you to be at peace with your emotions in return," Landen said.

I heard the truth in his words and shifted my emotion to calming bliss. Smiling, he kissed my lips softly and gently reached his fingertips to my eyes to close them. We rose at the foot of bed and for the first time in days we submitted to each other completely, taking in the healing power and blissful emotion.

Chapter Fourteen

We slept past dawn, which was unusual for us. When our hungry bodies woke us, Landen rolled to his side and let his fingers run across the base of my eye. "You look rested now," he said, smiling.

I smiled, feeling better. It wasn't until I thought about the day in front of me that my smile lessened.

"We don't have to take Beth back; Marc will," Landen said, judging my emotion.

"It's our place to negotiate against war – not Marc's," I said.

Landen's eyes grew serious. War was our conflict – not Venus. In the three days that we'd spent playing the devil's games, the tension between Delen and the surrounding world had grown. My wish for that day was to find a balance, to be thankful for what I'd accomplished and understand that I couldn't save them all at once. For my intent to come to life, I knew I'd have to have an alliance with Drake.

A smile came across Landen's face. "Have you learned patience?" he asked, slightly amused.

"I'm trying…don't get your hopes up," I said, winking at him.

In the distance, I could sense Brady's intent to come there and I knew he was getting close. As he felt it, too, Landen's eyes widened and he rushed out of the bed. "He's coming to help me build a wall around that passage in the yard," he said.

I kept forgetting about that passage. It was where we saw Evelyn for the first time. It led to Drake's doorstep. "No unwanted guests," I said under my breath.

"I just want to be able to have a little more warning if someone does pass through it," Landen said, pulling his clothes on and looking out the window. I rolled on my back and stared at the ceiling. Feeling Brady, my father, and Ashten coming with the intent to 'help,' I counted every emotion I could feel surrounding our home. I realized that Marc had brought Beth there and that they were all gathered at August's house; I smiled as I felt their bliss.

When Landen was done dressing, he smiled down at me. "Hungry?" he asked.

I was starving, but I wasn't up for company; I wanted to ease into this long day. I turned my head from side to side. "I just want to lay here for a while," I said.

Understanding, he leaned down and kissed me before he left. I listened as he let everyone in and they gathered in the kitchen for breakfast. I couldn't hear what they were saying, but from the fright I felt coming from Brady,

Ashten, and my father, I imagined that Landen was telling them everything that we'd lived through over the past few days. When I felt them go outside, I pulled myself out of the bed and dressed for the day. My growling stomach wouldn't give me time to make our bed.

I made myself a sandwich and watched as a stone wall in my side yard came to existence. It was going to be at least six feet high and two feet wide. I promised myself I'd plant a growing vine around it, or at least paint it. Paint…I hadn't painted in almost two weeks. I knew it would make me feel better, help me sort through my emotions.

My studio was at the top of the stairs. I opened all the doors and let the light flood in, then sat down in front of a blank canvas and stared. The only image in my mind was the evil angel – and I had to get it out. I picked up my brush and began to paint more vigorously than I ever have in my life; I painted so quickly, I wasn't even focusing on the image that was coming to life, just the utter details. Hours passed and I painted on, determined to leave it all on the canvas, to get out what I was I trying to say, trying to think.

When I couldn't find another detail that needed my attention, I stepped back, completely captured by what was in front of me. It was what I saw just before I took my life: images of me, Landen, and Drake – and the devil controlling us. As I stared, my mind replayed each second in vivid detail; the pain, the judgment – it was all so overwhelming.

I sensed that most of my family had gathered at my house, but I didn't realize how close Olivia had gotten to me.

"Wow," I heard her say.

I snapped out of my illusive stare and turned to smile at her. The pink in her Aura had faded -- I could tell that she hadn't had any new dreams lately.

"It's one thing to dream it – but to know it really happened…that freaks me out a little," Olivia said, stepping closer to the canvas.

I looked from her to the painting, then back at her, awestruck. "Your dream was *that* detailed?" I asked.

She tilted her head slightly. "Yeah…I mean, the only thing different is that I was focusing on the demon," she said.

I looked at the canvas: the demon was in the center of the painting. His wings stretched out to each side…they were the background.

"He *is* the focus," I said in a stunned tone, thinking that Olivia's eye for art was weaker than I'd given her credit for.

She pulled her eyebrows together. "Um…no…you – or who you were – is the focus," she said, rather sure of herself. She walked closer to me and put her arm around me. "Take another look, Willow."

I sighed, closed my eyes then opened them again. The demon was the center of painting just before him I'd painted Landen and Drake. The sides of the painting, framing Landen and Drake, were the images of Aliyanna and Jayda.

"The demon is the center," I replied, not wanting to see that the largest images were Aliyanna and Jayda.

"Half of your face is on each side of the painting. The demon is the last thing on your mind; Landen and Drake are the next largest images," Olivia argued.

Aggravated, I pulled her hand and took her closer to the canvas. "Do you see the ash wings? They're the entire background; you're just focusing on its body," I argued. I knew I'd spent more time painting the wings than anything else.

"No, I don't see the wings because the artist doesn't

see the wings because she can't get past a life she can't remember," Olivia said, looking me dead in the eye.

"What are you talking about?" I said, louder than I intended. "I *am* the artist," I said, patting my chest.

"I know, so you should recognize your own mind," she said, crossing her arms in front of her petite figure. "You painted to get it out of your head; now you can see what's causing you so much grief."

"I didn't need to paint to realize that I'd caused all of this – but thanks for pointing it out," I said.

I started putting my brushes away, a little more aggressively than needed. I wiped the paint off my hands and threw the towel at the canvas, then slouched in my chair. Olivia carefully pulled the towel off the damp canvas, then dabbed her fingers around the damage I had caused, trying to repair it.

"It's going in the trash. You're wasting your time," I said to her.

Olivia looked over her shoulder at me, cleaning her hands with my towel. "Not until you face it. When you do, I'll personally burn it," she said, stepping closer to me.

"What else do you want me to face? I've already stared the devil in the eyes," I said.

I stared at her, watching her struggle with her intent, her emotions; she didn't know if she should push me or give me the space the rest of my family had afforded me. I felt her sympathy, her anger, and her fear. I sighed and furrowed my eyebrows.

"Just push me – and start with the emotion of anger; I'm in the mood for that," I said shortly.

I knew that bluntly calling her out was irritating to her – and she had a right to be; as human beings, the only privacy we're granted is our intent, our emotions. My insights allowed me to invade that privacy, though, to make my own judgment – even before the person had come to one.

"Fine then; get over yourself," she said.

"What?" She was too blunt.

"Get over who you were – good or bad. Knowing you've lived before, conquered before, should make you stronger – not weaker," she said.

"That's not the issue; the issue is that somehow I've managed to become a target for the devil, that I've managed to entangle Landen and Drake in the same twisted fate – and no matter what I do, it's not good enough…someone gets hurt."

"I was under the impression that we were going to find your twin – the 'good soul mate' – and that that would solve the Drake issue," she said, mocking her hands in quotation.

"That's a broken heart; I'm talking about lost lives. Everything you went through, I went through; what I put Landen and Drake through will be pointless if Delen is overtaken by the rest of the dimension."

"Finding Chrispin, finding Stella, you having Landen – that's not pointless. Nothing you've done will be in vain," she argued.

"That still leaves Drake's broken heart," I said shortly.

"See, *you* are the issue," she argued.

"NO – *Drake* is," I said as the frustration made itself known in my Aura.

"Drake is because you are. Before you knew you had past lives with him, he was nothing to you; but now – knowing – you blame who you were. You blame yourself and that's just stupid," she said, enticed by my argument.

I glanced at the painting, to my images framing it: Drake, who stood behind Jayda, and Landen, who stood behind Aliyanna. Staring at the four of them I didn't see the demon. Olivia was right.

"How do I fix it?" I said, looking to the corner of my blank canvas.

Olivia stepped to her side to block my view. "In nineteen years, in this life as Willow Haywood, have you ever loved anyone beyond Landen?" she asked.

My eyes fell to the ground. Three days ago, I would have said no instantly – but knowing Drake, his perspective...I did have love for him...nothing that could compare to the way I loved Landen, but I did care about him and I did want him to be happy.

Olivia stepped closer to me and raised my chin. Her eyes searched my face. "You know what kind of love I'm talking about," she said quietly.

"What I feel for Landen can never be overshadowed," I answered, avoiding her eyes.

Olivia held up one finger to signify that I was one, one with Landen.

I could hear the laughter of everyone outside. The wall was finished and an aggressive game of football was underway. From my second story balcony, I could see Brady and Landen soaring through the air; all the privileges of controlling your energy were in full effect. Olivia debated taking me outside to show me why I should be happy, but her intent shifted as a new approach to deal with me came to her.

"You know, back home those girls we went to school with, they had boyfriend after boyfriend, but they managed to walk the halls, go to the same parties, and remain friends with them; surely there's enough room in this universe for you and Drake," Olivia said.

I found it odd that Olivia would point that out. We

were never those girls. We never understood them. I'd always feel their infatuation, excitement, sense of love, and then heartbreak. I remember being thankful that I'd have my gift of emotion to rely on when I committed to someone.

"We're not in high school anymore. My time with Drake was more intense than a few dates to the movies," I argued.

"That's my point: those girls could actually remember their relationships – but you can't. You're letting yourself mourn for a love you can't even remember," she argued.

"*He's* mourning," I said quietly.

"You can't feel him," she argued carefully.

"I can see it and it hurts me to know that I'm the cause of so much misery," I said.

"Listen," she said, taking a deep breath, "I feel sorry for him, too. I know it couldn't have been easy being raised around someone like Donalt. I'm more than sure that he escaped through you – thinking of you. He's in love with the idea of you. Who you were then and who he imagines you to be today. His day will come. He'll find the right girl. You can't wait for that day to forgive yourself…it's a distraction that will only hurt you."

I grinded my teeth as I took in her words. My eyes moved back to the canvas. I noticed that the images I'd painted seemed to reflect the truth in Olivia's words: Aliyanna's eyes were happy and blissful, and Jayda's were sorrowful. I let out a deep breath then looked to Olivia. "I understand. I'll work through this, but you have to understand that it's not a switch I can turn off. I have to see beyond what's in front of me, and I know that I've barely scratched the surface of what this soul has seen. The darkness is my focus…I promise," I said.

"You know, I admire you more every single day," Olivia said, smiling.

"Don't," I said, shaking my head from side to side.

I felt Clarissa, Felicity, and Stella making their way up the stairs. All of them had the intent of helping Olivia reach me, to pull me out of my self-destruction. I let out a breath.

"Backup is coming," I mocked, tilting my head to the doorway.

Felicity came in first. Her eyes were drawn to the portrait. She was full of every emotion imaginable. Clarissa and Stella then came to my side. I opened my arms and hugged Stella. I felt so bad for her. I'd thought I was saving her from some dark place, but the truth was she was still there – now forced to carry the stress I'd brought to my family.

As Felicity stepped closer to the painting I followed her eyes they were staring at the image of Drake. "I didn't realize how attractive he is," she said, almost to herself.

Stella blushed slightly as she let me go. I felt the resentment rise in Clarissa. She was a traveler. She'd seen him at a distance on more than one occasion.

"Olivia has done a good job of giving me a reality check. I'm afraid your work is done," I said, standing and stretching my back.

Felicity turned to look at me. "Then why do you still look horrible?" she asked, amused by her words.

"Thanks," I said, looking to the balcony. Landen and Brady had collided in mid-air. Laughter erupted from the ground below. I smiled slightly, glad that Landen was so relaxed.

I felt the tension rise in the room. None of them knew how to handle the mood I was in now. Felicity turned and walked to me. "Willow, every woman has her doubts from time to time. This is normal," she said in a sympathetic tone.

I looked at her like she was crazy. The others had surrounded me – dread and concern saturated their emotions. "Doubts about what?" I asked, trying to read them all at once.

"Listen," Clarissa said, putting her hand on my shoulder. "It's harder for you because Landen can feel you. The rest of us can struggle with our emotions in private, but you're forced to unveil yours to him."

"I don't hide anything from Landen," I said as clearly as I could.

"You've never pushed an emotion away because you didn't want him to know you had it?" Clarissa asked, raising one eyebrow.

"I push emotions away so I won't have to deal with *them* – not *him*," I said.

"Willow, we just want you to know that we're here for you and that we'll listen to you and not push you," Felicity said, moving in front of Clarissa.

"What has gotten into you guys? There's no doubt. I'm not struggling with my emotions. I've been through a lot. I think I have a right to sort through what's happened to me without my love for Landen being doubted," I said, louder than intended.

They all grew silent and looked away from me.

"Is this what you guys did for the last three days? Debated on if I'd 'choose' Landen or Drake? If that's the case, I want you to know that hurts," I said.

"No, no, no," Stella said, looking up at me. "We spent the last three days at Aora's side. She told us that we were your council." She pointed to herself and said, "Fire," to Felicity and said, "Air," to Clarissa and said, "Earth," and to Olivia and said, "Water. We make up the elements that will support you when you're faced with adversity."

The others had been nodding along with Stella's expressive explanation. I moved my head from side to side, frustrated with Aora and Pelhan's half-guided direction. "You should have just asked her who, what, when, and where – and then all of this would be over," I said sarcastically.

"They don't know," Olivia said in a frustrated tone. "They can tell you what you've done before and they can tell you where to put your thoughts. They can even tell you where the thoughts you're having 'may' lead you – but our fate isn't sealed."

"What are you guys so worked up about? Venus is over. Do you think I'm weaker? That with Mars I'll finally fall?" I asked.

"Aora has her doubts," Felicity answered.

"Does she?" I said sarcastically.

"She feels that the planets are a gateway for the darkness, that if you'd chosen to go with Drake during the Blue moon or Mercury, the darkness would have overtaken him. The only way both you and he would have survived would be if you truly did love him," Felicity said.

"And you don't," Olivia said. "Aora's fear – our fear – is that your sympathy for Esterious will cause you to sacrifice yourself into his arms. Without true love, you both will die. Esterious – the entire universe – will fall into darkness."

"All of you are insane," I said, frustrated. "I don't really care about planets or choosing – because that choice was made since before I can even remember. I'm sick and tired of the doubts all of you have."

"We don't doubt you, Willow," Felicity said. "We just

want you to know what we were told. Aora said she knew of one life that you had with Drake in detail. You married him because your father wanted you to – for the benefit of your family. She said you sacrificed your heart."

"The photo we found, that was the life she was talking about," Clarissa added.

The photo they were referring to was the one that was found in my old house in Franklin. It was the first time I realized that there might be truth to what Drake had said, that we'd loved before. It had caused me so much turmoil.

"No matter what, you have to be with the person who completes you – not the one that you think will benefit the world," Clarissa said.

My head started to spin; they were driving me crazy. I didn't know how many times or ways I had to say it; I just wanted them to get it through their heads that there was no reason to doubt me. I was more than sure that whatever de-cisions I'd made in past lives were what I had to do. I felt overwhelmed; one minute they were telling me to get over who I was – and the next they were telling me not to make the same mistakes I'd made before. Which way did they want it? If they wanted me to avoid my past mistakes, that meant I'd have to deal with who I was – and all of it in-cluded the way I felt about Drake then.

Suddenly, they all froze in place. A mischievous grin spread across my face. I looked over my shoulder and saw Landen standing on the balcony.

He smiled impishly at me. "*I thought you might need a break,*" he thought.

I carefully maneuvered around the girls and went to the balcony. Landen opened his arms and I fell into his em-brace, hiding my face in his chest. "I don't know what they want from me," I said quietly.

"To be happy, I'm sure," he answered, raising my chin so I'd have to look at him.

"You don't think I'm hiding anything, do you? That I have doubts?" I asked.

He turned his head from side to side, smiling. "They don't understand us, Willow; they're trying to place themselves in our shoes and imagine how they'd react. There's no one in this universe that's walked our path. I know you struggle with your emotions – not because you doubt our love, but because you're a good soul who wants everyone to be at peace, to feel the way we feel when we're together."

I turned in his arms and looked at the frozen figures of Stella, Felicity, Clarissa, and Olivia. "Maybe you should tell that to my council," I said, amused by my words.

"Sure, then you can tell mine," he answered. "Good luck with August, Marc, Brady, and Chrispin."

"Are they your elements?"

"So they tell me. Apparently, Pelhan was trying to give us some peace; he told them they all had a role and that they should stay in it and not overwhelm us."

"What about everybody else? Our fathers?"

"They were told to give us only the insight they were clear on, that their main focus is the children. Apparently, with each adversity there'll be something that at least one of our elements can help us with."

"If that were true, then we should have taken Olivia – not Dane." I said, staring at her frozen image.

"Maybe so; honestly, Drake protected you more than Dane did," Landen said, looking over the balcony.

"He kept me calm; he helped," I said, defending Dane.

Landen turned and smiled at me. He knew that I'd depended on Dane for strength before I found him. Dane was my best friend.

"I won't be able to keep Brady home again; his intent is strong," Landen said.

"He needs to take care of his daughter," I argued.

"He feels that by taking care of us, that's what he's doing."

Landen turned me in his arms, then leaned down, kissed me and held me as tight as he could. "*I love you, Willow. Don't let them get to you,*" he thought.

"*I love you.*"

He released me and smiled. He then nodded his head and time resumed. Behind me, I heard Clarissa continue her argument – only to be halted by the shock of not seeing me standing in front of her anymore. Their gaze found me on the balcony in Landen's arms. Their emotions of surprise and bewilderment made us both smile.

"Ladies," Landen said, looking at them, then down to me. "We both feel privileged to have you in our lives." He looked back to them and said, "Willow understands your concerns and so do I. We assure you that we know without a doubt that we belong together – no matter what adversities are put in front of us."

They all stared, unable to respond. I felt their confidence in me and Landen build. Our love for each other had them awestruck once again.

Landen squeezed his arms tighter around me and said, "Clarissa, do me a favor: burn the canvas; its purpose has been served," he glanced at me, "right?" I nodded and smiled.

"Let's go down. We need to leave soon," he said, putting his shield of energy around me and moving us over the balcony to fall gently to the ground below.

Chapter Fifteen

As we fell carefully to the ground, I saw Brady lying on the ground, gripping the ball. Marc and Chrispin were on top of him. My father, who was watching from the side, smiled up at us. He loved and trusted Landen and me so much.

"I don't think I'm fond of this new gift," Brady said as Marc helped him up. "Could you at least make sure I'm not in harm's way before you disappear?" he finished.

"Harm yes, a tackle – maybe not…sorry, man. I felt pulled somewhere else," Landen said, amused by his words.

Landen sat us down in front of our house. My mother and Rose were sitting on the steps. Beth and Aubrey were standing beside them. As Beth stepped closer to me, Landen released me and I hugged her.

"Are you glad you came home?" I said, hugging her tightly.

"I am, but its time for me to go," she answered, extending her arms to look at me.

"You still have a few hours before the sun sets," I argued.

"Marc is going to take me and Preston to Drake's estate. We'll meet you at the palace at sunset."

"You're taking Preston back to Esterious?" I said as fear overcame me.

"He just wants to see Drake; his home is here with all of you," Beth said, tucking a loose strand of my hair behind my ear.

I nodded in agreement with her; Preston needed to be here so he'd be guided and protected. It still made me sad that he'd be away from Beth - that she was pulled between her children.

"Chrispin is going, too," Landen added. "He'll bring Preston back to Chara. Marc wants to be with us at the palace."

Beth's eyes moved to Chrispin and Marc, who were in mid-play in the side field. Her eyes smiled and joy overcame her. "To have them all in one room at one time...Livingston said this day would come," she said, looking to Aubrey, who was at her side.

"I'm going to talk to Marc and Chrispin. I want to make sure they don't put Drake in a bad mood before we talk to him about Delen," Landen thought, tilting his head in their direction. I nodded.

In the distance, I could see Nyla and August approaching with Libby and Preston. Beth smiled and made her way to them. I sat down on the steps between Rose and my mother and watched as everyone began to prepare for us to leave again.

My mother let her hand run across my back. "Beth told me that she'd never met someone as strong and brave as you and that we should all be proud of how well you handle yourself when you're faced with a crisis," she said.

I smiled and leaned into her.

"You just keep being who you are, my Willow," she whispered to me.

Rose leaned forward to catch my gaze. "I want to go with you tonight, but I've been reassured that my role is here with the children," she said, smiling.

"I'm sure we'll be fine. No one seems to have any answers anyway; it would only frustrate you to watch them debate," I said bleakly.

Rose nodded and smiled. "I understand that you saw a different side of Perodine, that her image of an immortal was replaced with one of a woman whose simply lived a long time," she said to me.

I nodded and looked at my mother. I knew if I were her I'd be jealous of another woman claiming that I was her child in another life. But my mother, Grace Haywood, lived up to her name and was graceful with the thought of Perodine, as well as the thought of Libby belonging to Landen and me in another life. She cherished the role of being our mother in this life, to be our support.

"I'd suggest that you and Landen walk the streets of Delen before you go into the palace so they'll see that you're still there for them. Tomorrow, we'll all go and help them continue to build a new life," Rose said.

"That's a good idea. I can imagine they're a little nervous," I said.

Olivia and Stella opened the front door. I turned to

look at them and couldn't help smiling at their awestruck expression.

"We didn't mean to scare all of you; he just thought I was getting overwhelmed," I said to them.

Olivia nodded. "Honestly, I'm surprised it took him that long to stop us," she said, looking past me to the field.

I turned and smiled at Landen. August and Nyla had met him, Chrispin, and Marc in the field.

"We're going to say goodbye," Stella said as she stepped carefully around Rose.

"We'll be back tonight," I promised her. She nodded but didn't turn. Olivia followed her.

"Are you hungry? Do you want something to eat before you leave?" my mother asked as she stood.

"No. I ate a little while ago. Thanks for asking," I said, smiling up at her.

She leaned down and hugged me. "I'm going to take Libby home and give you your space. Be careful tonight," she said to me.

"Do you have room for two more?" Rose asked, standing.

"We'd love to have you and Karsten over," my mother said, smiling.

I watched as Libby hugged Preston goodbye, then ran to me. I tried to focus only on her emotion; she was blissful, carefree. I admired her so much. She came to my side short of breath from her run. "I would think you'd be sad; I don't think you and Preston have been apart since we brought him here," I said, reaching my arms around her.

"He'll be right back; he just wants to say hi and give his brother a hug," Libby answered.

I looked in Preston's direction. Marc had picked him up and was carrying him to the passage. Chrispin and Beth were at his side. August and Nyla were a few feet behind them. I could feel the excitement coming from Preston, the fears coming from Chrispin and Marc -- the hope coming from Beth.

"He does love his big brother, doesn't he?" I said, agreeing with her.

"We love everybody, Willow. That's how it's supposed to be," she said, looking at me like I should already know that.

"You're right," I said, smiling at the wisdom of an innocent child.

"Tell Willow goodbye, Libby. You can help me and Rose make a really big cake for Willow," my mother said, extending her arms out in each direction to demonstrate how big it could be.

Libby giggled and shook her from head side to side. "Her birthday was yesterday; she doesn't want a party," she looked up at me, "right, Willow?"

"Right," I said, laughing. "But I love cake," I said, encouraging her to go with my mother. She hugged me goodbye and went with Rose and my mother. As they walked away, the front door opened and Clarissa and Felicity stepped out. Felicity was carrying Allie. They sat down on either side of me.

"So, young lady, have you gotten caught up on your sleep?" I said, smiling at Allie. She smiled back and turned to hide her face in Felicity's chest.

"She just now woke up," Felicity said, relieved by Allie's happy mood.

I looked at Clarissa. "So, did you burn the canvas?" I asked, amused.

"It's on the back porch; I'm going to get Dane to help me with it," she answered.

I nodded and let my gaze settle on Landen, who was surrounded by Brady, Dane, and our fathers. I found myself wishing I could freeze time on his behalf. I knew he wasn't bothered by what they were saying; in fact, he seemed to have the same confidence he'd had throughout this whole experience.

"I didn't mean to upset you earlier," Clarissa said, feeling ashamed.

"Don't worry about it; sometimes it gets to be too much," I answered.

"That's what we want to help you with; we don't want to add to it, just help you sort it out," Clarissa said.

I leaned back and let my body rest on my elbows. Flashes of everything – from the day at the lake 'til now – came to me. I heard the voices of my family, Drake, Landen, and my own arguments.

"Right now, there's one thing I can't get around in my mind; maybe the two of you can make sense of it," I said to them.

I had Felicity and Clarissa's full attention. They both turned halfway on the step they were sitting on to see me better.

"OK. I've said over and over that it's always been Landen," I said. They nodded in agreement. "We found that photo, Drake showed me our lives, and Aora justified my fears by telling me that I'd loved him. We all came to the conclusion that you could love someone and not be in love with them," I said, looking between the two of them to make sure they were following me. They nodded, telling me to go on.

"Drake told Landen that he gained his strength by remembering when he was one with me. I argued that there was no way that I was one with him because I could only complete Landen, that his memories were of another who looked just like me, my twin…I'm losing that argument now, though, because I know that Jayda – myself – loved him. And that love was powerful enough to make the darkness leave Oba. So, explain to me how I can be 'one' with more than one person? Am I crazy to think that there's another girl for Drake? Is his fate to wait his 'turn,' as he puts it?"

They glanced at each other, then to me. I smiled as I felt them take on my confusion, knowing then that they understood where I was coming from.

"You're looking for one answer…what if there are two?" Felicity said as an excitement came through her.

"Go on," I said, amused by her energy.

"What if there's another 'you' that makes him complete? What if his dreams are of the two of you – and he can't tell the difference?" Felicity said.

"That makes sense," Clarissa said, sitting up straight. "He could have them crossed, mixing his passion with love."

"Did Jayda show you images of you and Drake joining?" Felicity asked.

I reached for my charm and let the memories she gave me play again in my mind. "No," I said quietly.

"But they found mediation; they left Analess through the string. They knew what you know about energy – yet she never showed you the most beautiful part about being aware of your energy?"

My eyes widened slightly. She had a point; it didn't make sense that Jayda wouldn't share that with me.

"I think there are two of you; that's the only way it would make sense," Felicity said.

"Then where is she?" I said under my breath.

"Ask him to tell you more. Maybe we'll be able to sort through his memories and find her," Clarissa said.

"I don't know how I feel about validating his memories. They're the rock he stands on, the reason he thinks Landen has me living in a 'web of lies,' as he puts it."

"Yes, but the more he tells you, the more information you'll have to help us all find this girl," Clarissa said, enforcing her point.

"He doesn't even know that I know he was Oba," I said with a smile. "Landen said he was waiting to be scorned when I told them that Jayda and Aliyanna showed me my past lives."

"That's good; catch him off guard. I'd be interested to know why he just didn't tell you," Felicity said.

I leaned back and played out the argument in my head. I was anxious to hear why he just didn't tell me who he was then, why he'd watch me struggle with the idea of me killing him. Anger swarmed deep inside of me as I assumed that he let me suffer in order to give himself the validation that I did love him.

"I'm going to be honest with you, Willow," Felicity said. I looked at her like she was crazy; she had no choice but to be honest with me. She raised her eyebrows and continued, "Let me rephrase that," she said, laughing at my expression. "I'm going to tell you what I think – and that is that you're standing in the center of a love triangle that no woman would want to be in." Her eyes found Landen. "Standing between Lust and Love, both of them are so perfect that it's hard not to stare."

I sighed and nodded. I'd never admitted aloud how attractive I found Drake; his presence alone was growing addictive.

"Stella told us how impactful Drake's touch is on you,"

Clarissa added.

"That's just my body; Landen reaches my soul," I said as my gaze caught his across the field.

"We're just trying to put ourselves in your place so we can help you – and when we try to imagine ourselves there, we find ourselves weak," Felicity said.

I looked to my side at her. "You'd never choose anyone above Brady," I promised her.

"My soul wouldn't, but we're all made of flesh; I can't tell you what I'd do if the 'bad' soul mate came to me and had a touch like Drake's, eyes like Drake's…I would never leave Brady, but I know my mind would at least play out the possibilities for me," Felicity said.

Her honesty was making me uncomfortable; in my opinion, some things, some desires should just be left unsaid.

"I'm not giving much credit to the 'bad' soul mate idea; I believe that August would agree with me on that point," I said, sitting forward.

I lied to them. I was starting to believe the idea; I just didn't want them to have any cause to fear my weakness. I knew Landen would feel their doubt in me. Right now, his confidence was what I was hiding behind.

Clarissa leaned forward -- her eyes searched over my face. "I believe it. I've seen it," she said.

"Where? How?" I asked, slightly amused by how sure she was.

"When I travel, it's everywhere. On more than one occasion, the person I was leading found someone who was already in a committed relationship. It's really common in Infante. I'm sure you've seen it more than you care to admit," she answered.

I knew in the world in which I was raised that it was

growing more and more uncommon for couples to join for a lifetime, that most of my friends had two sets of parents. I never saw that as a choice between passion and love. I saw it as one love dying and another being born…the children were just bystanders in the matter.

"I'd feel sorry for the one that was left behind when I escorted the new soul mates home, but I reasoned that the person left behind was now released from an illusion that the body gives; they were free to find the one that completed them," Clarissa said.

I sighed. "You know what would make me feel better?" I asked her. She raised her eyebrows, telling me to go on. "If you told me that you knew for sure that the person you left behind did find someone, that they weren't living a life of heartache that was left to them," I said, tilting my head.

I watched as Clarissa's eyes moved across her memory.

"Now, I'm going to have to check and see," she said, frustrated by her own words.

I smiled slightly. "Let me know if you find positive results," I said under my breath.

"Well, I won't know before we go to the palace, so you're going to just have to trust what Aora said about your past life: you can't sacrifice your heart for what you think is the greater good; you'll all die," Clarissa said as grief and doubt overcame her.

"What do you mean 'we'? You're not going?" I said under my breath.

"Dane's going; you said we weren't to be apart, so I am going," Clarissa said, standing and walking to Dane's side.

My eyes found Dane. I knew it would break his heart if I told him I thought it was Olivia who was supposed to protect me. I'd rather just let him come, keep the peace.

Landen looked up as he felt Clarissa's intent, then shook his head slightly, knowing it would be pointless to persuade her to stay.

"Well," Felicity said, "honestly, I feel better knowing she's going with you."

I looked at her with wide eyes, surprised by her words.

"You need a woman there, a woman as brave as you are," Felicity said.

"You're brave," I said, trying to make her see that she was just as much of an asset to me as the others.

"You and Clarissa are a lot alike. She's had to prove herself over and over to travelers outside of our family; she has a strong will and determination. I wasn't surprised when Aora said she'd travel at your side; in fact, it took everything Brady had to keep her with us after she heard Aora. She wanted to leave then for Esterious – not to see Dane, but to help you. I think she'll bring you balance when you're in the midst of turmoil," Felicity said.

I watched Clarissa approach Dane's side. He pulled her to him and held his eyes low. I could a feel an uneasy distance rising inside of him. I furrowed my eyebrows as I tried to understand it.

I took a deep breath then stood then leaned down to hug Felicity goodbye. I looked down at Allie's smiling eyes, then made my way across the field to meet the others.

Chapter Sixteen

As I made my way to Landen and the others, Brady passed me; he was going to say goodbye to Felicity and Allie. I started to tell him just to stay, that we were only going to talk to Drake – but I felt his solid intent and decided not to waste my breath. My father glanced up as I got closer. He stepped away from the others and moved toward me. His eyes were still green, but I could see a hint of hazel beginning to invade them. I watched as he looked over my body, stopping at my heart. He smiled slightly. I stopped just in front of him.

"Better?" I asked, reaching for my scar.

"Much better," he said, moving his head from side to side.

"What?" I asked.

"You and Landen just amaze me," he said.

I blushed slightly then let my gaze catch Landen's over my father's shoulder. "Are you coming with us?" I asked.

"No," he answered, staring into my eyes. "This truce must be between you and Drake."

"That isn't stopping the others from coming," I said, looking at Dane and Clarissa.

"Yes, but they won't remind him of his father as Ashten and I would," my father answered. "You'll need him to be calm if you're going to negotiate with him."

I looked down at the ground. Drake being calm was never the issue; he was always calm. In my opinion, that was one of the most frustrating traits he had.

"On the inside," my father said quietly. I looked up at him. "When you have a disagreement with someone, the only way to resolve it is to see their point of view – and for them to see yours," he said.

I nodded. My father reached his arms around me and held me as tight as he could. "I don't care how many birthdays you have; you'll always be my baby girl," he whispered. I squeezed him tighter and thought of how much I loved him.

As I felt Ashten getting closer, I let go. He wasn't as calm as my father, but I felt him trying to let go, to let me and Landen live our own lives. I smiled up at him. I could feel his overwhelming pride of having me in his family. He put his arm around my shoulder and hugged me. "You'll be home tonight, right?" he asked me.

"I don't think we'll be there long. It can only go one way or the other; either he'll help, or we'll have to find another way," I said, focusing on a calm emotion and giving it to Ashten.

Brady came up behind me. "Ready?" he asked.

I nodded and let go of Ashten, then smiled back at my father and began to walk at Brady's side toward Landen. "Did you get a chance to talk to Landen?" I asked him in a low tone.

Brady looked down at me and smiled slightly. "He talked; I listened," he answered.

"And...?" I asked, prepared to critique his response.

"I'm relieved to know that Drake isn't the devil I thought he was," he answered, raising his eyebrows.

"That was Landen's conclusion?" I said.

Brady nodded. "I have to give both Landen and Drake credit; I don't know that I'd be calm enough to let all of this unfold. If I was Landen, you'd be hidden away on a deserted island, far from any reality that Esterious could give you; and if I was Drake, I'd have stolen you away the first chance I got. The two of them prove that love isn't a selfish act – it's one that must come with some pain," he said.

My expression was solemn. It seemed that Drake had managed to reach my family; they now had sympathy for him, which made being angry and resentful toward him all the more difficult.

Brady reached his arm around my shoulder. "It's not a choice of who you love any longer; you've made that decision. Now, it's a choice of either fighting for the lost souls – or walking away," he said. His eyes looked somewhere inside me. "Landen and Drake aren't going to walk away. Neither are you."

We'd reached the others. As Landen reached his hand out for mine, Brady let his arm fall from around me. A smile came across my face as I felt his touch. He pulled me to his side and kissed my forehead.

"A member of my council wasn't trying to reach you,

was he?" he thought with an impish grin across his face. I looked over my shoulder at Brady and our fathers, who were walking toward their homes.

"Nope. Apparently, you've managed to convince them that Drake isn't such a bad guy," I answered, tightening my grip on him.

I looked past him to Olivia, who was standing near the passage to the string. As I felt her intent grow stronger, I tilted my head curiously; she wanted to go and was prepared to argue her point. Landen looked back at Dane, then to the passage at Olivia. I stepped away from him and slowly approached Olivia. As I got closer, she crossed her arms and stared into my eyes; her determination was so strong, I could see it waving through her energy.

Brady passed by me and stepped in the string. As they followed Brady, Dane and Clarissa looked curiously over at Olivia, who locked eyes with Dane and tightened her jaw. She was furious at him. He held her angry stare, then pulled Clarissa into the string with him. I looked back at Landen to see if he understood what was going on between them. I could feel a derision coming from him. He no longer thought that Dane was the one who was meant to protect me.

"Olivia, this isn't dangerous. I'm just going to talk to him," I said, trying to understand her determination – and fearing the worst.

She took a deep breath. "It's *my* place at your side – *not* Dane's," she said calmly.

The truth echoed in every word she spoke. Her certainty was terrifying. I looked at Landen for help. He felt guilty for not trusting her before, for asking Chrispin to stay behind. Landen's emotion was uncalled for, though, because we thought we were protecting them. I reached my hand out for his and let an emotion of peace flow through him.

"I'm sorry," he whispered to her. "I'd take you with us, but I know Chrispin wouldn't want you in Esterious without him."

"He knows I'm going with you. I told him this time I wouldn't take no for an answer, that one way or another, I'd be with you tonight," Olivia said.

Landen looked me. She believed every word she said.

"I'm the one who's always been at your side, Willow," she said tenderly.

"How are you so certain?" I asked, bewildered.

"I've always felt it – but now, my dreams…they prove that I've been," she said.

"You're dreaming of the past now?" I asked.

"My dreams move so fast, it's hard for me to know where I am in time – but I know that we've always been together."

"Did you dream something bad about tonight?" I asked.

"No," she said, looking down.

I looked back at Landen. *"What do you think?"* I thought.

"We'll take her; I just hope Chrispin doesn't kill me for it," he thought.

"According to her, he already knows she'll be there," I thought.

"Alright, I have no reason to doubt you. Come," Landen said, stepping halfway into the string.

A smile spread across Olivia's face. I felt hope rise in her soul. She stepped past Landen confidently and he let his hand rest on her back and guided her through. I followed, prepared to lead her through the darkness she'd see. When the glow of string had surrounded me and I felt the gentle current of energy, I focused my eyes on Olivia; she was staring back at me.

"You see me?" I said in an astonished tone.

As confidence consumed her, a grin grew across her beautiful face. Brady, Clarissa, and Dane surrounded us. Dane stepped between Olivia and me. "What is this? Why is she here?" he asked in an appalled tone.

Brady raised his hand to silence Dane then pushed him back. His eyes then raced between Olivia, Landen, and me. "You can see in here?" he asked.

Olivia breathed in and smiled. "Chrispin has managed to bring sight to me once again," she said.

A smile echoed in my eyes as I remembered that it was Chrispin's love for Olivia that brought her sight back when Drake took her. We'd never really acknowledged how powerful the love between Chrispin and Olivia had to be; we were too focused on saving the lives of my other friends, trying to figure out who we were.

"How?" Landen asked.

"Over the past three days, we stood in the string just in front of Pelhan's dimension. I meditated and listened to Chrispin's words as they created what I should see. It took time, but slowly I began to see the glow, to see him smiling proudly at me," Olivia explained.

"You were told to stay in Pelhan's world," Dane said shortly.

Clarissa stepped in front of Dane with an angry scowl. "Is that where you kept disappearing to? Aora told us you were meditating – you lied to me," she said in a tone that expressed the betrayal she was feeling.

"I didn't lie; I just didn't tell you where," Olivia said shortly.

"Wait a minute," Brady said with wide eyes. "Why do you care if she didn't tell you? That's not the point." His face showed the utter amazement he felt. "The point is, she can see; that's absolutely remarkable – do you have any idea how incredible it would be if we could teach our family to see in here?"

Clarissa rolled her eyes and crossed her arms. Olivia smiled as she took in the overwhelming sense of accomplishment she felt. She looked at me. "I told you that one way or another, Chrispin knew I'd be in Esterious," she said.

I looked up at Landen. He raised his eyebrows and smiled slightly. *"She reminds me of you sometimes,"* he thought.

He wasn't the first person to come to that conclusion. Throughout our childhood, Olivia and I had been mistaken for one another. Not only did we have the same disconnected feeling for the world around us, we were both petite with olive skin, long dark hair, and unique green eyes. My idea of having a twin somewhere in the world was fading. I feared that Olivia just may be her – and that she, without a doubt, belonged to Chrispin. A grief that I'd never find the one who belonged to Drake began to seep into my soul. Landen's smile fell, then he reached his arms around me and pulled me to him; I felt hope come through him.

We slowly began to lead the others to Esterious. Olivia came to my side and followed silently. I felt the disdain inside of Dane, but I couldn't understand it.

I took in Landen's emotion and made myself focus on a beautiful outcome. He tightened his arm around me. *"You may be the one that has to talk to Drake – alone,"* he thought.

I felt my stomach begin to turn. I wasn't afraid of

Drake, but I didn't trust myself alone with him – not after everything I knew now. Landen sensed it and through his touch I felt a calm. *"You're the only one he trusts, Willow; he'll do as you ask if it's in his power,"* he thought.

I looked up at him. *"What do you want me to do – play with his emotions so we can have our way?"* I thought as resentment began to surface in me.

"No," Landen said. I looked over my shoulder to find the others staring at us. My cheeks flushed with the anger I was starting to feel.

"Listen to me," Landen said, pressing his lips against the side of my head. *"He is the path to what we need: the path to the safety of Delen, the path to his soul mate, the path to defeating that demon. You know I believe there's a reason for everything – so there has to be a reason that we're both in this life. I don't want you to toy with him; I want you to be honest with him, tell him what we need."*

"I just don't like being in the middle," I thought.

"I don't want you in the middle either. Beyond this truce, you need to let that anger out. I don't want you to mull over why he didn't tell you he was Oba. Ask him, fight it out; there's a very good chance that his dreams are the only reliable source we have for the next trials. The scroll didn't do us much good this time," Landen thought.

"The scrolls had everything right except who the knife would go through," I thought, trying to find a way around talking to Drake alone.

A spark of grief and horror raced through Landen's emotion. I immediately felt guilty for bringing that moment to his memory.

"I don't know if Drake knew that part or not and I doubt he'd tell me – but I'm sure he'd tell you. He's a part of this, Willow. August is right: we can't afford to be di-

vided when we're faced with a demon like this," Landen thought.

As I reached my hand out and let it rest on his chest, images of the darkness pushing through him raced through my memory. I wanted to forget it all, to push it down.

"The only way to move past it – is to face it," Landen thought, reading my intent.

I nodded. *"Can we try to talk to him together first? Then, if that doesn't work, I'll talk to him alone,"* I thought.

"That's what I was planning on doing; I just wanted you to be prepared to be alone with him," Landen thought.

"I am as ready as I'm going to be," I thought, leaning into him.

We stopped at the passage that led to Patrick's home; we wanted the people in Delen to see us, to know that we hadn't abandoned them. As the haze moved past us, we smelled the fresh flowers that they'd laid on the staircase. For once, we were happy to see them leading our path, happy that they still had faith in us.

I led us up the stairs. When I opened the door, I saw Patrick staring out his window at the streets; he felt solemn. He turned as we entered the room. A smile filled his face – but his mood didn't shift as I expected it to.

"Did something happen?" Landen asked, reading his emotion.

Patrick's eyes filled with sorrow. "A mass of people tried to escape over the wall last night; they didn't make it," he said in a low tone.

The solemn mood Patrick had spread into all of us; I tried not to think of the lives that were lost while I rested contently in my own world.

"The morale is down in the city," Patrick said. "Seeing all of you should bring back their hope."

"We plan to see if we can reach a truce tonight," Landen said.

"Tread carefully...Drake has the same enemies that you do," Patrick answered.

Landen nodded then looked down at me. It was as if we were the last ones to realize the thin line Drake walked on.

As we stepped out on the street, people stopped what they were doing and watched us pass. I felt their joy and hope. Landen and I reached our hands out to touch them and returned what we felt as we walked by. I could see the wall and hear the builders in the distance. It had grown another foot since we'd left. I wondered how high they were going to take it.

The palace looked beautiful at sunset. It was almost completely painted white now. Flowers were on every balcony. My willow tree, the one that had grown in the center court after my first trial, swayed in the autumn breeze. I smiled as I watched the energy of light dance around it. It was my first mark on this world. I was determined to make another.

As we approached, the doors opened. The woman who'd shadowed Perodine during our stay was waiting on us. She still wore a solid black dress, but she'd pinned a red rose to her chest; the color gave me hope that even those most loyal to the court could find a way to change.

As we followed her up the stairs to Perodine's study, I looked back at Brady and Clarissa to see their take on the palace. Clarissa was eyeing all the paintings along the walls. Brady was more focused on where we were going.

"I wouldn't have thought you'd have wanted to come back to this place," Dane said to Olivia.

Olivia hesitated. I glared at Dane; I couldn't believe he

would have wanted her to remember the time she was held here, the time she lost her sight. Olivia turned on the step where she stood; Dane was just behind her. Her gaze eased across his stone cold image. A content smile then spread across her face. "This palace was a doorway I walked through. I don't fear it. It was simply a small stepping stone on my path to Chrispin," she stated all to coolly.

She turned and looked at me, and I reached my hand out for her to come to my side. Dane looked up at me, and I felt his emotion of disdain grow. It bothered me that they were being distant with each other. They'd never been close. Growing up, I was the one friend that linked them. At times, I'd feel pulled between them – and right now, that was last thing I needed on my plate.

Landen reached his arm around me. *"I'll talk to him when I get a chance. He's only acting that way because his pride is hurt; he sees her as a threat,"* he thought.

"He always has; I just don't know why he's putting me through this right now," I thought as I began to climb the steps again.

When we reached the study, we found Perodine staring out the window at the wall that was growing taller by the moment. Brady and Landen went to her side. I made my way to the table to see if she'd made any more notes on what she'd found in the scroll. The others followed me there. The books that Alamos and August had brought were stacked neatly at one end of the table. The scroll was in the center. A note pad with a mathematic equation was sitting just below it. When she saw Brady and Landen at her side, Perodine turned and reached her arm around Landen. He pulled her close to him I could feel the flooding calm he was giving her. I smiled, wondering how close they were in my first life.

Perodine's eyes moved to me. "Did you have a good birthday?" she asked.

I tried to smile. "I just rested, painted," I answered.

She nodded. "I have a gift for you," she said, crossing the room to the table that centered the couches.

I watched her with anticipation. I knew that whatever she gave me would be perfect. On the table was a long box made of cherry wood. The hinges were silver and so was the lock that closed it. Perodine carefully picked up the box and walked to the table in front of which I was standing. I stared at her, wondering what was inside.

"I am afraid it is not new; it was once yours," she said, smiling.

Landen and Brady came closer to see what was in the box. I carefully reached for the silver latch, then opened and pulled the lid up slowly. Inside, there were paint brushes – every kind imaginable – in perfect condition.

Perodine traced her finger across the box. "I have no idea where the talent of art came from, but it most definitely has always been your passion," she said as she watched me gently pick up the brush that lay on top. They felt like they were mine. I remembered them. I smiled as images I must have painted long ago came to me.

"You told me that when you painted, you let your soul speak to you. Each time you had a problem that seemed too big for you to comprehend, you would paint; when the painting was complete, you had resolved whatever was tormenting you," Perodine said.

Olivia and Landen looked at each other, then at me. "I assure you that's her way of sorting through her conflicts today," Landen said. I felt how proud he was of me, how much he loved me.

I gently laid down the brush I was holding and carefully closed the box. I then extended my arms to hug Perodine and in her embrace I felt the kind of love my mother, Grace, gave me: unconditional. Perodine was abundantly thankful I was in her life. I let the gratitude I felt flow through my emotion. I then leaned back and let my arms fall.

"Did you have a peaceful night?" I asked.

She looked over her shoulder at the wall, then down at the scrolls. "No demons; just the wake of his evil," she answered. I knew she was referring to the lives that were lost last night, the innocent people who just wanted to escape. An uneasy breath escaped me. I fell into the chair I was standing in front of and tried to pull my thoughts together; there had to be a way around war, a way that Drake wouldn't be overtaken by evil.

Landen reached for the math equation. "Are we sure that Venus is done now?" he asked Perodine.

"I want August and Alamos to check my math, but I am almost certain that the timing was right," Perodine said.

Landen handed the pad to Brady, who picked up a pen and started going over the equation. I looked at Landen curiously. *"Math is a universal language that Brady has always spoken well,"* Landen thought. I raised my eyebrows, showing the surprise I felt. *"It's always been too black-and-white for me,"* Landen thought." *I try to find a way to prove the theories wrong – and it annoys him,"* he finished, smiling at Brady.

I felt August, Nyla, Beth, and Marc approaching from the other direction. My insides started to tie themselves in knots. Adrenaline rushed through my veins. Landen walked around the table and reached for my hand. I felt his calm as he pulled me up and led me to the couch that faced the fireplace.

"He's not with them," he thought. With his thoughts and his emotion of calm, the knots started to unwind. A numb feeling came in the wake of the adrenaline.

"I don't think I can talk to him. I won't be able to control my anger – I'll only make it worse," I said, leaning forward and letting my head rest on my knees.

I felt Landen gently run his hand across my back and Clarissa take a seat next to me. Olivia sat on the table in front of me. *"I don't want you to hide anything from him. Anger, fear – he has the same emotions. The two of you are going to have to face them."*

As the dread built in me, I turned my head from side to side. I knew that if I were to release any kind of emotion, Landen would feel it. I was struggling to protect him from any doubt that I loved him. I just wanted to hide. Brady's idea of a deserted island was sounding better and better as the seconds crept by.

"There's nothing you'll feel that will make me doubt what we have. We are not running," Landen thought.

I looked up at him to find him smiling at me. "I promise," he whispered.

I leaned into him and took a deep breath. August and Nyla appeared first in the doorway. Beth and Marc were behind them. They had so many emotions running through them that it was hard for me to judge them. Marc and August looked curiously at Olivia. Nyla and Beth just smiled. I knew then that they were more than aware that Olivia had found a way to see in the string, a way to travel.

"Did something happen?" Landen asked August.

"Drake had a meeting with his court, so we had to leave," August said as he took a seat on the couch next to ours. Nyla sat down next to him. Beth came to Olivia's side and let her arm drape around her. I watched as Beth whispered something to Olivia; I couldn't hear her words, but I knew they filled Olivia with pride.

Marc let his hands rest on his hips then raised his eyebrows. "I knew Chrispin was hiding something from me," he said, looking between Olivia and Beth.

"He wasn't hiding anything; he wanted to tell you, but you've been distant," Olivia said.

Guilt absorbed Marc and Landen. The last thing they intended to do was push anyone away. Landen looked over his shoulder at Brady then to Olivia. "I won't leave them behind again – I promise," he said.

Marc nodded in agreement. "Does he know you're here? Should I go and tell him?" he asked.

"He'll be here soon," Olivia said, turning to smile at me. Clarissa shook her head from side to side and she couldn't hide the betrayal she was feeling. Olivia and Clarissa had grown close over the last few months. Right now they couldn't feel more distant.

"Where is he?" Landen asked.

"He led Preston home," August answered, leaning forward and burying his head in his hands.

"You're concerned...did the court see you?" Landen asked.

August leaned back, shaking his head slowly from side to side. He then sighed and stared into space. "He's in a dark place. The only one on his side for sure is Alamos," he answered. His eyes then moved quickly to Landen. "He's on his side. You can feel he wants to help him, right?" he asked, looking for validation.

"He loves him as if he were his son; he won't betray him," Landen answered, confident in his words.

August sighed and extended his arm around Nyla.

"How was it having all of them in the same room?"

Landen asked, nodding his head in Marc's direction.

Marc looked down and walked to the table with the others. August smiled as he watched Marc walk away.

"Tense at first, but Preston eased it over. They were all civil," August answered.

I felt an overwhelming pride coursing through Beth. I could feel Chrispin approaching. I glanced over my shoulder a second later he appeared in the doorway. He glanced at Marc and Brady and smiled boyishly. His eyes then found Olivia and he walked quickly to sit by her side. He wrapped his arm around her and smiled at me.

"Is she not the most amazing woman you've ever met?" he asked Beth.

Beth smiled and nodded. "One of four, hopefully," she said under her breath. Remorse began to seep into her; I knew her thoughts were with Drake at that time.

Clarissa's body tensed next to mine. A dense jealously began to absorb her. Perodine slowly walked to the couch next to ours then leaned against the edge and stared curiously at Olivia.

"How did you get here so quickly?" Landen asked, grinning proudly at Chrispin.

"Rose and Libby were at the gate. Preston had that look in his eye. You know the one: like something life-changing is about to happen," Chrispin said, raising his eyebrows.

Landen's smile fell and the room filled with a sense of dread. Perodine stood up straight then looked at Dane and Olivia.

"You're a Cancer," Perodine said to Olivia. Olivia smiled and bowed her head. "Have you always had a sense of optimism – even in the darkest hour?" Perodine asked.

Olivia looked at me and I nodded. In my opinion, she

had too many dark hours. When we were only children, she lost both of her parents – but even though grief consumed her, she still found a way to smile and to make me smile.

"And you are the dreamer?" Perodine said under her breath.

Chrispin looked past me at Dane and I felt a tension rise between them. Landen stretched his hand out for Chrispin's knee, drawing his attention away from Dane and giving himself a sense of calm. Chrispin broke his stare and pulled Olivia closer to him. I could feel Perodine's emotions racing. It terrified her to know that if it weren't for August insisting that we allow Drake to stay, I could have been easily overcome by the demon. Drake had been the only thing standing between me and the darkness that chased me.

"Water is every part of your chart," Perodine said to Olivia. "It gives you the ability to see beyond the moment you are in…you are the one the demon fears the most – for you can see it coming," she said slowly.

I felt Dane come to the edge of the couch, but I didn't look at him; I knew if I did, his eyes would make me feel guilty for not thinking he was the one who was supposed to protect me.

"I feel better now," Perodine said, smiling slightly. We all looked at her curiously. "I could not figure out how he was able to cause the illusion in the bathroom or get as close as he did inside of Drake. I thought he had somehow grown more powerful than the shield, but that was not the case," Perodine looked at Landen, then to me. "The shield was simply misplaced."

"To admit you were wrong is the same as admitting that you could be wrong again," Dane said through his teeth; anger and jealously were engulfing him.

August leaned forward and raised his hands as if to calm the room. "Then we'll just make sure that in the future they're both with Willow; that way, we have no doubts – and Willow is protected."

I felt Landen's anticipation. I glanced to my side at him then followed his eyes to the doorway August had come through. "It must have been a short meeting," Landen said aloud, watching the doorway.

I felt him sorting through the emotions and intent of Alamos and Drake. I still couldn't feel them. I could only feel Landen's response to what he felt – and at that moment, he had sorrow, fear, and anger.

Adrenaline spread through me. I unknowingly held my breath, waiting for the moment when I'd look into Drake's dark eyes.

"Is it bad?" I thought.

He glanced at me. "They're just very overwhelmed and apparently they aren't thinking clearly."

I drew in an uneasy breath and waited for them to enter the room. Alamos came in first. His eyes moved across the room, first finding me, then Perodine. He passed by me and stood at Perodine's side. He felt Olivia's gaze and stared curiously back at her. Drake appeared in the doorway. He looked passed everyone at me. Our eyes locked and for a second I thought time had stopped. I couldn't hear or feel anything – I could only see his captivating dark eyes outlined in dark circles. He looked so tired. The sleeves on his button up shirt were rolled up. My eyes fell to his tattoo of the dragon covered by a willow tree on the inside of his arm. He carefully rolled his sleeves down when he saw the tattoo had once again taken my attention, then kept his eyes on me as he took a seat on the couch next to August. I was calmer than I thought I would be in his presence.

Clarissa reached for my hand and held it tight. I felt how uncomfortable she was around Drake. Like every young girl in his presence, she was completely captivated by him.

Olivia turned to look at him. He smiled slightly, noticing her for the first time. "I was wondering where you were," he said to Olivia as he relaxed into the couch.

His eyes moved to Alamos.

"I thought that was her," Alamos said.

Marc walked behind Landen. "You should recognize her; are you not the one who held her captive, the one who took her sight?" he said shortly.

Alamos smiled slightly, then looked at Drake and Marc. "Son, the priest you seek revenge on has since lost his life; beyond that, it's impossible to take her sight. If anything, they caused her to find her third eye more suddenly than expected," he said.

"Third eye?" Marc repeated sarcastically, shaking his head.

Alamos looked at Perodine. "The only one that really matters," he said. "What we see with our minds is far more important that what our eyes see; this child has the ability to see clearly without concentration."

You'd think Olivia would be afraid of the power they were telling her she had, but she wasn't; it was like she'd known all along. I envied her calm state. I looked at Drake to see his eyes barely open. He broke our gaze and gently shut his eyes.

"Why didn't you just tell us that before?" Marc asked. It terrified him to think that we'd made a bad decision, that in our haste we'd left behind the one that could guide us clearly.

Alamos looked at Perodine, then to Marc. "I was under

the impression that you already knew," he said, tilting his head in Perodine's direction.

Perodine shook her head from side to side and tried to suppress her anger. "You only have to worry about Drake; I have to guide the children, Landen and my daughter," she said, looking apologetically at me.

"My thoughts are always with 'our' daughter," Alamos retorted.

I raised my hands and closed my eyes; the emotions of the room were starting to drain me – and Dane's feeling of betrayal was killing me. "I know all of you are here for me," I said, daring to look over my shoulder at Dane, "but when you battle over who's known me longer or who has the best intentions for me, you lose your focus; you forget that this demon has a power beyond our imagination. Stop fighting. Let's resolve this."

Alamos cleared his throat. "Well then...what shall we discuss first? The end of Venus? The impending influence of Mars? The proclamation of war? Or Drake's awaiting assassination?" Alamos said to the room.

His last words reached inside of me and ripped my soul in two. I couldn't hide the grief I felt for Drake. I looked to see him resting peacefully. Landen reached his arm around me and pulled me as close to him as he could. He wanted to move my emotion, but it was too strong; my sorrow remained.

"Is it that serious over there?" August asked Alamos.

"The only way he survived the night was by executing those proven to plot his overturn," Alamos said.

I closed my eyes and thought of the innocents that had lost their lives last night as they tried to cross the wall. If Drake had taken their life, there would be no way for me to forgive him. Landen's eyes moved to the wall.

Alamos must have known what we were thinking. "We had no part in that; they were all priest," he said to Landen. "They were shared enemies of yours, I assure you."

I glanced at Drake. He opened his eyes slightly, just as I did. I'm sure he was judging my response. I let the sorrow I was feeling reflect itself in my eyes. He sighed before he gently closed his eyes again.

Beth stood and walked behind the couch he was sitting on then ran her fingers through his hair. Her only desire was to calm him. Her eyes found mine, but I couldn't look at her long. It hurt too bad.

"We just need to look over the math for Venus. If we're right, then we can move on to more pressing matters," Perodine said as she gently pulled Alamos' arm to the table.

"More pressing matters than Drake's death?" Alamos said in a disgusted tone, refusing to look at the equation.

"That is not what I meant," Perodine said defensively. "I would like to know that there is not a demon pulling the strings, causing him the turmoil he is living through."

"Trust me, 'it' will pull the strings until Willow stands at his side," Alamos said.

Unable to take another word, Beth leaned down and kissed Drake's forehead, then left the room. Nyla looked at me, then stood to follow her. August stood and went to the table to help Brady look at the equation. Landen kissed the side of my head, then followed August. I leaned a little closer to Clarissa, then glanced up at her, she was watching Drake as he seemed to drift to sleep.

"Willow," she whispered, "you're stronger than I'd imagined."

Chrispin rolled his eyes at Clarissa then stood to follow Landen. As Olivia studied Drake's sleeping body, her eyes seemed to go to another time. I felt a sea of emotions, varying from happiness to grief. I wanted to pull her aside and make her tell me every dream she's had, but I knew right now my past wasn't the issue – it was my future.

"I'm not," I whispered back, trying to make myself look away from Drake. I wanted to make him feel better. To give him a peace I was sure was escaping him. I stood abruptly, wanting to hide at Landen's side. As I turned, I caught Landen's gaze.

"You're fine," Landen thought, reaching his arm out for me to come to his side.

August was checking over what Brady had already reviewed while Marc and Dane sat at the table, watching patiently. Perodine and Alamos were locked in a daring stare.

"I feel the trial...the moment Willow's heart was pierced occurred at the moment the scroll indicated, but the influence of the Venus in retrograde is still in the air. We must be careful with the decisions we make right now," August said as he checked the last part of the equation.

Alamos broke his stare with Perodine and looked at August. "I think we should take advantage of the influence of the retrograde. We must stop making selfish choices of our own hearts and use logic to save lives," he said, walking to August's side.

"And what do you mean by that?" Perodine said coldly, following Alamos to the table.

He turned abruptly to find Perodine inches from his face. "I mean, he will die if she doesn't stand at his side. I'm not asking that she gives her heart to him; I just want her to stand next to him in front of the court, in front of the world," Alamos said as he pulled his shoulders back.

Marc and Dane both stood abruptly. Clarissa turned and caught my stare. She then stood slowly and walked to my side. She was screaming at me with her emotions, her panic, fear, and determination not to let me take that path. Olivia and Chrispin were the only ones that remained calm. I knew then that Aora had predicted what choice I'd be forced to make next.

"You are a fool. You may deceive the world – but you will never fool the devil," Perodine said, pushing against Alamos' chest.

He caught her hands and held them tightly. "You may hate me right now," Alamos said, "but you loved me at one time. You know I'm not an evil man. I'm trying to save his life, the lives of innocent bystanders. How many people must die before you see that I'm right?" Alamos said.

Perodine looked away from him and pulled her hands from him. As her eyes caught mine, the tension in the room began to rise.

"I'm sorry," Perodine said, looking at me.

A single tear fell from my eye. Landen pulled me closer to him, but I couldn't bring myself to look at him. I could feel his solid intent of saving lives, of putting the world's needs in front of his.

Brady moved passed August to Alamos. Marc and Dane were close behind him. "Listen, I don't know you. I have no way of knowing what your intent is, but I know that this isn't the answer. Willow belongs at Landen's side," he said in a calm tone.

Alamos shook his head in disgust. "You're defending your brother's heart. A noble thing to do. But you get to go home and live in a world of peace. We're left here to hear the blood-curdling screams of those who lose their lives based on Willow's choices."

Marc pushed in front of Brady. "And you're defending a tragedy that you caused. You'd think that a man that's lived as long as you wouldn't have brought more harm than good," he said as loud as he could.

Marc's tone startled Drake out of his rest and he sat forward and surveyed the room.

"Aww, look – he's awake now," Marc said sarcastically, looking at Drake. "Let me fill you in: your latest plot to get Willow has failed; she will *not* stand at your side – no matter what the risk is."

Drake stood with an angry scowl on his face. Alamos looked away from him; it was clear he wanted no part of Alamos' reasoning. Landen looked at Drake, then sighed and moved his eyes to Marc. "This is a decision that Willow and I must make – not you," Landen said.

"Have you lost your mind?!" Marc yelled. "I refuse to let you make this choice!"

"You're causing more harm than good," Brady said to Marc.

Clarissa rushed to my side and gripped my shoulders; her eyes showed the anger she felt. "Mistakes are only made once; don't do this. Remember what I told you: you will die in vain," she warned me.

I gently pulled her arms from my shoulders, then looked over my shoulder to see Olivia still seated calmly; I wished the others would just follow her lead and let me think.

"I never realized how selfish the souls of Chara were," Alamos said bleakly into the room.

As arguments from every direction erupted, I felt like my head was going to explode. I turned to Landen and buried my face in his chest – then silence. I slowly leaned my head up and found that time had once again been frozen. I looked up at Landen and saw that he was looking over his shoulder at Drake.

"Was that you or me?" Drake asked.

"I think we made the decision to stop and think at the same time," Landen said, looking down at me.

"Well," Drake said, "how long do you intend to keep them frozen?"

"Long enough for you and Willow to leave the room and work this out in private," Landen answered.

"Don't make me do this," I thought in a pleading tone.

"Willow, I love you and would never make you do anything that makes you unhappy. I just want us to make a decision and not regret it," he thought.

"Then the three of us need to make it," I thought.

"Talk to him alone, then the three of us will decide. You need to clear your mind and get your anger and grief under control," he thought.

He leaned down and kissed my lips tenderly, then slowly stepped away. Behind him, Drake was standing staring at me with exhausted eyes.

"Take her far enough away that the emotions of this room are muffled. They know she can feel them and they'll do everything in their power to distract her," Landen said.

Drake turned and walked to the doorway. I glanced up at Landen he smiled at me then tilted his head, telling me to follow Drake. I held my breath and told myself to put one foot in front of the other. My heart began to thunder. The exhausting adrenaline raced through me once again.

Chapter Seventeen

We walked silently to the other side of the palace. Drake opened a double doorway that led to a beautiful open bedroom. I hesitated, trying to remember to breathe. I then stepped cautiously forward. He walked to the window and stood with his hands on his waist, then let his head fall. I stepped guardedly closer to him.

"Would it save your life – the souls in Delen – if I stood at your side before the court?" I asked in a careful tone.

His shoulders tensed, then he turned to look at me, tightening his jaw and swallowing before he answered. "We won't lead them to truth with a lie," he said quietly.

"You didn't answer my question. Will it save your life?"

"Listen to me," he said, stepping forward. "Preston told me no less than two hours ago that if you came to my side, you must come completely. Otherwise, the demon would consume me and you wouldn't know any different. That's not going to happen."

"I've looked the devil in the eye. I would know," I said, offended by the lack of confidence Preston had in me.

"He's never been wrong before," Drake said, looking away from me.

"You want to know what I think?" I said in a sharp tone. "I think you just have a death wish that you're determined to end your life and make it my fault – to make me suffer."

His eyes shot to mine. The intensity behind them took my breath away. "Death is *not* my wish," he said calmly.

"Then tell me why you didn't tell me you were Oba?"

He walked past me and paced in front of the elegant bed.

"Why didn't you just tell me?" I asked again.

"I didn't know until it was almost over," he answered in a frustrated tone.

"You knew in enough time to put your mother to sleep...you watched me suffer with the idea...you felt my grief," I argued.

"What did you want me to tell you – that I'd seen you hold a diamond blade against your chest more times than I care to recall?"

"You knew it wasn't you that had to die – why would you make me suffer like that?"

"I didn't know. The scroll, Alamos, Perodine...they all said it would move through the blood of Jayda."

I stepped closer to him and pointed my finger at his chest. "My children stayed with my sister. I raised yours.

You knew that. You knew the descendants never moved – only the sisters."

He held my hand against his chest. My breath became measured as I felt his addictive sensation. I glared up into his dark eyes, which were shadowed by dark circles.

"You want to know what I remember?" he asked. I nodded. "I remember an old man looking into a small pool of water. He told us that evil would consume Jayda and subdue the power. You were Jayda. I was the power. You were determined to take your life to protect mine – to protect our world. You demanded that every diamond be shaped into a blade. Frankly, I'm surprised that every table in Analess doesn't have one." He ran his fingers through his hair and sighed. "The worst part is, every time a shadow would cross our path, you'd raise a blade to your chest." His eyes began to glisten. I knew he was holding back tears. "We lived in terror – terror that we'd be taken from one another," he said in a voice just above a whisper. "I admit I was relieved to hear that in this life I was the blood of Jayda and you were the power…I wouldn't have to watch you end your life."

"You could have told us the children were never moved," I said, wanting to be angry with him but finding it harder by the moment.

"How was I to know that our children never told their children? We didn't hide it from them. They knew our family was divided," he said.

"You had to have known," I retorted.

"This may be hard for someone like you to understand," he said slowly.

I stepped back, offended. I felt like he was talking down to me.

He stepped forward and put his hands on my shoulders. "Listen to me before you lose your temper. This is hard for you to understand because you don't dream like the rest of us. Dreams aren't lucid. They shift forward, backward, side-to-side. Sometimes you live them sometimes you observe them. You can have hundreds in one night. You're asking me to put all my dreams in order. You think that they're clear to me? That I can recall them without any uncertainty? I'm only nineteen. It would be impossible for me to have lived all those lives in detail."

He was right: I *didn't* know how to dream like the rest of the world. The only dreams I remember having in my entire life were the ones I had inside Evelyn's body – and they were out of control.

"They have to be clear enough for you to believe them soundly," I said, staring back at him.

"You're clear. You. Are. Always. Clear," he said as he let his hands fall from my shoulders. "Do you want to know how I reason that this hell is reality?" he asked.

I stared back at him. He let his fingers run through the energy that was surrounding me. "Because in this life your energy, your power, is stronger than ever before – leaving me no choice but to believe that the worlds I go to in my dreams are in a distant past," he said.

"Was Landen in that life? Did I leave him for you? Do you remember?" I asked with pleading eyes. He stared back at me and turned his head slowly from side to side. "There was another man. I had children," I argued.

"It was Dane," Drake said as he tightened his jaw.

"What?!"

"Why do you think I can't stand the sight of him near you? He was the one that refused to let your children come and live with us. You cried endlessly over them. There was nothing I could do to help you."

"Dane?" I said making a face. I loved Dane, but not in that way.

"He's been in several of our lives," Drake said.

"He's a good guy," I said – even though Dane's behavior that day had been a bit off.

"He's never wanted me to be with you – that's for sure," Drake answered.

"Have you ever seen Landen in your dreams?" I asked.

"Never," Drake said in a serious tone. "There's never been a doubt that you belonged to me," he finished.

"You have doubt now," I said, staring back at him.

Drake pointed in the direction of the study. "I can see how much he loves you," he said. "It wasn't clear to me until the demon stood between us." He reached for my chest and let his hand rest where my wound was. "When you did this, I wasn't strong enough to hold the darkness in myself so he could help you. He saw that and held it in himself so at least one of us could go to you."

Tears surfaced as I heard his words. "His love was strong enough to hold the demon inside of himself and strong enough to push him out – and after all that, he found the strength to heal you. He doesn't puts himself before the rest of the world. I have no choice but to respect him."

"There's someone that can love you the way he loves me," I said, prepared to argue with him.

He let himself fall on the edge of the bed and buried his hands in his face. I knelt down before him. "I just want to help. For all we know, we may need her to beat this demon," I whispered.

He looked up from his hands into my eyes. His stare reached somewhere inside my soul and pulled at my core. He reached for my face and gently cradled me with his mesmerizing touch. "You are the only thing keeping me sane. You're the only thing that's real to me," he said, leaning his forehead to mine.

"You deserve to be one with someone in this life, to feel the energy in reality. I can't do that for you."

He leaned back slightly so he could stare into my eyes. "You don't believe you've ever completed me?" he whispered.

I let my eyes tell him no.

"Hold still," he whispered, holding my stare.

I held my breath terrified something was wrong. He closed his eyes and in that second I felt his energy move inside of me. I gasped, closing my eyes as I took it in. I felt so warm that I was cold. Every part of me hummed. It was powerful, addictive, blissful, and beautiful. My head started to spin. My mind went blank – then all at once, the sensation was gone. I opened my eyes to see him staring back at me. The dark circles under his eyes had vanished.

"Do you believe me now?" he asked as his thumb traced the bottom of my eye.

I fell back on my knees and let my head fall, trying to catch my breath and make the room stand still. I felt his lips on the top of my head. His hypnotic touch coursed through me. I looked up, hiding behind the glass of tears that wanted to fall.

"That wasn't the same. That's not how Landen and I join," I said, trying to comprehend him.

"I'm not Landen," he whispered, running his hands through my hair.

"I can't love you the way you need me to."

"The impasse remains," he said, kissing my forehead before he stood.

"We should just run...all of us," I said, almost to myself.

"I told you I'm not going to betray them," Drake said, extending his hand to help me up.

I took his hand and slowly stood, finding it difficult to balance after his rush of energy. He smiled and let his hands rest on my hips, trying to help me. I gently slid them off.

"I don't think you're making it any better," I said under my breath.

He sighed and his grin grew wider. I stepped closer to the bed and sat down carefully, then laid back and closed my eyes. I was so dizzy, the room was spinning out of control. A moment later, I felt him sit down next to me.

"Are you OK?" he asked.

I opened my eyes to see him looking carefully over me. I turned my head from side to side. "I don't want you to die," I whispered.

"Tell me what to do, Love. My purpose in this life – in every life – is you."

I stared at him. An impasse. That's what we were all living in. It was as if the devil had trapped us in a web of emotions that can't be explained. There had to be a way. There's always a way when you have the best intentions. The people in the city, their smiles, danced in my mind. The darkness of the world beyond the wall terrified me. I felt like I was trying to redeem hell itself; without the light Delen gave the dimension, it could very well be mistaken as such a place. I pondered if there were a way to give the darkness a home and take the light to a new one.

"Do you think I could find a dimension that could hold the number of people that live in Delen?" I asked, pulling myself up.

His eyes questioned my words.

"I meant it. We should all run, all of us – and the entire

city of Delen," I said.

He looked at me like I was insane. "Do you wish to leave all those who are struggling to get into this city to suffer? Save some and betray most?" he asked.

"I'm only trying to solve what's in front of me now. I'll find a way to save the rest of the dimension," I said, growing more confident with my idea.

"I don't know of any dimension that would be large enough to take on such a mass of people, or even a place that wouldn't terrify them. This dimension is light years behind others," he said.

"We could save some," I said.

"And how would you choose? Women and children? Leave their fathers and husbands behind? That's not the answer. This is their home and you're teaching them to run from their fears – not face them."

"Drake, some is better than none. They're going to charge the wall. Even if you managed to hold them back, the people who try to cross it will be executed."

His eyes left mine and shifted from side to side. He then stood and began to pace in front of the bed, ultimately stopping and smiling down at me.

"They'll be executed by me," he said in an excited tone.

"Are you insane?" I said, standing – full of rage.

His hands gripped my shoulders his sensation swarmed through me. "Listen," he said, capturing my eyes. "I'll tell the court that I will personally execute anyone who strays from the life Donalt created for us, that their bodies must be banished from the world – into the string. You can find them there, then take them to Delen or wherever you wish; in the mind of the dark side of the dimension, though, they will be executed."

"What about Delen? The war?" I asked, feeling empowered by his excitement.

"If I'm executing mass numbers of people, the court will no longer think that I'm weak. I'll tell them that Delen wants us to attack them; they know that if we cross the wall, we'll be demented as well. I can even order a five-hundred-mile radius around the city, claiming the ground the crops grow in is demented," he said.

"Is that enough room?" I asked, trying to imagine the distance.

He raised his eyebrows and his grin widened. "That'll depend on how many people I'm forced to execute. It will buy us time – time we didn't have when we walked into this room."

"Will they believe you?"

He let his smile leave, then his eyes turned dark and his jaw locked. "I can be scary if I need to be," he said, letting his smile return.

A smile spread across my face. His eyes softened and he tilted his head.

"What?" I asked.

"You've never smiled at me in this life before."

My smile grew wider and I felt my cheeks blush. "It's hard to find a reason to smile sometimes," I said, looking away from him.

"Will you smile when I lead the executed into the string?" he asked. My smile grew wider. "Well then, I suppose I'm going to have to execute not only those who try to pass the wall – but all who show a desire to know you as well," he said.

I reached my arms around his shoulders and hugged him as tightly as I could. I felt an overwhelming joy come through me and I let that emotion flow through my touch.

"I can feel you," he whispered. "I want to make you feel like this all the time."

I let my arms slowly fall from around his neck. I was afraid I was giving him false hope.

His eyes danced across my face, and his smile remained. "We should tell the others. I'm interested to see what Alamos thinks about our resolution," Drake said. He then took my hand and led me back to the others, back to Landen.

Chapter Eighteen

The closer we got to the study, the more intensely I could feel the emotions of the room; with the exception of August, Chrispin, and Olivia, my family was angry with me and Landen. The doorway to the study was in sight and I saw Landen appear in the threshold and begin to walk in our direction. I looked up at Drake and saw that he was looking down at me. I let a small smile come across my face. When he saw it, he grinned and a sparkle came to his dark eyes. We stopped and waited for Landen to reach us. When he did, he reached his hand out for me to come to his side. I stepped forward and wrapped my arm around him. When he felt my peace, a relieved smile brought his dimples to life.

"You both look better," Landen said, looking from me

to Drake.

Drake nodded. "I think we have a solution that will buy us some time."

"He wants to talk to me alone," Landen thought.

I nodded and looked back at Drake, then up at Landen before I walked past them. I was feverish about stepping into the swarm of emotions that were stirring in the study. I walked as slowly as I could, hoping that Landen and Drake's discussion wouldn't be long. When I reached the threshold I found the entire room staring at me. Dane walked to my side, then reached down, grabbed my legs and threw me over his shoulders.

"This is for your own good," he said, turning to go to the opposite doorway. Chrispin and Brady moved to block him, but Clarissa pushed against Brady.

"You two are out of control," Brady said, pulling Clarissa's arms away from him and reaching for me. "If Landen sees this, the two of you will be on the other side of the universe with one push of his anger."

I felt Landen rushing in my direction as arguments erupted all around me. I closed my eyes and focused on my energy, making it as solid as I could as I flung myself out of Dane's arms and suspended myself in mid-air – just out of reach of his powerful long arms.

"If I were you, I'd back away. She's barely using the power her energy has," Alamos said. I looked at him to see an intriguing smile across his aged face.

Marc pushed Dane back, and Clarissa glared up at me. Olivia shook her head with disgust; she felt for them. Perodine nodded for me to come down and I slowly lowered myself. She then walked cautiously to where I landed. Her green eyes sparkled. Anticipation consumed her.

August walked to my side, guarding Dane and

Clarissa's sight from me. He then held his hand up, telling Chrispin to remain calm. As I felt Landen just feet away, I let my shield of energy fall.

"I can see the resolve in your expression. What did you decide?" Perodine asked.

My eyes looked to the table where Alamos was standing. "Drake will prove to the court that he's not weak by executing those who chose to know me," I said, feeling the horrified gaze of my family. "By 'executing,' I mean he'll push them into the string and Landen and I will retrieve them."

"Absolute genius," August said under his breath.

Alamos looked past me and I followed his gaze to see Drake and Landen standing just inside the doorway. Rage was in Drake's eyes -- a disbelieving rage was consuming Landen as he stared at his sister, Clarissa.

"And where do you intend on taking them? Into a city that will be overcome by war?" Alamos said, clearly not fond of our solution.

"Drake can prevent war," I said shortly.

"Drake brings nothing but destruction," Dane said in an angry tone.

Drake took a dominant step in Dane's direction, but Landen held him back. Marc then pushed Dane out of the room. Clarissa followed, shaking her head at me in disgust. When Dane was out of sight Drake let the tension in his body release then stared into Landen's eyes as is if he were trying to give him a guarded message.

Alamos looked sympathetically out the window. "I'm afraid, my dear, that he'll have no choice but to evoke it," he said.

Drake broke his stare with Landen and looked at Alamos. "I will not evoke war – I will cause the world to fear this city."

"They will not fear it; it's nothing compared to the mass outside the walls," Alamos said.

"They fear the demented. In their eyes Delen is just that," Drake argued.

"Yes. And they will destroy it just to give them peace of mind," Alamos said.

"We must give them reason to believe that they cannot destroy it," Perodine said. I felt her excitement and relief as she took ownership of the path I'd chosen.

The room was still. Each of us were lost in our own thoughts, what we thought would be enough to terrify an entire world. Brady looked to the window, then to Landen. "Do you think you can lift that wall – push it back?" he asked.

Landen looked down at me, then to Drake. We'd never moved something so enormous.

Alamos looked over his shoulder at the wall, then to Drake. "Drake, Willow, and Landen could," he said.

I felt an excitement rise in the room as we all looked at one another.

"If you lift that wall, that would give them enough fear to buy us time," Perodine said.

"Hold on," Alamos said. "Drake can't be seen helping Landen."

"Then we'll do it by nightfall," Drake said.

"Do you not realize that they're watching your every move? Someone will realize that you were missing at the moment the wall was moved," Alamos said.

My eyes looked to the doorway through which Marc had just left. Drake looked at me and smiled slightly; he had the same thought I had: Marc could pose as Drake.

"We'll do this tonight. Marc will stay in my chambers

with you and my mother at his side. Once the wall is moved, Landen and I will stop time. I'll be back before they alert me that Delen is attacking."

"And what if you're not back in time? What if they choose to speak to you about a different matter?" Alamos argued.

"I'm sure you'll think of something. We're only talking about moments," Drake said.

"I'm going to get some of your clothes for Marc," Perodine said, leaving the room.

I looked at Drake. I knew if the chamber were dark enough, if the priest didn't come close enough, they'd be convinced.

I could feel the immediate intent of Dane and Clarissa – they were leaving. I knew I wouldn't be able to focus if I thought for a moment that I hurt them.

I began to walk to the doorway and Landen stepped closer to me and reached for my hand. *"I don't want you around him without me,"* he thought.

"Then come," I thought, pulling his hand to the doorway.

Landen looked at Brady and asked him to follow us. Chrispin began to follow us, but August reached his arm out, telling him to stay.

In the hallway, we found Marc trying to reason with Dane and Clarissa. Their violent whispers halted when they saw us.

"Marc, I need your help," Landen said. Marc nodded and Landen tilted his head toward the study. "They'll explain," Landen said.

Without hesitation, Marc returned to the study. Dane crossed his arms across his chest. Clarissa refused to look any of us in the eye.

"It seems we're not needed here…we're leaving," Dane said.

I felt Landen suppressing the anger he felt for Dane. He pulled me closer to his side and stared at Dane.

I looked at Dane. "Dane, you crossed a line. What I need from my family and friends is trust – not doubt. I'm not choosing between the two of you and Olivia and Chrispin; I'm simply listening to my soul…you have to trust me," I said.

Dane's jaw tightened and he took in a deep breath. "The devil has a way of dancing in your mind, a way of changing your perception – and right now you're playing the part of a fool," he said as he leaned forward and locked eyes with me. I couldn't understand what had happened to him. I've never known this person staring back at me – which was terrifying. Landen held me tighter as he leaned forward, breaking Dane's stare.

"Dane," Brady said, "I don't know how Landen is remaining as calm as he is – because if you'd even thought of touching Felicity that way, I would have killed you."

"I think Dane's right: all of you are blind to the devil in there," Clarissa said in support of Dane. "You can't even see that Drake is right where he wants to be – with Willow."

Landen looked at Clarissa. "Last time I checked, I was the only one that could read Drake's intent," he said calmly.

"You know what? I don't even care anymore. I'm leaving," Clarissa said.

"I'm not going to stop you," Landen promised. "I think you're too close to all of this. You both need a break."

Clarissa looked at me, wanting me to stop them and send Olivia and Chrispin away.

"I love the both of you," I said, catching Dane's stare.

"We all do – and I refuse to choose between people I love. I think a break would be good. I promise when this is over, you'll see that my intent led my path to peace."

Dane reached for Clarissa's hand and pulled her toward the stairs. It broke my heart to see them walk away, but the tension in all the energy around us was finally leaving. I knew this was best for now.

Brady looked at Landen and said, "I promise next time I'll make sure I'm closer to her when you're gone. I had no idea they were planning that."

"They hid it well," Landen said in a harsh tone.

He pulled me closer to him then we turned and went back into the study. Marc and Drake were standing side by side in the center of the room. I looked between them with growing confidence that Marc would most definitely pass for Drake, even at a slight distance. I gently let go of Landen's hand and went to the table to retrieve a black pen. I then nodded my head for them to come to my side. Drake smiled slightly, then unbuttoned his cuff and rolled his sleeve up – revealing the dragon covered by the willow tree as he made his way to me. Marc looked curiously at me. I reached for his arm -- understanding then came to him.

Alamos looked up from the scroll to see what I was doing. When he saw me begin to outline the long dragon, he stepped closer to me. "You are a brilliant young woman," he said, "They'll have no doubt if they see this mark on him."

Marc extended his right arm so I could reach him. "Did Dane go home?" he whispered.

"They left, but their intent wasn't to go home. They were going somewhere to be alone," I answered, not looking up.

I could see the tension leave Drake's body. Marc

glanced at him as he sensed it. Marc's eyes then moved across the room and found Olivia. She was sitting calmly on the couch in Chrispin's arms. I hated the crack that was appearing in our picture perfect family, but I knew it would heal itself in time. Dane just needed to cool off. I knew once he was alone somewhere with Clarissa he'd see how brash his actions were and undoubtedly would ask for my forgiveness – even though I'd already forgiven him.

I began to add in the details of the willow tree on top of the dragon – which I'd seen in every nightmare since I was a child. While I was working, I seldom glanced to Drake's arm, only to make sure I was remembering it clearly. The head of the dragon started below the wrist. The body stretched to the crease of the elbow. Its body twisted into an S-like shape. Small spikes lined its back. The willow tree was a vague mask to the eerier image beneath it.

Alamos let his hand rest on Drake's shoulder. "This act will weaken you. You must begin to recall the memories that will give you the strength you need to make it back to the estate," he said to Drake.

Drake's eyes moved to mine. I could see his determination.

Alamos looked at August. "They'll be weak as well, so you must guide them home so they can regain their strength," he said.

I looked away from Drake and began to fill in the last details of the willow tree. Perodine returned. Nyla and Beth were with her.

I checked my work once more before releasing Marc's arm. "Let it dry for a moment. Be careful when you change," I said to him.

"Willow, come with me for a moment," Landen thought.

I turned to see that he was still standing near the door-way. I turned back, glanced between Marc and Dane once more then went to Landen's side.

"We'll be right back," Landen said to the room.

Landen put his arm around me and led me down the hall. We stopped in the first room and he closed the door behind him. I felt his calm, but I also knew he thought what he was going to say would make me angry. As my eyes questioned him, he came to my side and gently wrapped his arms around my waist.

"I'm going to ask you to do something. If you refuse, I understand...I'm only asking because I'm concerned about Drake making it back safely – to protect Marc from being discovered as an impostor." I didn't say anything. I just waited for him to go on.

"One of the things Drake wanted to talk to me about was when he moved his energy inside of you," Landen thought, raising his eyebrows.

I felt my stomach suddenly tie into knots. I hadn't had a chance to feel guilty for that act – and now it was wash-ing me away.

Landen let his lips rest on my forehead and held me as tight as he could. I felt a numbing calm come from him. *"I'm not angry. I'm not jealous – I'm relieved,* "he thought.

I leaned back and looked at him as if he were insane.

"I'm relieved because Drake was wrong: we don't find our strength from the same place. I find it in your soul, and he finds it in your energy."

"I don't understand."

"When we're one, we both feel empowered. When it's over, our strength is renewed. Drake said he only moved in for a second and it drained you – meaning he can't restore you...only I can."

"It's because you and I are one and I love you," I said, wiping away a stray tear.

"I love you," he thought.

"I don't understand…what are you asking me to do?"

"After we move that wall, I'll be surprised if he's able to stand. I'm asking you to give him what strength you can, then I'll carry you home and we'll restore ourselves."

"This feels wrong," I thought, looking away from him.

Landen turned my head gently and let his hand fall to rest on my chest. His eyes settled deep in mine.

"We're cheating the devil. It's the last thing that demon would expect me to ask you to do," Landen thought.

I raised my hand to rest on his. I knew he honestly believed that we'd stumbled onto a hidden power, that with my heart I could empower the ones that would bring an end to the demon that had lived inside of Donalt for so long.

"You are the power. I fear if you don't restore him, even if he made it back – he'd be too weak to act as they'd expect him to. I understand that this is your body, your energy, your choice. I'm only encouraging you to save lives."

I looked down and took a deep breath. Landen gently raised my head so I'd have to look into his perfect blue eyes.

"If I have the strength, I'll help him," I thought.

A small smile came to his face, just barely showing his dimples. He pulled me to him and let his lips frame mine. He had innocent intentions but I could not hold myself back. I pulled him tightly against me inviting him into a passionate embrace. Before we lost control he released me slowly. His eyes fell into mine as his thumb gently traced my lips. I could feel an odd wonder coming from him. I couldn't fathom why.

He took my hand and began to lead me back to the

study. As I felt the emotions of the room, I remembered the doubt Dane and Clarissa had for me.

"No one will understand why I'm doing this. It'll only give them reason to doubt the way I feel about you," I thought.

"They won't know. When we stop time, that's when you'll help. This is a secret that'll stay between us and Drake."

"You trust him?" I asked.

"I'll pull him aside. If he gives me any reason to doubt him, I'll tell you. He honestly wants to redeem this dimension – that's all he's every wanted."

As we stepped into the study, I wrapped my arm around his waist and leaned into him. In the distance, I felt my father and Ashten. I glanced up at Landen he was questioning why they were there as well. We stepped inside the study. Alamos and August were at the window with Drake, discussing the wall. The others had left the room. Our fathers came through the opposite doorway; I could feel they were anxious about being there. Ashten surveyed the room then looked at Landen.

"Preston told us to come. He said you needed our help," Ashten explained.

Drake turned at the sound of a new voice then moved his head from side to side. "I just wish sometimes he'd tell me what he knows in the first place, save time and energy," he said.

I smiled, slightly understanding his frustration. Alamos put his hand on Drake's shoulder. "The children can only navigate through the choices you make. You had to decide to do this before they could send help," Alamos explained.

My father walked in my direction. As he approached, I saw him survey my body. "Did something happen?" he asked me.

I didn't want to lie to my father, but I didn't want to tell him that Drake had drained me either.

"It's just been an emotional evening," Landen answered, protecting me from having to lie.

My father nodded. Landen looked at Drake and nodded his head, telling him to come with him; unwavering, Drake followed Landen out of the room. August then called our fathers to the table to explain our plan.

Alamos extended his arm, telling me to come to his side. When I reached him, he smiled at me then looked to the wall. My eyes followed his. "I want you to study every part of this wall that you can see," he said.

My eyes moved across the wall. It was just as tall as I was. The stones were close to four feet in width shaped into a half circle. It looked enormous.

"Now I want you to see it as a gray cloud, weightless, diminutive," he said. I focused again on the wall and let my mind make the stones look like pillows then I turned them into innocent rain clouds.

"Do you see it that way now?" Alamos asked me. I nodded. "Hold that image. Even when you step away from this window, in your mind see it in that manner."

"How am I going to lift it? I can't do the things Landen and Drake can. I don't have control like they do."

Alamos chuckled quietly. "I'd say that you're stronger than the two of them combined," he said, smiling proudly at me.

As I stared at the wall, I blushed slightly.

"You must see your energy as a force. When the moment comes, you'll take your energy and push it forward with your mind. Do not release it. When it reaches the wall, you'll then raise your energy and push back again."

"With my mind," I said, sighing.

"The mind is powerful. It can create or destroy anything we wish it to," Alamos said.

"How far can we move it?"

"If you were walking on the ground, you could take it as far as you wish. For your safety, you'll be on the roof of the palace. You should be able to move it until it leaves your sight."

"I'm afraid it'll crumble, hurt the ones beneath it," I said, looking at the workers around the wall.

"Your energy will hold it together when it's in the air. When you set it down, some stones may fall. I wouldn't raise it more than six feet in the air. The workers will scatter as it begins to move, but I don't think you'll bring them any harm."

I looked to my side at him. "Are you having a change of heart? I thought, in your opinion, that I brought destruction," I said quietly.

Alamos looked down, took in a breath then looked up at me. "I yearn for the day that my soul will rise above this life, the day that I can look back over the chapters of my time and understand why we're all put through so much turmoil."

"We're not meant to live in turmoil. I believe we decide if we're happy," I said, looking at him.

"Maybe so, but I've seen more tragedy than good," Alamos said bleakly.

"Think of the good that'll come, not the tragedy that's occurred – and you'll find a peace that's escaped you," I said to him.

He smiled at me. "I just wish you could feel how much I love you…how much Drake loves you," he said, looking back at the wall.

"I don't doubt the way the both of you feel about me. You know my insight is rare. The rest of the world has the pleasure of discovering the emotions in others by their actions, their words; I sense an emotion and make a judgment. It's not my place to judge. Sometimes I feel the insight is more of a curse."

Alamos looked down at me, his aged eyes studying my every feature. "Aliyanna couldn't feel others as clearly as you can, but she understood others' emotions more deeply than any other soul I've met. It's a blessing, not a curse. You have the ability to understand what drives the emotion, which would make you a sound ruler."

"I'm not going to rule anyone," I said in a tranquil tone.

"That is growing more and more clear with each passing moment," Alamos said.

"I need you to stop pushing me in Drake's direction; you cause him more stress than peace when you do so."

"I only want him to be happy. He deserves to have at least one life of complete contentment," Alamos said.

My eyes questioned his words as he looked away.

"He *will* have that life," I answered.

As I felt Landen enter the room, I turned. *"Well?"* I thought.

"I had to convince him. He's afraid it will hurt you."

I glanced at Drake. He was staring at me with a solemn face. I smiled at him and moved my head from side to side. I wanted him to know that I wanted him safe and that I'd be fine. He let a smile come across his face.

Alamos called Landen to his side and Landen eagerly came, wanting any council he could get on moving the wall. When Alamos began the same lesson I'd just heard, I walked to the table. My father extended his arm for me to come to his side. The others were seated around the table.

"This is a brilliant plan. I'm proud of you," my father said.

"It was Drake's idea," I said, looking around the table and judging the others' emotions. Overall, they were pleased that we'd found a peace with Drake – but they feared it, too. They thought Landen trusted him too much.

Marc and Brady came in the room. Marc had changed into Drake's clothes. He had his hair tossed back in the same manner that Drake wore his. The sleeves on his shirt were rolled up, revealing the dragon I'd drawn on him.

Drake looked him over carefully and smiled. "You nearly fooled me. This is going to work," he said. "Come, there's a room here that looks like my chambers. I'll show you where I sit and how I act in there in case anyone's watching."

Marc nodded and followed Drake out of the room. Brady was smiling at our fathers. "I was just thinking that I should go and get you so you can help us get them home – and now here you are. Let me guess: Libby and Preston?" Brady said, amused by his words.

They smiled back at him. August waved Brady to the table and Landen came to my side. Alamos appeared at my other side.

August cleared his throat. "Alright. On the roof, there's a weather vane a passage is beneath it. All of us will go to the roof with them. Once the wall is moved, they'll stop time. When it resumes, Drake will already be in the string. Ashten, you need to step into the string. Follow Drake's path; there's a chance he'll be too weak to have made it all the way back. You must make sure he gets to the chamber and that Marc is out safely. Alamos and Beth are going to try and stall the members of the court long enough for

Drake to gain some kind of strength."

I glanced up at Landen. He was trying not to smile, not to seem overconfident. We both knew that if Drake used me as a source, he wouldn't need any time to gain his strength. By the time Ashten made it to the string, he'd more than likely be standing in front of the court – mocking rage at Delen.

"Landen and Willow are going to be weak as well," August continued. "They'll need to go home immediately. Brady, Chrispin, and Jason will need to guide them, carry them – whatever they need. Nyla, Olivia, and I will stay here and walk the streets; the people in Delen are going to be terrified. Once you've gotten Landen, Willow, and Drake where they need to be, all of you need to return here and make your presence known in the streets; the more of us they see, the calmer they'll be. It's going to be a long night," he finished.

Everyone nodded, taking responsibility for their roles.

"I want someone to take Beth and me back now," Alamos said. "We've already been gone longer than I thought we'd be. Someone is sure to be looking for us."

Brady extended his arm, telling Alamos to come. "I'll take you," he said, looking at Landen.

"Come, we'll find Beth and leave immediately. Wait for him to return before you move the wall," Alamos said.

"You should just take Marc now," August said.

Alamos nodded, then looked at Landen. "While you wait on their return, call on your memories. I'll tell Drake to do the same. You need all the power you can obtain."

Landen took my hand and led me to one of the couches. I collapsed in his arms then through my touch I let the emotion of love that could only belong to him flow. I watched as his energy brightened, then he let his fingers run through my hair and gently pressed his lips against the side of my temple.

Chapter Nineteen

I wondered for a moment if I could gain strength from the memory of being one with Landen, like he did. I closed my eyes and leaned into him and he pulled me closer to him. My mind drifted and my soul brought forth the emotion of absolute bliss. Time stood still. The world – in that moment – was perfect.

"It's time," Landen thought.

I opened my eyes. I could feel Brady approaching. I turned to see the others surrounding the table. Perodine and August were showing my father and Ashten the scroll and their notes; I felt their intent of wanting to unravel the influence of Mars before it came. I sighed, not wanting to know what that planet would bring.

I searched the room for Drake, not finding him.

"He's in the observatory," Landen thought, answering my question.

I nodded then he stood and gently pulled me up. The others looked up from the table.

"Brady's back?" August asked.

Landen nodded. August walked around the table with the intent of telling Drake it was time. As he left the room, Brady came through the opposite doorway.

"Did you have any problems?" Perodine asked.

"No," Brady answered. "This is a well thought-out plan," he said, looking at me. I smiled back at him.

Drake and August came back into the room. "Alright, is everyone clear?" August said into the room.

My eyes moved to each of them; I felt their confidence in us and took ownership of it. They all seem to nod at once. Landen took my hand and we crossed the room to meet Drake. His eyes found mine. He looked strong, confident eager to move forward with our plan. When we reached him, he turned to lead us to the rooftop. I felt the others follow behind us. As Drake led us to the observatory, on the back wall there was a wide metal door. Landen let go of my hand and helped Drake open it. When the door was opened, it revealed a stone staircase.

At the top of the stairs, I heard the wind whistling. The stars made a beautiful backdrop to the night sky. Once on the roof, I realized just how high we were. The buildings in the city reminded me of miniature toys.

We were at the far end of the palace. Drake led us along the roof to the weather vane in the center. As we walked, I studied the sky above: above the city of Delen, the stars sparkled – but on the edge the gray clouds hid them. It was as if the city were trapped in a snow globe, a world of their own.

I could see the weather vane in the distance. It was almost twenty feet high at the base. I could see the night air move, and the passage we were told about was there. Landen looked down at me to make sure it was clear. We stopped just before it, and the others surrounded us.

"Do all of you see the passage clearly?" Landen asked.

They looked at him like he was a fool, but Landen had reason to ask. There were several passages we could see that they couldn't.

"Spread out, then," Landen said.

They all moved across the roof. My father kept his eyes on me; I knew he feared this would hurt me.

Drake glanced down at me, then to Landen. "I haven't moved anything this big before either; all I have is Alamos' direction," he said.

I looked past them down to the wall. Doing as Alamos had instructed me, I saw it as a cloud.

"I can't imagine it being any more difficult than blocking the force of darkness," Landen said to Drake.

Drake nodded. "Or holding it in, forcing it out, then finding the energy to heal," he said to Landen.

I smiled, proud that they were encouraging one another, recognizing each other's strength. It was a moment I never would have believed would have occurred just a few short days ago. Drake and Landen both smiled at me and my grin grew wider. I knew the logical emotion for me to have right then was anxiety, fear – but I was calm, confident. I had them both peacefully at my side and my family supporting me what more could I ask for?

I stepped nearer to the edge of the roof and they followed me closely. From there, you could clearly see that the wall was nothing more than a giant U. The workers had yet to close in the city completely.

"Willow," Drake said, "you focus on the center. It's the most stable. Landen and I will focus on the ends of the wall."

The wind picked up and blew my long hair out of my face. I felt like I was standing on top of the world.

"Tell me when," I said, not losing my focus on the innocent rain clouds my mind had created for me.

Landen and Drake moved away from me, facing their section of the wall.

"Now," Landen said.

As I kept the wall in sight, my focus moved to the energy around me. I pushed my energy forward slowly; as it stretched out from me, I could see it joining with Landen and Drake's. I stepped forward as they did -- our energy flowed down to the wall. When the energy met the wall, a rumble could be heard from where we stood. I heard screams below; it took everything I had to block them out. I envisioned the wall of clouds rising and urged my energy to pull it up; gracefully, the wall began to rise. Dust rained down as the workers scattered, screaming in every direction. From our height, it was hard to judge how high we'd brought it. I looked across the wall to make sure that Landen and Drake were holding the sides at the same height that I was holding the center. As I took in the wonder of this massive wall being suspended in thin air, a smile came across my face; what had caused me so much worry was now in the palm of my hand. I pushed forward and watched the wall glide through the air. I then stepped closer to the edge, wanting to be able to push it as far back as possible. I could still hear the screams of the ones below, but everyone had managed to move out of the path of the wall. As it moved away, it was growing smaller and smaller, fading into the darkness.

I felt my mind and body begin to drain. A dizzy sensation crawled through me. Suddenly, I felt my father's fear; I knew he was watching me closely and that I must be approaching a dangerous point. I stopped the push of energy against the wall and it halted its glide. Slowly, the three of us let it fall to the ground. It was just inches from the earth when I had no choice but to call my energy back to me. I heard it collide with a brutal force. The palace shook with the vibration. I fell to my knees and tried to catch my breath. My eyes searched the ground as I frantically judged the emotions around me, hoping we hadn't hurt anyone.

Silence came. I looked to my right side and saw Landen on his knees. He looked up at me and nodded his head in Drake's direction; I turned to my left to find him on his knees as well. He held his head down. I could see him fighting to catch his breath. I crawled across the short distance between us. It was only a few feet, but it might as well have been a mile. I felt so heavy, so weak.

When I reached him, I pulled my body up onto my knees and he looked up at me. "You can't do this. It'll hurt you. We'll just keep time frozen long enough for me to find my memories," he said.

I reached up for his face and pulled his forehead to meet mine. "You don't have the strength to keep time frozen. Let me help you." I whispered.

He sighed and reached out his hand to cradle my face; his numbing touch helped me find my breath. Within that second, I felt his energy inside of me, his addictive rush. A second later, he leaned back and I fell forward. He caught me in his embrace. "You are my life," he whispered into my ear.

He stood, lifting me. Landen had found his way to his feet. Drake nodded in the direction of the weather vane.

Landen took the few steps to it then leaned against the metal rod. Drake gently set me down in Landen's arms. Landen held me as tightly as he could, protecting me from falling.

"Maybe I should take the two of you home first," Drake said, clearly energized with my power.

"No. Go," Landen said, smiling slightly. "Remember to be fierce."

Drake grinned, finding the idea pleasurable. "Be in the string at mid-day. Make sure others are there to help you. I don't know how many I'll push through."

Landen nodded, then Drake looked at me. It took the last bit of strength I had to smile at him. He vanished into the string. Landen's arms then tightened around me and we slid to ground. I knew he was trying to keep time still for as long as possible, so I focused on a calm emotion: the blissful love I felt for him.

It felt like an hour, but I'm sure it wasn't more than ten minutes before I heard the screams from below again. I raised my head up to look at Landen, and he leaned down and kissed my lips. I felt our family rush to our side.

"Brady, carry her," Landen said.

I felt Brady's arms around me and leaned my head back to see Chrispin and Ashten helping Landen up. Landen leaned into Chrispin, letting him support him. I felt a pride rise in Chrispin; he felt needed, appreciated. I felt my father's overwhelming concern and imagined that we looked as bad as we felt on the inside. I closed my eyes and leaned into Brady. A second later, I felt the hum of the string and the gentle flow of energy.

Brady carried me home. They'd left Jeeps by the passage, but I don't know who drove us to our house. I felt myself drifting in and out of consciousness.

"Willow," I heard my father say. I opened my eyes to
see that I was in my room and that Landen was next to me.
"I want you to drink this water before you fall asleep.
You're very dehydrated."

I pulled myself up and looked to my side. Rose was
handing Landen a glass of water. My father brought the
glass to my lips. I took in what I could then fell back. I felt
myself drifting and focused on my room. It didn't take long
for me to find myself at the foot of my bed. Landen was
still drinking. His perfect blue eyes saw my soul. He smiled
as he gently let himself fall back to the bed. He held my
gaze until his eyes grew too heavy to remain open.

As Rose pulled the covers over our bodies, Landen's
soul appeared at my side. My father kissed my forehead
and turned off the lamp -- we watched them leave. We
could feel the urgency of Chara all around us, but even in
this state, we still felt weak. Landen moved away from me
to the window. I followed, curious to see why we could feel
so many people so close.

When we pulled back the curtains, we could see a line
of hundreds of travelers waiting their turn to step into the
string; their intent was to bring calm to Delen. Landen
turned to smile at me. Our world was reaching out once
again; it was an amazing sight.

He turned to me and slowly let his hand rest next to my
heart. As his energy joined mine, a beautiful sensation
raced through me. I felt as if life itself was finding its way
back into my soul. I reached for his heart and watched as
the glow around him grew. He slowly pulled me to him. In
that moment, everything I'd been through seemed worth it.

When the sunlight peered through our window, we
brought ourselves back to our bodies. I pulled myself to the
warmth of Landen's body and he turned to his side and

pulled me closer to him. We stared at each other for a moment; I couldn't understand how it was possible to love one person as much as I loved him.

I could feel Landen's emotions drifting through the last few days. Overall, he felt victorious – yet he feared what was still to come.

"Do I get the pleasure of telling you that we have nothing to fear?" I thought. He was always the one who never showed any fear.

"Maybe so," he thought, bringing his dimples to life.

"What are you afraid of?" I asked.

He raised his hand to trace my eyes. *"When I was talking to Drake yesterday, he told me that he'd seen Dane in a lot of your lives,"* he thought.

"I really don't want to think about that. It's just too weird," I thought, making a face.

Landen didn't smile. I felt a dread build in him.

"Why are you upset? Are you still upset with him about yesterday? He was just being protective," I thought, pulling myself up on one arm and searching through his emotions and intent.

Landen sighed and rolled to his back. *"I'm sure I'm overreacting,"* he thought.

"I don't understand," I thought, turning his chin so he'd have to look at me.

"Drake said that in the life of Jayda and Oba he didn't choose to fight for Jayda's children because their father, Dane, practiced dark magic. He was known for controlling the elements of the land. Jayda feared that a drought would kill them all if they took the children by force," Landen thought.

"He must have his memories crossed, or he's just seeing it from his point of view. Dane couldn't be dark. He

doesn't know how," I thought, finding the idea farfetched.

"He remembers him being dark several times. Drake spoke the truth when he told me," Landen said.

I didn't say anything. I just sat up and pulled my knees to my body. I didn't like seeing Dane in a dark light.

Landen moved his hand slowly across my back. *"Drake fears that because Dane's soul is old and that it's practiced with the devil before that he could become possessed. He wanted me to watch him closely. He wants me to watch everyone closely. He said you're the only one that he and I could trust completely."*

"Dane loves Clarissa. You know that and I know that. Our family would never hurt us," I thought.

"I'm not saying he'll fight for your heart. I'm saying that if he were possessed, he could manipulate you into thinking or doing something you wouldn't normally do," Landen thought.

"He didn't change my point of view yesterday. I think both of you are overreacting," I argued.

"If it's possible for Drake and I to be overtaken by the darkness, then it's possible for our family as well," Landen thought.

I looked back at him. His blue eyes reflected the concern in his thoughts. *"Are you going to say something to them?"* I asked.

"No. They're already upset with the alliance we've formed with Drake. They feel that I'm letting my guard down around him and that it's too dangerous right now to do so. They'd say that Drake is trying to divide us," Landen thought.

"I don't think anyone in our family is capable of bringing harm to us – possessed or not," I thought.

"I never thought Dane would use force against you

either," Landen thought, raising his eyebrows.

"He didn't think we were thinking clearly."

"I know that. But when I was alone with them the entire time you were with Drake, he didn't say one thing to me. I felt how nervous they were, but he hid his intent – and that action brought validation to Drake's fears."

I tried to remember if I'd overlooked their intent when I walked into the room. I remembered their emotions, but Dane's intent escaped me.

"See what I mean?" Landen thought as he felt the betrayal come through me.

"I still don't think he meant any harm," I said, looking down at him.

"You may be right, but when they make decisions like that, they're endangering both our lives. If Dane had made it to the string, it would have hurt you. They thought of you being in pain. Even if only for a moment, it's just too much to bear," Landen thought.

He pulled me to him and reached for the scar on my chest. I placed my hand above his heart and nestled by his side.

"From this point on, if we find a power or a new insight – we're keeping it to ourselves. Not only to protect us, but to protect them. Whatever they know, the devil would know the moment he took over," he thought.

My eyes met his. *"You never told me what it was like when the darkness entered you,"* I thought.

He sighed as his eyes searched every part of my face. "I felt the contentment Drake spoke of, but I fought against it – and when I fought it, it felt like my body was tearing apart. Horrible images came to my mind. At first, I thought the blade in your heart was an illusion; it wasn't until I saw Drake's panic that I knew it was real. I just wanted someone to hold you to take your pain away," Landen said.

I pulled him closer. "I'm sorry I put you through that. I would have found another way if could have," I said.

As his arms tightened around me, I felt his fear and grief as the memory played out in his mind.

"When I was in that state, I felt our love more intensely. I knew that we'd never be apart, that this body would end where it began and my soul would rise."

"Dust to dust," Landen whispered.

As we lay in silence, I understood why Landen condoned me to empower Drake. I knew at that moment that he trusted his insight and planned to use Drake's dreams as navigation through what lie before us. Both Drake and Landen trusted me, only me. The irony was that I didn't trust myself.

"I trust the children," I thought as Libby, Preston, and Allie came to my mind.

"They deserve our trust. They've never once told us what to do. They do as Alamos said: they guide us through the choices we make."

Realizing that Landen was right, I felt confidence come back to me. My only concern now was how I'd protect our family from the darkness that could threaten their soul.

Feeling my father and Rose approaching the house, I pulled myself up and began to dress for the day. Landen got up as well, then pulled the curtains back and looked out the passage into the field.

"Everyone's gone except for your dad, Rose, Felicity, and the children," he said once he'd stretched out his insights.

The screams from the night before came to my memory and I wondered if our world had managed to calm Delen, if Drake had managed to convince the court that he was a fierce leader.

We were dressed and waiting by the door when my father and Rose reached the porch. As my father surveyed us, his hazel eyes turned to green. "Once again, you're restored," he said to us.

"What happened after we left?" Landed asked them.

"Delen was scared for a few hours. Once they saw all of us, though, they calmed down and went to their homes and slept. Everything on the other side of the wall has been silent," my father said.

I looked past them and saw Libby and Preston running in our direction. Felicity was walking behind them, carrying Allie.

"I brought food here last night," Rose said. "I want to feed the two of you before you go into the string again."

We led them into the kitchen. Rose began to unload the refrigerator while my father pulled out plates. Libby and Preston crashed through front door and ran to Landen and me. I picked up Preston, Landen picked up Libby and we spun them around, absorbing their innocent laughter.

"So, did they leave you in charge, little man?" I asked Preston.

"No. Felicity said she's the boss," Preston said.

Felicity came into the kitchen, a little breathless from keeping up with them. "Easier said than done," she said, smiling at me.

I let Preston fall, then reached out for Allie. She smiled at me and reached her tiny hands in my direction. After Rose and my father set the table, I sat down, nestling Allie in my lap.

"So, everyone's in Delen?" Landen asked.

They all nodded.

"The travelers are going to meet you in the string. Your mothers, Olivia, Stella, along with others who can't travel, will be waiting by the passage in Patrick's home; they want to make sure they see a friendly face when the darkness in the string passes," Rose said.

I looked at Landen. We both knew that right then there were people who thought their lives would end soon; it made me angry that – no matter what – they'd have to live through something like that. I pushed my plate away. My stomach was turning. The anticipation was eating me alive.

"This is a good day," Libby said, pushing the plate back to me.

I reached my arm out for her to come to my side.

"Are you happy with all that we've done?" I asked her, looking for validation.

A smile came across her face as she looked across the table at Preston.

"We've just begun," Preston said, looking at me.

I tried to smile, but I couldn't. My mind was trying to imagine how much harder it could be.

"Well, I'm happy," Rose said, standing to clear away the plates.

"I couldn't be more proud of either of you," my father said, smiling at me.

I took in a deep breath, then hugged Libby and stood. I gently handed Allie to Felicity and said, "I wish you could come."

"My place is with them. Trust me, they paint a beautiful picture with their words. I see it all as if I were there," Felicity said just before she kissed Allie's head.

"Are you staying, too?" I asked Rose.

"I am. I know in my heart I'm helping you by protecting the children," she said, walking to my side. I reached up and hugged her.

"We should go. It's almost mid-day there," my father said.

Preston hugged me goodbye as Libby hugged Landen goodbye. We then climbed into the Jeep with my father and drove to the passage in the distant field. When we stepped out, I took Landen's hand.

"How many people do you think will come through?" I asked him.

"Even if it's only one soul, it'll be a victory," he said, smiling down at me.

"Knowing how fond Esterious is of executions, I'm sure it's more than one," my father answered.

"There will be enough food and shelter, right?" I asked them.

"The land in Delen is producing faster because of the sun, so we'll have plenty for now; but, this is only a temporary solution," my father answered.

Landen stepped in, pulling me behind him. My father followed us. Inside the string, we could feel the emotions of hundreds of people; they were excited and eager. Travelers from Chara were lined between Patrick's passage and the passage that led to Drake's estate. We smiled and let our hands run across them as we passed, wanting them to feel the gratitude flow through us.

At the end of the line was our family. Marc's grin grew as we walked closer.

"Was he back before they noticed?" Landen asked him.

"When we first got there, Alamos wanted me to walk through the hall. Only one person tried to approach me. I just raised my arm with the tattoo on it and turned my head. They left us alone after that. Drake was back a few minutes later," Marc said.

Landen smiled and put his arm around me.

"Chrispin said you were really weak – but Drake... when I saw him, he looked strong. How come it bothered you and not him?" Marc asked.

August stepped forward. "Landen suspended time, allowing Drake to return. I'm sure that's why he lost his strength," he said.

Marc nodded and August looked at us and smiled slightly. It was as if he knew I'd helped Drake.

My eyes searched for Dane and Clarissa, but they weren't there. I felt my heart sink as the division in our family made itself known.

"We told them to take a break. That's what they're doing," Landen thought as he felt my grief.

When Landen approached Chrispin, he reached out his hand and placed it on his shoulder.

"I'm glad you were there for me last night," Landen said to Chrispin.

"Always here for you, man," Chrispin said, grinning.

We moved past him and saw Ashten and Brady next to the passage.

"You look good," Brady said to Landen.

"Thank you for carrying her home," Landen said to him.

While Ashten began to tell Landen about the preparations that they'd made in Delen, I focused on the wall. Through the excitement of the ones in the string, I felt a horror behind the wall of the string, I knew there were people living in a nightmare. I felt Landen's hand on my back, as well as the calm he was giving me, but it couldn't hinder the desire to step inside and bring them peace.

When the others saw that our attention was focused on the gray haze, they fell silent. Everyone stepped behind us and lined the wall, prepared to lead the lost through the passage. From the haze, an arm stretched through: Drake's arm; I'd never been so happy to see that tattoo. As I reached out and held his hand, I felt his rush. He knew I was there waiting.

He let go of my hand, then I stepped closer the haze, just inches from moving through it. My eyes searched, wanting to touch whoever was to come first and give them peace. In that second, I saw a small figure begin to emerge. I reached my hand out, finding Drake's hand on their shoulder. I gently pulled them through. As the haze fell a beautiful little girl no more than four years old was standing in front of me. I leaned down and hugged her, sending joy through her soul. I then brushed her long dark hair out of her eyes – only to find them searching blindly.

"There's more coming. Give her to Brady," Landen said in a tone that was pure joy.

I handed the little girl to Brady and turned to see Landen holding a little boy. Before he could hand him to his father, another little girl came through. I was so happy that I started to cry. Travelers carried the children to Patrick's passage. There must have been more than a hundred of them. The women began to come next. Landen and I stood on either side of the passage and calmed them before passing them to the other travelers. Once the women had passed, the men came; they were more full of sorrow and defeat than the women and children.

Landen said over and over again, "Your family is safe, you're safe." With the sound of his voice – and the emotion we were sending them – they found peace. When the flow of people stopped, our family and the travelers escorted the last of them into Patrick's passage. Landen and I waited, hoping that Drake would emerge so we could thank him.

A moment later, he stretched his arm through once again; Landen gripped it and showed him his gratitude. Landen look at me, then smiled and stepped away. I reached for Drake's hand and smiled as I felt his rush of energy. I pulled his hand to my face and let him feel my smile. Every joyful emotion I could call forth, I gave to him. I gently kissed his hand and let him go, then stepped out of the haze and smiled up at Landen.

"He felt your emotion. You made him happy," Landen said, grinning at me. "He wants us to return tomorrow. He's expecting just as many – if not more."

My grin grew and I reached my arms around his shoulders and pulled him to me. He smiled and slowly leaned in to kiss me.

"I want you to always be this happy," he thought.

Through my embrace, I let the love I felt for only him flow. I felt him push his undying love through me. I felt strong, victorious – and I knew that with him at my side, there was nothing I couldn't do.

Acknowledgments

Gratitude is an emotion I've always felt simply because I have a wonderful family that loves and supports each of my crazy ambitions. I never realized that emotion could amplify as much as it has over the past few years of my life. I am still eternally grateful for each person that encouraged me to bring Insight to life. Today, I must thank so many more. Embody & Image would not be here today without the support and acknowledgement from countless book reviews, bloggers, and most importantly the readers who took a chance on a debut author. I thank each of you from the bottom of my heart.

About the Author

Jamie Magee has always believed that each of us have a defining gift that sets us apart from the rest of the world, she has always envied those who have known from their first breath what their gift was. Not knowing hers, she began a career in the fast paced world of business. Raising a young family, and competing to rise higher in that field would drive some to the point of insanity, but she always found a moment of escape in a passing daydream. Her imagination would take her to places she'd never been, introduce her to people she's never known. Insight, her debuting novel, is a result of that powerful imagination. Today, she is grateful that not knowing what defined her, led her on a path of discovery that would always be a part of her.

The fun Bio: I'm an obsessive daydreamer. Lover of loud alternative music. Addicted to Red Bull. I love to laugh until it hurts. Fall is my favorite season. Black is my favorite 'shade.' Strong believer in the saying: there is a reason for everything, therefore I search for 'marked moments' every moment of everyday...and I find them. Life is beautiful!

http://www.facebook.com/Insight.Jamie.Magee?ref=hl

https://twitter.com/Jamie_Magee

http://authorjamiemagee.blogspot.com

Made in the USA
San Bernardino, CA
14 August 2013